Touch of Darkness

The Síoraí Legacy, Book II

by

Victoria Noxon

Touch of Darkness: The Síoraí Legacy, Book II

COPYRIGHT © 2012 by Victoria M. Noxon

Cover Art by *Rae Monet, Inc. Design*

The Wild Rose Press, Inc.
PO Box 708
Adams Basin, NY 14410-0708
Visit us at www.thewildrosepress.com

Publishing History
First Black Rose Edition, 2012
Print ISBN 978-1-61217-209-5
Digital ISBN 978-1-61217-210-1

Published in the United States of America

Aiyanna kept her features composed while she studied the man who looked scrumptious enough to eat. She found it increasingly difficult to maintain her stoic posture. He was drop dead gorgeous. A natural strength radiated in his perfect, tanned face. Lips, firm and sensual. Thick tawny-gold hair tapered neatly to the collar of a long black leather jacket.

His eyes drew her full attention, extraordinary eyes the color of amber, flecked and ringed with gold reminding her of tiger eyes. Fascinating, almost hypnotic.

He towered above her by at least six inches. Aiyanna always thought herself tall for a woman, especially at five-foot-six, but beside him, some might consider her elfin.

Her gaze moved over him.

Holy crap, the man's body reminded her of a solid brick house, built to perfection. Beneath his black leather jacket, a dark T-shirt accentuated the hard rock bulges of his abs, and tight blue jeans complemented strong, muscular thighs.

She lifted her gaze to find him watching her, a devilish gleam in his eyes.

"Do ye like what ye see?"

Once again, Aiyanna forced a blank expression on her face. She shrugged. Using her best bored tone, she answered, "I guess it's okay if you're into that kind of thing."

No way would she tell him that just his sexy voice, deep and accented, made her heart beat a mamba against her breast or that the sight of his masculinity made her stomach do flip flops. Nor would she admit, even to herself, she suffered from a deep physical magnetism to a man she didn't know. .

Dedication

To all the readers who dare to enter
my world...Thank you for playing with me.
To my husband
for his unending support and patience,
I love you.

"From Findias was brought the sword of Nuadu: no man could escape from it; when it was drawn from its battle-scabbard, there was no resisting it."
                                                          ~*The Yellow Book of Lecan*

Prologue

Ireland, 1750 AD

"Blessed Jesu! Spare me!" Sarah MacLean cried in a frightened whimper.

Staggering through the forest, she sought to escape those who chased her. Tears streamed down her cheeks, and the sound of her own ragged breathing filled her ears. She sucked at the thick air and blinked hard, swiping the back of her hand over her eyes.

Pain flared across her upper arm, and she stifled a sob at the burning sting that lanced her skin. She glanced down and discovered a tear in the sleeve of her dress. A trail of blood seeped through the white material altering the fabric to a bright shade of crimson.

From the corner of her eye, movement drew her attention. One lone limb swung back and forth, slowing until it stilled...evidence of its guilt.

She clasped a hand over the throbbing injury, shielding it from the bitter winds, and stumbled onward. All around her, trees swayed against the blustery breeze.

The sun completed its cycle and vanished over the horizon, transforming the forest into a dark and sinister visage. A mist, thick and dense, blanketed the ground and stretched across the meadows into the trees to cover the woodland floor. With it came a sharp blast of wintry, frigid air.

She struggled through a cluster of brambles.

The barbed undergrowth scratched and clawed at her skin. Blood trickled from the wounds, but she pushed forward heedless of the pain that plagued her flesh.

Suddenly, her skirt hitched, wrenching her to a standstill. Fear tightened and squeezed her chest. She swallowed and squared her shoulders before looking behind her. A bitter sigh of relief escaped her lips at the sight of her skirt tangled in the thorn bushes. Choking back a moan, she bit her bottom lip and gave the material a fierce tug. The sound of splitting fabric filled the air, releasing her.

With a stifled cry, she stumbled over a fallen log and dropped to her hands and knees. She rocked back on her knees and strained to hold her breath, listening for the sounds of those who tracked her.

Faint, but they roamed nearby. Mingled with the noises she and her pursuers made, the winds lashed among the trees creating an eerie echo that swirled through the forest.

Why hadn't she stayed with the girls? She'd simply planned to be away for a few moments...just a few moments. At home, no one cared for her babes. She'd left them, alone and defenseless, to check on the village elder across the meadow. The knowledge twisted and turned her insides, and she swallowed the anguish that rose in her throat.

Why had she gone to Agnes'? A gnawing fear crept into her stomach. She gripped her bruised arm and looked at the marks the village magistrate's vice-like grip had left on her skin. Why had her friends and neighbors taken it in turn to beat the old woman? And why did they now want to do the same to her?

A god-fearing woman, Sarah lived her life in peace. But Agnes' brutal murder brought a dread she never experienced before. She closed her eyes against the memory and told herself she did what any frightened woman would do. She ran as far and as fast as her wee legs would carry her.

That had been hours ago.

Cameron! She mentally screamed her husband's name. In her heart, she knew he wouldn't hear her cry, nor would he be able to help her. Maybe he would be there for their girls.

She pushed herself to her feet, gathering heavy skirts in shaky hands. Her legs trembled, prickling with exhaustion, but thoughts of her family pushed her forward. The longer she kept going, the better the chance Cameron would return in time from his trip.

Her hair, free from the chignon she'd wrapped it in earlier, hung in long sweat-drenched strands around her face. Her ankles throbbed, and with certainty, her feet swelled in boots laced too tight.

The mob of villagers closed in on her. Boisterous shouts pierced the air. Bloodlust surrounded them like an evil cloud ready to burst with retribution. Their vengeance aimed at her.

Her breasts rose and fell under labored breathing. Her lungs burned, and she gasped for breath, lightheaded with fatigue. She needed to rest for a moment and stopped, so tired her nerves throbbed.

Drained, she collapsed against an ancient oak tree, grimacing when the rough bark grazed her back through her bodice. She released an unsteady breath, allowing herself only a few precious moments to ease the weariness of her body.

Blood, mixed with sweat, dirt, and tears poured down her face. With a trembling hand, she swept the wayward locks of hair from her vision.

Horses' hooves thundered in the darkening forest. The snorting and neighing of the great beasts ricocheted around her.

Oh, blessed Jesu. They were everywhere.

With a burst of determination, she pushed herself away from the tree and moved forward. Scarcely able to pick up her feet, she continued to trip and stumble through the forest.

When she broke through the hedgerow, her legs collapsed beneath her. She fell forward and sprawled face first on a bed of dried leaves and twigs.

She spit the crushed foliage from her mouth and gulped in a quick breath of air waiting for the strength to raise her head. When she did, the smooth, satin black hair of a horse's legs came into view. Higher, her gaze traveled until she met the cold, dark expression of the village magistrate. His lips twisted beneath a crooked nose. Reddish hair peeked from under his tam and grazed his cheeks.

He leaned over her. His saddle groaned in protest. "Stop yer running, wench. It wilna do ye any good."

His voice, raspy and coarse, sent chills up her spine. Goose bumps flared across her skin.

"Why are ye doing this to me?"

His jaw clenched, and rust-colored brows drew together in an angry frown. "Doona play the innocent with me. I have been well versed in the ways of black magic. I seek to protect man from those who violate God's laws. 'Tis why I am here. We seek yer confession."

"Black magic? Confession? I doona understand what ye wish me to confess to, for I have done no wrong."

"Confess as the witch ye are, and God will surely forgive yer sins."

She gasped, realizing a shiver of panic. Sweet blessed Jesu! They thought her a witch.

"I am no' a witch." Apprehension surged through her with each palpitation of her heart.

"Ye defended the old one against us." He waved a hand toward the four men who entered the meadow from the trees. He rubbed his chin. "Why is that, do ye suppose?" Without waiting for her reply, he continued, "Let me tell ye why. 'Tis because the two of ye are in league with the devil."

She swallowed hard and lifted her chin, hoping the gesture would not look as defensive as it felt. "Nay, I but cared for her. She had no one else."

"Confess!" he demanded again, pinning her with his steady gaze. His eyes darkened with malice, and evil glinted in their depths.

"I wilna! I have nothing to confess."

In the next instant, a second man she didn't recognize rode up beside the magistrate. With dark hair and a shadow of facial hair, Sarah guessed him to be barely twenty...so young to be tainted by the likes of their leader. The lad's suspicious gaze watched her when he spoke. "Her lips speak lies. The villagers saw the old woman this morn mixing up her witching potions."

"Aye. We shall have this one's confession afore we leave this place. If no', we'll cleanse her tainted soul," he said, in a voice heavy with sarcasm.

"She has children, milord. What of them?" the lad asked.

"Spawn of a witch." The magistrate's voice deepened...heartless. Sinister eyes turned to her, taunting her with an arrogant grin. "When we are through here, they, too, shall need to be purified."

Sarah envisioned her two wee girls, their bonny golden curls, innocent smiles and beautiful faces. They were only babies. One still suckled from her breast. Tears coursed down her cheeks and, with a moan of distress, she screamed and jumped to her feet. "Nay! Leave them be. They are innocent babes and have done naught to ye. Doona harm them!"

The magistrate's gaze met hers. A hard, cold smile lit his features, and his expression grew hard and resentful.

"Shut up, witch!" he said in a harsh, raw voice.

"And her husband? What of him?" the other man asked.

Sarah grabbed the magistrate's leg and pleaded, "I beg of ye, sir—"

"I told ye to shut up," he said, with a snarl. He lifted his booted foot and with a quick kick against her shoulder sent her sailing across the ground.

The side of her face struck a small boulder before she rolled to the ground. Her teeth punctured the inside of her lip, and the coppery taste of blood filled her mouth.

She sat up, dazed, and lifted a hand to her already swollen cheek. With her fingertips, she swiped at the liquid that spilled from the corner of her lips and ran down her chin.

The magistrate lowered his hand in a decisive gesture to his followers and ordered, "Seize her!"

The four men glanced at their leader. Their brows rose in surprise. No one moved. When the magistrate glanced up, they dropped their gaze. Beneath dark lashes, they exchanged looks of uneasiness.

With an impatient grunt, the magistrate withdrew a coil of rope from his saddle horn. Deft fingers knotted the end and hurled the loop over the top of Sarah's head. She slipped her fingers between it and her throat a mere second before he kicked the horse's flanks and urged the animal into the woods at a gallop, dragging her behind.

Pain pummeled her body. He dragged her across rocks and over downed branches. She closed her eyes, protecting her face in the crook of one arm, for fear of losing her vision to one of the sharp limbs littering the ground. Her lower body slammed against a mound of rocks displaced from the nearby stone fence by last year's flood. Little could be done to shield her legs that burned in pain from the onslaught.

When he slowed his steed, she scratched out a quick word of gratitude to the heavens. She pushed herself to her feet, wobbled on unsteady legs, and labored to release the rope. Breathing in shallow, quick gasps, she clawed at the knot. Her fingernails dug into her flesh and splintered, but the tether stretched taut. She choked back a frightened cry.

"I am no' a witch," she screamed again, her voice hoarse from the pressure of the rope across her windpipe. "No legal trial will prove me guilty of yer accusations."

"I am the law here. Evil deserves no trial." The magistrate's voice, though quiet, held an ominous quality. He glanced toward his supporters as if daring them to refute his words. When no one did, he beat his horse into a gallop.

Sarah staggered behind him. Her fingers throbbed, her throat burned, and she was so dizzy she strived to stay on her feet. Less than five minutes later, she dropped to the ground, unable to maintain his harsh pace any longer. Her hands jammed between her neck and the rope preventing the course fiber from choking the life from her body.

When he stopped, Sarah lay motionless. Her muscles throbbed, her head ached, and the fingers on both hands were broken. Burning pain raged through her, robbing her of the ability to maintain coherent thought.

Rough hands seized her hair and yanked her to her feet. She had no strength to even cry out when they bound her bloodied hands behind her back and tied her feet together. By this time, any thought of fight deserted her, and the last traces of resistance vanished.

"Do ye confess?"

Her body refused to support her weight, and she lurched forward. Rough hands caught her, preventing her from crashing to the ground. With a violent jerk, they pulled her up and forced her to stand on legs that shook. She lifted her gaze to the magistrate, barely able to do more than shake her head in denial.

A self-satisfied expression hardened his face before he turned to his followers and nodded. The rope tightened around her neck, and she gasped, powerless to thwart its astringent grip.

With little regard to her body's shattered condition, two men yanked her by the arms and dumped her onto the horse's back. Another man hurled the other end of the rope over the branch above them, jerking it until she slouched across the horse's neck.

She gagged, struggling for air.

Images of her impending death sent terror racing through her veins.

Her body numbed by pain, she mustered the strength to raise her head up and shoot them a withering glance. She refused to cower from her fate and whispered a quick prayer.

May God forgive her evil thoughts, but she hoped he sent these bastards straight to hell.

From the forest, a bright, shining light drifted from the heavens through the branches, gliding in her direction. The illumination embraced her and eased her pain, filling her with indescribably peace. From the depths of the glow, a pale, luminous hand reached for her, and Sarah smiled, no longer afraid. A warm sensation swelled inside, drawing her spirit from her body.

For a few moments, she hovered above her body, and then she soared into the sky.

A sharp "yah" and the slap of a palm against the horse's rump sounded below. High above the meadow, she glanced down where her body hung from the big oak tree. The empty shell that once housed her spirit twisted, then stilled.

No pain now, only a blessed tranquility. Her lips curved, and she turned back to the angel who carried her to heaven.

****

"Sarah!" Cameron MacLean crashed through the brush, numb against the pain of the thorns cutting into his flesh.

"Sarah," his voice broke. "Where are ye, love?"

Tears fell unheeded down his face. He'd come home an hour ago to discover his two wee girls dead, their throats slit, in their beds and his wife missing.

He pushed through the forest's undergrowth, his actions growing more and more frantic. "Sarah." On the other side of the bushes, he dropped to his knees. "Please answer me." His voice rose slightly above a choked whisper.

Then, the soft touch of her hand caressed his cheek.

Thank the gods!

He lifted his eyes expecting to see his beloved Sarah standing over him.

Instead, her lifeless body swung from an oak tree in the center of the meadow. He looked into his wife's blank, staring eyes. A strangled cry escaped him.

"No!" His bellow echoed through the trees.

They were gone. His wife. His children. His world. Dead.

He had nothing to live for. Not now, not ever, and there, in the meadow, before his wife's hanging body, he fell to the ground and beat the soil with his fists. Great sobs shook his frame.

A light entered his peripheral vision and surrounded him. He lifted his head, assured he would come face to face with his wife's murderers.

He stiffened, drawing a quick sharp breath. A slender woman towered over him, her brown eyes kind. Silver hair curled around a face with rosy red cheeks. Soft creases lined her eyes and mouth, an indication she must be close to eighty or ninety years of age. A glorious light embraced her, cascading around her.

"Cameron MacLean, your time has come to return to the land of your birth and become what you were born to become." A gentle smile graced her wrinkled face.

Baffled by her sudden appearance, he shook his head in indecision. Awkwardly, he cleared his throat. "I have no wish to go anywhere except beside my wife and children. Are ye an angel? Can ye take me there?"

The woman's eyes filled with sympathy, and she shook her head. "I'm sorry, I cannot."

He pushed himself to his feet. "Then go away, and leave me be," he muttered.

"It is not your time. If you would let me, I can help ease the pain of your loss."

"Ye canna make me forget them. That wilna happen. They were my life and shall always remain," Cameron pointed to his head, then his heart, "within me. I shall find whoever has done this and make them pay for—"

Cameron's words caught in his throat when the woman shook her head.

"You cannot. The men responsible for this heinous crime shall pay the ultimate price, milord, but it will not be by your hands. Your destiny leads you elsewhere."

"I wilna rest until those bloody bastards are dead, just as my sweet Sarah—" Cameron choked off with a sob.

"You shall never forget, but you will move forward with your life. You have been chosen by the gods to protect the lives of those who cannot protect themselves, against a great evil that will rise from the sand to threaten the souls of humanity."

"Gods?"

"Aye, the gods of the great ancient tribe of the Tuatha Dé Danann, the *people of the goddess Danu.*"

"Tell them they have chosen the wrong man. I couldna protect my own wife and children. Why would they believe I'm capable of protecting innocent strangers?"

"You were not meant to save your family, Cameron MacLean. They were destined to die this day," she remarked, in a compassionate tone.

He hesitated, blinking with bafflement. "Ye tell me this is destiny? I doona understand."

"They were put on this earth to serve a purpose."

Cameron swiped a hand across his face, wiping the tears from his cheeks. Anger at her words surged over him. "Purpose? What bloody purpose could the cruelty of their deaths serve?" He took a step back, his jaw tightening.

"Their deaths were meant to spark an immortal fire within your soul. Once you have embraced their loss, the gods shall grant you immeasurable powers for all time."

"Embrace the death of my wife? My children? Do ye jest?" His voice rose until he drew a deep breath, gritting out between his teeth, "There is nothing they can do or say that will erase what I'm feeling." His heart clenched in anguish, and then his temper flared. His anger became a scalding fury, and his hands fisted at his sides. "So tell yer precious gods to shove their power up their arses, and go to bloody hell."

Two deep lines of apprehension appeared between her eyes, and she stepped forward, placing a hand on his arm.

"Let me help ye. Do not let this be for naught?" she said, her voice soft, sympathetic.

11

"Who are ye?"

"I am the Druid Uiscias of Findias, and I have come to take you home."

The sharp stab of pain that disappeared during his burst of anger returned three-fold. Agony ripped through him at the thought of going back to the dwelling he shared with Sarah. He would be forced to bury his girls, but not right now. He needed a wee bit of time and shook his head. "Nay, I canna go back there. No' yet."

"We go not to your home here in Ireland, milord, but to the place of your birth. We go to Scotland, where you shall learn to become a Síoraí Guardian. That is where the path of destiny leads you, Cameron MacLean."

Uiscias held out a wrinkled hand. "Take my hand."

Cameron glimpsed into her eyes and read compassion in their depths. What remained of his anger dissipated at the gentleness of her expression.

He looked at her hand and shook his head. "I canna leave my Sarah like this."

When he raised his gaze to her, Uiscias stepped from his line of sight. His eyes widened at the tree, where his wife's body hung moments before, to see an empty rope dangle from the trees, swaying in the breeze.

His gaze shot to the elder's face. "Where is she?"

She smiled. "Home, milord. Your wife has gone home. Do not fear, for she is holding your daughters tucked in her loving embrace. They are safe and happy."

Uiscias wiggled her fingers. "Come."

Hesitant, Cameron rose to his feet and slipped his hand in hers. Nothing held him here any longer.

Chapter One

Present Day
Arlington, Virginia

Hidden in the shadows, Aiyanna Grey smiled.

She'd arrived at the warehouse two hours before sundown and waited. Her patience paid off when five blue-veined, ashen skinned, bony-assed vampires exited the side door of the lumber depot. The stench of decay infiltrated her nose, and she grimaced.

Nasty blood-suckers!

Even as she struggled to keep the bile from rising into her throat, every fiber of her person vibrated with anticipation. Adrenaline rushed through her veins.

"Howdy boys!" she said, in a silky voice, and slid from behind the forklift parked alongside the building.

To the far right, a female vampire with long-flowing black hair inched closer to the pack. Aiyanna's lips curved at the creature's attempts at looking human. The ruby red lipstick she wore did nothing to flatter the azure tint of her pale flesh. "Sorry, I didn't see you. Miss." She inclined her head in acknowledgement. Not waiting for a response, Aiyanna's gaze shifted back to the men. In a low, composed voice, she asked, "Stepping out on the town, eh?"

A silly question, but Aiyanna held the same conversations every time before a fight. This little chat provided her the opportunity to size up her opponents. By her way of thinking, she could deal with this group hands down.

From the center of the group, a male vampire, approximately five-ten, took a step forward. He brushed black hair, tinged with gray streaks, from his face. Dark circles rimmed scarlet-colored eyes. His mouth spread into a thin-lipped smile before he replied, "We were headed out for a bite to eat. What's it to you?"

Aiyanna bit her lip to stifle a grin at the telltale act identifying him as the leader of this misfit bunch of vampires. He frowned, his eyes level under drawn brows. His mouth took on an unpleasant twist. Her arrival must have interrupted their plans for the evening.

"Hasn't anyone ever told you it's not safe to wander the streets alone at night, little girl?" Salt-and-pepper brows rose in question.

She rubbed her chin. "Hmmm, piece of advice sounds vaguely familiar." She shrugged. "But I have a deplorable habit of not listening to the counsel of others."

"Judging from the situation you're in now, I'd say your bad habit has gotten you killed."

Her lips parted into a curved, stiff smile. "You don't say?"

He stepped forward. "I do."

She held up a hand. "I have one question before I kick your asses," Aiyanna said, her gaze fixed on the group.

The vamp's eyebrow arched for the briefest of instants, but his advance stopped.

"Confident, aren't you?"

Aiyanna tilted her head in a nod. "That's one of my many other flaws. Now, that question."

He laughed. The clamor, a mix between a growl and chuckle, grated on Aiyanna's nerves. "Yeah, all right." He held up his index finger. "But just one, and make it quick. We don't have all night."

"Where's my sister?" she asked, her voice laced with tenacity. She lifted her chin and met his icy gaze straight on.

His eyes widened. A look of comprehension crossed his face, and he said, "You're the one we've heard so much about? The witch the Queen searches for?"

"Queen, huh?"

"You should be honored."

"Sorry to disappoint you, but I'm not. Why don't you tell me about this *Queen*?" Aiyanna stressed the last word, sure to add a hint of disgust to her tone. "She has my sister, doesn't she?"

His lips twisted into a smile, displaying rotten teeth and yellowing fangs.

Aiyanna grimaced. "Don't you guys ever brush?" she asked. "*Damn!* That is just plain nauseating." Her shoulders imitated a grossed out shudder, and her lips curled in revulsion.

His smile vanished, and sudden anger blazed in his eyes.

She bit the corner of her lip to stifle her grin and shrugged. "Oops, sorry, I don't know what came over me. I'm usually not that rude." She took a deep breath and forced a demure smile. "I'm still waiting for an answer."

He folded his arms across his chest. "What makes you think I would tell you anything?" he asked, with a significant lifting of one brow.

"I did ask nicely. What more do you want?"

The vampire threw his head back and released a bellow of laughter that ended on a sharp note. His eyes narrowed. "Lady, I don't know who taught you manners, but something must have been lost in the translation. You call that nice?"

Aiyanna reached into her jacket and withdrew a wooden stake. Without taking her gaze from the leader, she threw it at the woman, striking her in the heart. A sharp intake of breath echoed before she evaporated into dust that coated the vamp next to her in smoke-colored ash.

The vampire leader followed her motion where he witnessed the woman's demise. His eyes, now a deep, angry burgundy, shot back to hers and held her gaze. "Damn it, what the hell did you do that for?"

She leaned against the apron guard of the forklift and flicked an imaginary speck of dirt from her pants. "To show you what happens when I get pissed," she replied with indifference. Stepping away from the lift, she straightened her shoulders and cleared her throat. "Now, where is my sister?"

The remaining four vampires spread out in front of her.

The leader gestured in a sweeping motion with one arm. "Look around you, lady. Do you see your sister here?"

"You know where she's being held, and you're going to tell me."

"You're in no position to make demands." His gaze shot around the circle and flashed crimson. "Try not to kill her. The Queen wants her alive, but I'm sure she'll understand if she's roughed up a bit."

Aiyanna's hand reached to the back of her jacket where she pulled a whip from the waistband of her leather pants. She snapped the long rawhide strap across the pavement. The noise bounced off the walls like the crack of thunder, jerking the vampires to a standstill. She grabbed a wooden stake from the inside pocket of her jacket with her other hand.

The bloodsuckers rushed again. This time Aiyanna twirled in a circle. With a quick flick of her wrist, she snapped the whip, aiming for their legs. The force behind her strike knocked all of the vampires, except the boss-man, off their feet. With surprised groans, they landed on their scrawny asses in the middle of the parking lot.

They shook their heads in confusion. While they labored to regain their composure, Aiyanna spun around and shot the stake at the leader where it landed in the center of his chest. He evaporated into a cloud of sooty dust that scattered across the pavement.

The alley fell silent.

The remaining vampires rose to their feet and glanced at each other in indecision. A giggle bubbled into her throat at the bewilderment in their expressions.

With no one to guide them, they were lost.

Over the years, she'd learned that most demons, whether vampire, shape shifter, or werewolf, didn't possess an ounce of intelligence. There was always one amongst the faction stupid enough to take on the leadership role.

They looked to the darkness of the alleyway, their only avenue of escape, primed to dart. She couldn't let them get away and snapped the whip, catching one of the vamps around the neck. With a quick snap of her wrist, she gave a fierce tug. Unsteady on his feet, the force of the whip sent him shooting toward her like a rocket. Prepared, Aiyanna kicked her foot up where a blade appeared from the black-toed tip of her boot. The vampire landed on the razor-sharp point.

Without waiting for the explosion, she spun around and punched the vampire who attempted to sneak up behind her in the chest. He fell backward. She yanked another stake from her pocket and flung it into his heart.

Gymnastics had been her favorite sport in high school, and she flipped backward, landing in front of the last remaining vampire, nose to nose. His mouth opened in surprise. Fear lit up his eyes. She stared into his face with a triumphant smile. In the space of a heartbeat, she whipped a knife from the sleeve of her leather jacket and caught him across the neck, slitting his throat. Before he disintegrated, she awarded him an exaggerated wink and said, "See ya."

She brushed her hands together. The dust floated away on the wind erasing all evidence of battle. Content with the knowledge that she'd taken care of the demons in the area, she gathered her weapons. She didn't feel like carving any stakes tonight.

Damn, she hoped to uncover some information about her sister from these bastards before she destroyed them.

Realization rushed over her, and she hesitated.

Perhaps she had.

This *Queen* had to be involved. Her investigation just took a new course...discovering the identity of the *Queen*.

****

Cameron MacLean sat on the rooftop overlooking the alley below, impressed with the woman who single-handedly took on the whole den of vampires. At first, he assumed they were friends, especially since she spoke to them with such a charming smile. When she vanquished the woman vampire, he concluded she didn't run with this coven.

He should have offered his assistance, but she appeared to do quite well on her own.

Instead, he sat back and admired the view.

Her lithe figure in all that black, *tight* leather...oh, what a tiger. Standing about 5'7", instinct warned him that his hands would fit nice and snug around her slender waist. Her breasts accentuated the smallness of her waist. And her hips...by the gods, they would make perfect handles to grab onto and pull her body against his.

At that moment, the woman bent over, and Cameron caught his breath. What a derriere, well-defined, tight, and round.

He shook his head. Damn, what the hell was he thinking?

Magnetism to the woman flared inside him, and he froze, his breath trapped in his lungs. When she turned in his direction, he exhaled a long sigh. Golden skin, the color of milky crème chocolate, showed from beneath the black mask that covered her face. Shoulder length black hair curled at the ends around a face that appeared, from this distance, oval in shape.

She picked up the remaining weapons and reached for her whip. The way she fought reminded him of Cara, the only female guardian. With four Síoraí in existence, himself included, he rest assured this woman wasn't one.

But, then, who was she?

He couldn't resist the temptation to uncover her identity any longer. To safeguard his own secrets, he rose from his crouch, spun, and walked to the alley side of the building, out of her line of vision. He glanced over the area below him as well as the surrounding vicinity.

Reassured that the locale was unoccupied, he swung his legs over the edge of the rooftop and jumped. His body jerked at the impact on the concrete pavement, knees bent, but his landing was silent. He stood to his full height, adjusted his clothing, and ran his hands through his hair.

A moment later, he rounded the corner.

He came to a sudden stop. His gaze dropped from her shoulders down her back to her tight arse, tracing every delicious curve. His heartbeat exploded into a series of rapid thuds in his chest. A hot ache grew in his throat, and he resisted the urge to snatch her up in his arms, toss her on the stack of lumber, and make wild, passionate love to her. Slivers be damned.

Startled by the thoughts that flashed through his mind, he shook his head.

Damn, but this woman was hot.

He grinned at his foolishness, straightened his shoulders, and walked into the circle of light from the lamppost.

"Who are ye, lass? Cat woman?" he asked in a low, yet loud enough for her to hear, voice.

Her body tensed.

Without a word, the woman twirled. Her hand rose. The leather whip held firmly in her grasp. With a quick flick of her wrist, she snapped the whip, catching him around the neck.

He clutched at the unbreakable strap wrapped around his throat, choking the life out of him.

Bloody hell!

With a swift tug, she pulled him toward her. Caught off guard by the attack, Cameron lost his footing and sprawled on his back to the pavement in front of her. Before he could jump to his feet, she rushed at him and placed her foot in the center of his chest. The sharp two-inch heel of her boot jabbed him in the ribcage and held him immobile.

"Meow."

Cameron peered up into her face and caught a glint of humor in her eyes beneath her mask. He laughed and then groaned when the spikes of her heels pressed deeper into his ribs. She eased her weight off a bit but maintained enough pressure to hold him still.

He grinned and replied, "I'm sure ye have a cute wee purr as well."

With a slight smile, she rolled the lariat into a loop and hung it from her belt. Only then did she lift her foot off his chest. She turned away. Over her shoulder, she asked, "Who are you? And where did you come from?"

He rose to his feet and brushed the dirt from his pants. He lifted his gaze to follow her movements.

When he didn't answer right away, she stopped, faced him and demanded, "Well?" One ebony eyebrow rose in question while she waited for his response. An attractive trait.

Unsure whether she would understand that he leapt five stories from the building behind her, he opted for another explanation. He inclined his head toward the shadows of the alley. "I came around the corner over there." Not exactly a lie. "I heard the commotion. I would have helped, but ye seemed to have everything under control. I hung around in case ye needed me."

"Oh you did, huh?" She tilted her head. A soft curve touched her lips. "My hero." She bent over to pick up a sharp piece of timber. "You really shouldn't be out in this area. It's not safe."

"I thank ye for the warning, but I've been known to take care of myself in sticky situations."

She stood, tucked the wood in a pocket of her jacket, and then glanced his way. One of her delicate eyebrows rose, and she smirked. "Yeah, I noticed how well you do that. I think."

He refused to comment at the subtle mention of his downfall at the hands of her whip. Instead, he stepped toward her and held out a hand. "My name's Cameron, and ye are?"

She slipped her fingers in his. A burst of electric shock shot through his body at the contact, and he almost jerked away.

Damn.

Up close, her pixie-like face stirred his insides. Fire and intelligence burned deep in large chestnut eyes.

She snatched her hand from his. A mysterious

look of withdrawal came over her face.

This woman radiated strength, yet beneath her harsh exterior, he sensed a vulnerability she desperately wanted to keep hidden.

He fought the overwhelming need to yank her into his arms. The impulse to taste her, to feel her lips pressed against his overpowered all other sensations.

What the bloody hell was wrong with him?

Chapter Two

The man hadn't even touched her in a sexual way, yet there was enough warmth in his golden eyes to set her body on fire. Her heart pounded an erratic rhythm at the molten lava pooling between her thighs.

She gave herself a mental slap.

She cleared her throat and pretended not to be affected by his strong...golden...sexy...hot...

Another slap!

"My name's Aiyanna," she said quickly over her choking, beating heart.

Amusement flickered in the eyes that met hers. He nodded. "Aiyanna, unusual, yet attractive. It isna a common name."

His hand massaged his neck in a circular motion.

Her lips trembled with the need to smile. He was probably trying to ease the pain of her whiplash. But gosh darn it; he deserved it, sneaking up on her like that. He was lucky she hadn't sensed a vampire, or she would have staked him. She could pick up on a bloodsucker miles away by their vibes alone, and her sense of smell was fantastic.

"It's Cherokee."

"Cherokee? Isna that the name of a bird or something of the likes?" he asked, a probing query in his eyes.

"Ha, very amusing." Her stomach leapt with disappointment.

He was cute but just another jerk. In spite of her

reserve, a tinge of annoyance crept into her voice when she asked, "I bet you think you're a funny man, don't you?"

His brows dipped into a frown. "No' really. Why would ye say that?"

She turned and stomped away, but his footsteps echoed close behind.

"Hey, if I said something to offend ye, I'm sorry. I dinna mean anything, and I wasna trying to be funny."

She spun around to face him, her hands clenched at her sides.

His eyes pleaded, melting her anger to a dull simmer.

He shrugged, offering her a small, apologetic smile. "I doona even know what I said to cause ye such distress."

She shook her head, released a deep sigh, and glanced around the grounds for weapons she might have missed. Discovering none, she looked at him and explained, "A parakeet is the name of a pet bird. Our names were chosen according to my mother's heritage."

"Were?"

She hesitated, swallowed hard, and replied, "Our parents are dead." Tears stung her eyes. She waved a hand through the air trying to appear casual. "Anyway, Mom was Cherokee Indian and Dad American. When we were born, they chose to name us according to our mother's heritage.

"Our?" he asked in an odd, yet gentle tone.

Aiyanna hadn't realized she'd included her sister in the conversation. Too late to take it back, she said, "My sister, Cheyenne, and I."

"I'm sorry for the loss of yer parents."

"Thank you, but it was a long time ago," she murmured with a forced smile.

He angled his head to one side and stole a

slanted look at her. "Still a hard loss to handle at any age. And I'm sorry for the remark earlier. Ye were right to defend yer heritage. 'Tis all a person has that rightfully belongs to them."

"Thank you." She offered him a small, shy smile. "I'm sorry for over-reacting."

He nodded, leaning against the three-foot high pile of two-by-fours, his arms crossed over his chest. "No harm done. Now can I ask ye a more personal question?"

Aiyanna arched her brow, looking at him uncertainly. "Sure, why not?"

"Does yer sister hunt vampires, too?"

Her body stiffened in shock, and her mouth dropped open in surprise. She stared at him, speechless. Her heart pounded. A tumble of confused thoughts ranging from confusion, doubt, and, finally fear, assailed her, and she struggled to get her swirling emotions under control.

After a few moments, she clamped her mouth shut and managed a choking laugh. "Vampires, huh? Read a lot of comics, do you?" Aiyanna asked, struck by indecision. How much did she dare tell this man? When she'd pinned him to the ground, no vamp vibes radiated from him, and he smelled too much like a human, doused by the fresh scent of sandalwood oils, to be considered dead meat. In fact, his essence was clean, almost too pure, so how did he know of vampires?

"I'm quite capable of identifying a vampire when I see one. I can also tell you about shape shifters, werewolves, and ghosts..." His eyebrows rose up then down with each name. Then he leaned forward, his mouth twitched with amusement. "Oh my," he finished on a conspiratorial whisper.

Aiyanna was barely able to keep the laughter from her voice. "Funny, ha, ha. You are an amusing man."

He folded his arms across his stomach and bowed. When he returned to an upright position, his face grew serious. "So, why were ye fighting them, lass?"

"Why do you care?"

His mouth thinned with displeasure, and lines of concern deepened along his brows and under his eyes.

She laughed at his expression. "You don't even know me."

Leisurely, his gaze roamed the length of her body. When his eyes met hers, his brow quirked up in question. "Are ye daft, woman? Ye could have gotten hurt. Look at ye." Throwing up his hands, he muttered, "A wee bonny lass meant to be at home, tending the babes, no' fighting spawn of the devil."

She didn't fail to catch the note of sarcasm in his voice.

Her teeth clenched, eyes narrowed. Anger swept over her. "As I said before, you don't know me. Who the hell do you think you are? You have a lot of nerve to presume—"

He held up a hand to still her angry tirade. "Ye're right, I doona know ye." He shrugged, sighing loudly. "Acting the bastard, I am, and I'm sorry. In my defense, I tell ye I speak out of concern for yer welfare."

His deep-timbered voice softened and pulled at her heartstrings. She hesitated, torn by conflicting emotions. Her anger dissipated at the genuine remorse in his expression.

She released a long, audible breath breaching the silence of the night. "If you must know, I was looking for information."

"Can I ask what information ye expect to gain from a vampire?"

At his innocent inquisitive question, she muttered a reply. "You can ask."

"Will I get an answer?"

"Probably not."

"Fair enough, but ye do know they're cunning and devious creatures, doona ye? I wouldna trust a word any of them said."

Aiyanna kept her features composed while she studied the man who looked scrumptious enough to eat. She found it increasingly difficult to maintain her stoic posture. He was drop dead gorgeous. A natural strength radiated in his perfect, tanned face. Lips, firm and sensual. Thick tawny-gold hair tapered neatly to the collar of a long black leather jacket.

His eyes drew her full attention, extraordinary eyes the color of amber, flecked and ringed with gold reminding her of tiger eyes. Fascinating, almost hypnotic.

He towered above her by at least six inches. Aiyanna always thought herself tall for a woman, especially at five-foot-six, but beside him, some might consider her elfin.

Her gaze moved over him.

Holy crap, the man's body reminded her of a solid brick house, built to perfection. Beneath his black leather jacket, a dark T-shirt accentuated the hard rock bulges of his abs, and tight blue jeans complemented strong, muscular thighs.

She lifted her gaze to find him watching her, a devilish gleam in his eyes.

"Do ye like what ye see?"

Once again, Aiyanna forced a blank expression on her face. She shrugged. Using her best bored tone, she answered, "I guess it's okay if you're into that kind of thing."

No way would she tell him that just his sexy voice, deep and accented, made her heart beat a mamba against her breast or that the sight of his masculinity made her stomach do flip flops. Nor would she admit, even to herself, she suffered from a deep physical magnetism to a man she didn't know.

Worse than that, he called her a *bird*.

He stepped forward, stopping in front of her where he peered at her, his face intense. Her insides quivered when his eyes glowed with a sensual flame.

And then, his eyes rolled, and his body jerked as if he'd been struck from behind.

"Bloody hell!" he muttered, gazing upward. He closed his eyes and swallowed. The veins protruded from his neck. "Let it go already, will ye?"

Instinct sent Aiyanna's gaze shooting around the lot before they returned to his face. She had no clue who he spoke to.

"Who are you talking to?" Her question went unanswered.

He opened his eyes and glanced at her. A crooked grin twisted his lips. And then his body wobbled, and, in slow motion, he fell. She rushed forward to catch him, and they collided.

His arms wrapped around her, using her as an anchor, but the size of the man and force of the contact were too much for Aiyanna to handle. Her feet rolled back on her heels, and she tilted. He followed until neither one of them could regain their balance. They landed on the concrete with an audible *thud*.

Cameron kept his arms around her protecting her head and upper body from smashing against the hard pavement. Yet that didn't stop her ass from landing with a solid thump.

She groaned. Damn it! She hadn't gotten a scratch from fighting demons, but, within the space of ten minutes, this man blacked and blued her butt cheeks.

Go figure.

She struggled from beneath Cameron's shoulder but found herself locked in his embrace.

"What the hell was that? Get off me." She shoved him again, but he didn't budge. "You have to move. We're under attack."

"'Tis okay, lass. We're no' under attack." He rested his forehead against her shoulder as if trying to regain his composure. "Are ye okay?"

"Fine," she snapped. "If we're not under attack, then what clobbered you like that?"

Cameron lifted his head, his eyes glazed. A sheepish grin curled his lips. "A long time ago, I made a bet with a god. I lost. This is his way of reminding me that I'm no' invincible."

She hesitated, blinking with bafflement. It was hard to remain coherent with him so close, but she managed to say, "I don't understand."

Leaning up, he rested his cheek against the knuckles of a curved hand. With his other hand, he peeled up the corner of her mask and pushed the disguise from her face.

He gulped in a swift intake of breath.

"Has anyone ever told ye that ye're a verra beautiful woman?" he whispered, his mouth inches from her own. "Aiyanna—"

She had to say something, anything, tell him to get off, but the words wouldn't come. Her brain deciphered the sense of her thoughts, but her body had ideas of its own. She attempted to throttle the dizzying currents racing through her but realized she'd lost the battle when her arms, of their own accord, wrapped around his lean, muscular waist.

She smelled the crisp, clean scent of man, sandalwood and musk, a lethal combination. Her heart fluttered when she gazed into eyes filled with desire. A deep guttural groan rumbled from his throat, and his face lowered to hers.

The gentle touch of his lips sent shock waves sprinting across her skin. The touch and taste of him engulfed her in a craze of need she never considered possible. Her body arched toward his, and she moaned.

Leaning away, he stared into her eyes. His hand explored the soft curves of her waist and hips, sliding upward to stroke the area below her breast. A calloused thumb traced a path over her leather top. He lowered his head and pressed featherlike kisses to the corner of her eye before moving across her jaw. Her flesh erupted into a myriad of goose bumps.

His uneven breathing brushed her cheek before his lips claimed hers again. This time, his assault bore a savage intensity, and he forced her mouth open with his thrusting tongue. Shocked by her eager response to his touch, she met him with a passion that matched his.

His hand explored her back, her waist, and over her hip. Waves of electric currents streamed through her blood. When he moved away, Aiyanna burned in the aftermath of his fiery possession. He continued to trail light kisses to the sensitive hollow at the base of her throat until her insides tingled with pleasure. Molten tension surged through her veins.

"Cameron," she murmured. Desire assailed her, and she arched her back.

One of his hands stole beneath her top to reveal a portion of her belly. She shivered when the cool evening air touched her burning skin. His hand drifted higher until he cupped her breast, sweeping the sensitive nipple with his thumb. Her skin tingled.

His mouth moved over her. Heat swirled in her groin, expanding outward across her skin. His lips traveled across her cheek, to her neck where he spread sizzling kisses over her. The warmth of his breath fanned the flames inside her to unbearable heights.

Oh God, she wanted this man, and she knew

nothing about him. How could she want a complete stranger this much?

A sudden spasm pricked her neck. Waves of ecstasy throbbed through her, and she convulsed.

He lifted his head to peer into her face. The intense sadness in his golden eyes jolted her with surprise.

"What's the matter?" she asked, breathless.

A sliver of blood trickled from the corner of his mouth and caught Aiyanna's attention a second before his eyes glazed over.

"I'm sorry," he whispered, before he fell unconscious, his weight a cinder block on top of her.

Stunned, she laid motionless trying to come to grips with what just happened. It took all of her strength to shove Cameron off. He landed with a *clunk* beside her. Aiyanna jumped to her feet, turned and stared at the man in disbelief.

Damn! The man was hot, and his kisses even hotter.

She massaged the aching muscle of her neck. Hell of a time for a muscle cramp. But when she pulled her hand away, a sticky substance coated her fingertips. She held it up to the light of the lamppost. A cold knot formed in her stomach, and her breath solidified in her throat. Blood.

She was bleeding!

The bastard bit her!

Her eyes widened, and for a long moment, she watched him for any sign that this handsome, delectable, mouthwatering man was a vampire. Her heart jumped at the sight of the inch long fang, dripping with blood that slipped out from between his lips.

How? Why hadn't she sensed that before?

Her nerves tensed, and her heart refused to believe what her mind told her.

This man was one of the monsters she swore to

spend her life destroying. Aiyanna understood what needed to be done and reached inside her jacket to withdraw a wooden stake from the pocket.

He had to be destroyed. Stab him in the heart and wait for the explosion of dust.

She studied his face. One word came to mind, absolute perfection. Well, two, but Aiyanna didn't care. His face, perfectly sculptured, high, arching brows that accentuated wickedly long eyelashes and his lips...oh my, what she wouldn't do to...

Sandy brown eyebrows arched over closed eyes, his face ruggedly delectable. Even out cold, he stirred long buried visions of desire within her.

Oh, and his smell, even now, his warm masculine scent lingered on her skin, making her ache to do inappropriate things to his body even as he lay unconscious. His powerful body made her mouth water, and she throbbed with need. Never in her life had she ever seen a man's body so hard and well defined.

The man should have been a god.

With a start, she pulled herself from her fantasy. She had to do this before he woke. To her annoyance, she hesitated. Her hands shook.

What was the matter with her?

She knelt beside him and pushed aside his jacket. The stake held between her palms, she raised her hands to strike. Once again, the woman in her snapped to the front, and her gaze darted over his lean muscular ribs and abs so tight and well-formed Aiyanna knew if she were to drop a quarter, it would bounce right back up into her hand.

She wavered, her eyes catching sight of a dark stain high on his shoulder. It started as the size of a half dollar, but while she watched, it quickly grew and spread across his chest.

Blood. Was that blood?

She lowered her hands. Vampires didn't bleed.

Aiyanna leaned over him and yanked his T-shirt up.

Her eyes widened. Surprise sent her falling on her backside to the pavement.

The Mark of Luna.

Aiyanna read about the goddess' mark but never believed she would see it in her lifetime.

She stole a peek at the mark. The simple tattoo depicted creeping vines of a willow tree with the moonlight shining through the limbs from behind.

Just above that, another object. One she hadn't read about.

Another moon. A blue moon.

What did the two moons symbolize? Was there a special connection to the slight imprint of a woman's face centered in the middle?

Without thought, she ran a hand over the markings, tracing the intricate design, until a warning sounded in her brain.

This man was a Síoraí Guardian, pledged a warrior of the Tuatha Dé Danann. She'd read of the guardians, the prophecy, and the threat of evil that would arrive at a time undetermined by the prophets.

She released a deep sigh of frustration. Truth was found in prediction, not some fantasy concocted by the ancient muses.

Aiyanna sprung to her feet. Her gaze scanned the area searching for the others.

Legend read the gods created four, but the vacancy of the alleyway indicated no others in the vicinity.

A Síoraí Guardian? Here in Arlington?

Then another more frightening reality struck her. A guardian here, in Arlington, could mean one thing. Deidra, the Queen of the Undead, had escaped from her recorded prison.

Queen!

Oh crap!

That must have been who the vampire leader referred to when he'd said "Queen". Worse yet, that must have been the presence she'd felt in her thoughts over the past couple of days.

And now, an ominous cloud eclipsed the city of Arlington.

Warning spasms of alarm erupted within her, and she glanced back at Cameron. She had to get him the hell out of here. Aiyanna couldn't let anything happen to this man.

She'd save him regardless of what he'd done to her, if only she knew what that was.

Chapter Three

Deidra Sidhe drew a deep breath then gagged on the copious stench of honeysuckle that drifted across the evening breeze.

Free of her daytime prison, she strolled through the burial ground. Her hand traced the jagged crowns of each grave marker she passed. She cared not for the bodies that lay beneath the soil; simply what she gained from their existence.

She hesitated before an aged headstone, its surface covered with moss and lichens. Her hand moved across the top of the pitted limestone marker. Sections of the stone were worn, the owner's name obliterated by time.

Closing her eyes, she inhaled, trapping the essence of the young man whose body resided beneath the soil. Visions appeared behind her closed eyes, and she fed from the power of his memories.

Battle raged around him. Hidden behind a tree stump surrounded by brush, the young man wore a gray uniform. His hands tightened around the butt of a long pointed weapon.

He aimed it at a man dressed in a blue coat who ran from the thicket, his own weapon raised. The man in gray squeezed his finger. The tip of the barrel exploded with a puff of white smoke.

The man's body jerked. The blue of his jacket turned the color of plums as blood saturated the material. His eyes widened, and he came to a standstill. After a moment, he dropped to his knees and collapsed to a heap in a bed of wood ferns.

Another man dressed in blue appeared from the trees. He shouted, racing toward his downed comrade. He brandished a similar weapon, took aim toward the young man who'd killed his companion, and squeezed the trigger. A loud crack resounded through the trees. Birds scattered from their perches with loud *squawks*. A cloud of brume filled the air.

The gray coat's body jolted with a pain so fierce and brutal, it stole Deidra's breath, a pinnacle of gratification.

The fear at the time of his death produced a delightful snack, a delicious blend of vulnerability and despair that fed her ego.

Deidra opened her eyes, refreshed by the burst of energy that coursed through her veins. Her gaze moved around the grounds. Here, in this cemetery, she found shelter and the remnants of the life she once had.

Centuries ago, her position as succubus to the powerful Fomorian ruler Ághmach granted her access to unimaginable pleasure. Not only was he a commanding leader, Ághmach was a magnificent lover. Deidra deemed him her soul mate, and she missed his strong arms around her, his body inside hers.

Together, they created and ruled the Camarilla, their Crimson Kingdom. Side by side, they became a force to reckon with, but now, her people were dead and her kingdom destroyed by the gods of the Tuatha Dé Danann.

Images of blood and violence flicked through her mind. She closed her eyes and attempted to block the memory.

She failed.

Her stomach churned. Bile rose in her throat, and she clenched her hands into fists at her sides. She envisioned that day, the pictures forming behind her closed eyelids.

The ground trembled. Her temple crumbled into a million pieces that buckled into a cloud of dust and odd-shaped pieces of cinder. Lightning zigzagged through the clouds. Fireballs shot from the skies. Their destructive forces annihilated her world.

What occurred next was a blurry gathering of recollections. Judge and jury, the gods claimed Ághmach's practices were immoral, a crime against humanity, but Deidra knew the real reason behind their actions. The almighty deities were afraid of the Camarilla, and out of fear, they banished them, shattering their world in the process.

The gods sentenced Ághmach to life in the underworld where he has remained in a virtual prison ever since. She, herself, had been imprisoned beneath the earth's surface.

Deidra clawed her way through the realms, across dimensions, arriving here. It was a different world, a new time, but her purpose was more potent than ever...revenge on those who sabotaged her life. She vowed to reclaim what she'd lost and return Ághmach to rule by her side.

She arrived in this place called Arlington a few weeks ago, drawn by the overwhelming power of not one, but two white witches. With the power of both witches combined with her own, Deidra would be able to release Ághmach and transport him into this realm.

Deidra already possessed one of them, but she needed both for her plan to be successful.

During the day, a human who called himself Jack Stannard searched for the other sister. Jack followed Deidra to this place from the city of her rising in Michigan where he'd worked as a city coroner, whatever that meant. The man offered his assistance in exchange for immortality and power.

For Deidra, Jack symbolized the sniveling humans of this time and deemed him unworthy of what he sought. For the moment, he proved useful, this place still new. She would learn from the knowledge he readily shared. When she no longer needed him, he would make an agreeable bite.

At night, her minions searched for the sister witch, but that one proved to be elusive. So far, they had been unable to get a solid fix on her location. The witch popped up in the strangest places, often destroying many of her minions.

Deidra attempted to steal into the sister's thoughts, using her twin's link, but her efforts proved unsuccessful. A solid white wall blocked her way, but it wouldn't be long before her search brought her to the witch's doorstep.

Deidra breathed the faint vibrations and drank in the old terrors and confusion that filtered through the air. The Camarilla had been formed of these very emotions, from the needs of long existence without pain. These sentiments gave them life and sustained them through the centuries, and it would be these same things that would bring them into a new future.

She thought fleetingly of the Princess who brazenly stood against her, and of the Síoraí. When she first arrived on this plane, she searched for the Talisman of Destiny with the hopes to use the stone and the Princess to release Aghmach. The gods planned well in advance for her return. Their guardian creations foiled her plot that time, but she vowed it wouldn't happen again.

She seethed with vengeance, seeing red. Fear and death held dominion as always, and she would see the forces of darkness prevail.

Deidra glanced up to the skies. "I shall triumph over you," she proclaimed, in a voice as soft as silk.

Chapter Four

It was close to four in the morning when Aiyanna steered her small sedan onto the asphalt driveway of the two-story house she shared with her sister when Cheyenne wasn't traveling on business. She followed the short drive around the back of the building where she parked in an isolated area ten feet from the backdoor steps.

It had taken her an hour to drag the man from the lot to her car, and she didn't relish the idea of hauling his big ass into the house. Although the streets rang with the silence of the night, she couldn't chance exposing her magic to the public.

She switched off the ignition and gripped the steering wheel in both hands. Her gaze took in her surroundings. The lawn, less than an acre, held a birdbath, a wooden swing, and a small garden. The vegetable plants wilted in response to the cooler nights of autumn.

A six-foot white picket fence acted as the boundary between their property and acres of woodlands.

A lamppost near the garage filtered the darkness to soft shadows.

Pride flooded over her.

Privacy was one of the reasons Cheyenne and Aiyanna chose this house. On the west side of town, far from the busy metropolitan, with few neighbors, the scenario proved ideal for two witches who wanted to be left alone.

The house, itself, was much too large for the two

women, but they loved the solitude it offered.

The dwelling positioned away from the road on a huge corner lot, a chestnut tan frame building with cinnamon-colored shutters, surrounded by maple trees. Leaves of bright yellows, vibrant reds and oranges blanketed the ground and floated across the breeze. Even with the loss of foliage, the structure remained concealed against the prying eyes of those passing by. Gray cement steps, a glimpse of cerise-colored shingles and the silver mailbox at the end of the sidewalk were the only visible signs that a house existed on the land.

Here, in this place, the sisters found the seclusion they lacked in the two-room apartment they shared in downtown Arlington. And here, Aiyanna vowed to remain.

Three weeks ago when she'd arrived home to discover the front door smashed in, and Cheyenne missing, Aiyanna placed an invisibility spell of protection around the house.

Drawing a deep breath of damp air, she glanced at the unconscious man beside her. She wavered, trying to comprehend what she saw. The bleeding had stopped, and his wound healed. The only noticeable indication an injury existed was the slight pinkish line that ran across his shoulder.

She shouldn't be surprised. After all, as a guardian of the ancient Tuatha Dé Danann, he had supernatural talents. Why not miraculous recovery?

A handsome man, to be certain, and his nearness made her senses spin. Just the sight of his finely-tuned muscles made her heart jolt, her pulse pound, and created a tingling in the pit of her stomach.

Aiyanna reached across the center console, patted his arm, and said, "Stay put. I'll be back."

She slid from the seat.

Patterns of shadows shifted over the back yard.

Leaves rustled and whispered in the night wind. The slam of her car door shattered the stillness of the grounds, and she glanced in at her unconscious guardian.

"Oops! Sorry," she murmured. Her blood pounded, and her face grew hot with humiliation.

She walked around the front of the car to the two steps leading into the house. Opening the outside storm door, she strode onto the back porch where a night light in the corner lit up the small area. Squinting, she peered around the room until she located a five-pound box of detergent, which she used to prop the storm door open. Satisfied it would hold, she walked to the heavy oak door that entered into the kitchen. She settled the key into the dead bolt and turned, hearing the catch release on the other side.

Once inside, her palm located the light switches on the wall. With a swift upward motion of her hand, the room brightened. Flicking up the second lever, the floodlights lining the drive sputtered to life.

"Anya, I sense an unusual power."

Aiyanna's heart jumped, and she spun around.

A large white Himalayan cat sat in the center of the table.

Aiyanna's hand covered her breast in an attempt to still her rapid heartbeat. "Starr! You scared the hell out of me."

Starr had been with Cheyenne and Aiyanna since they turned eighteen and received their witching powers. The cat possessed supernatural powers of her own, including the ability to speak.

Orphaned as toddlers, the girls spent their childhood in and out of foster homes. Throughout their teenage years, she and Cheyenne often saw the cat out of the corner of their eyes; however it wasn't until they'd received their gifts that the cat showed up outside their apartment door in New York. By that time, the girls were adults and sought their own ways in the world.

As part of their transition to their new lives as witches, Starr taught them everything they needed to know, even the reason for her appearance into their lives. Most *familiars* took the form of a black cat, toad, dog or owl, but she chose an unusual shape...a *white* cat meant to complement her white witch companions.

Familiar or not, this large fluffy ball of fur became as much a sister to them as they were for each other and taught them what it meant to be a witch.

Except Starr needed to be reminded of her manners.

Aiyanna lifted her arms to cover her breasts, her brows drawn. "Starr, I thought I told you to stay off the table."

"Anya—"

"I know about the power you sense."

Starr tilted her head. "Then you have an idea what is causing it?"

"As a matter of fact, I do."

When Aiyanna hesitated, Starr stood up on her hind legs and crossed her paws over her upper body. Aiyanna giggled. Starr may be a cat, but sometimes she acted human.

"Well," Starr asked in an impatient tone, tapping her back paw against the table.

"I've brought someone home with me." Starr grimaced, and opened her mouth. "He needs our help," Aiyanna interjected before the cat spoke.

"And you are too trusting, Anya. People do not understand your powers. Have you forgotten—?"

In frustration, Aiyanna ran her fingers through her hair. Her lips tightened, but she managed to reply, "I've forgotten nothing."

"Then, how can you think to bring a human

here?"

Her hands dropped and slapped against her thighs. She kept her features deceptively composed. "Starr, he's a guardian."

Starr's hackles rose, and she hissed. "You cannot mean what I think you mean."

Aiyanna nodded her head. "I see you remember the prophecy well."

"If he is here, that means Deidra Sidhe has risen."

"I'm sure of it."

"Oh, crap!" Starr slumped to the table and covered her green eyes with her paws.

In spite of the dangerous situation they found themselves in, Aiyanna chuckled at the cat's reaction. "My sentiments exactly, but I hope he'll be able to help us."

A paw lowered, and Starr peeked through one eye to look at her. "Do you think he can help find Shy?"

Aiyanna smiled at Starr's nickname for Cheyenne. Her sister could never be described as "shy." In fact, just the opposite, Cheyenne's nature spoke of fun-loving flamboyancy; although she could be bitchy at times.

Not to mention, her sister hated the pet name.

Aiyanna bent her head and studied her hands. After a moment, she glanced up and bobbed her shoulders. "Maybe, I'm not certain."

"But you're helping him. Why wouldn't he return the favor?"

Aiyanna walked to the sink, grabbing a cup from a nearby cabinet. She flipped on the tap, waited for the water to chill then filled the glass half full. Spinning around, she faced Starr. "Starr, I think Deidra is the one who has taken Cheyenne," she said, raising the cup and taking a sip of water. She swallowed. The cool liquid slid down her parched throat.

Starr released a seething hiss. "Why would that witch want Shy?"

"For her power." Aiyanna set the glass on the counter with a sharp *click*, raised her hand, and ran a frustrated hand through her hair. "I haven't mentioned it before, but I've been receiving trivial taps against my psyche. A woman dressed in black sends me erratic visions that make no sense. I've been able to block them, but—"

Starr's tail flicked a quick motion. "You think it's her?"

Aiyanna strolled toward the table, resting her hands on the back of the table chair. "I do now. Before this man's appearance, she was no more than a nuisance. But it makes sense. Imagine the power she'd gain if she captured two white witches instead of one."

"Anya, if what you say is true, you're in grave danger." Starr hissed, in a tone laced with concern.

Aiyanna pushed the chair under the table. "Only if she captures me, but I'm not going to let that happen. We must think of the positive side."

Starr straightened, her ears twitched. "And what's that?"

"Cheyenne is still alive. Deidra won't harm her."

"What makes you so sure?"

"She's trying to use our link as twins to get inside my head. And if you think about it...if Cheyenne's power were enough for her, she wouldn't need me. Gut instinct tells me she's after our combined powers."

"Anya."

Starr's voice cracked, shaking with fear, and Aiyanna ran a soothing hand through the cat's feather-soft fur. "Don't worry, Starr. I don't know what her plans are, but I will. Besides, I plan on finding Cheyenne long before she puts it into motion." Aiyanna turned away, not waiting for a response. "Now, I'd better get this man inside before his essence draws some unwanted visitors."

She headed out of the kitchen, propping the kitchen door open with a chair on her way through. The springs could be touchy at times, and she didn't want it slamming shut before she had him in the house.

Over her shoulder, she called, "And Starr, please get off the table."

She smiled at the soft thud of Starr's four paws hitting the floor.

Aiyanna walked to the car and opened the passenger door.

After a quick glance around, Aiyanna raised her hands and chanted. As she did, the unconscious man levitated from the seat. Following close behind, she moved him from the car, up the steps, and into the house where she lowered him on the sofa in the living room.

He never stirred.

Aiyanna settled a crocheted couch pillow beneath his head. Starr perched on the back of the couch and watched.

"What happened to him, Anya? I thought the guardians were indestructible?"

Aiyanna managed a choking laugh. "Sorta, kinda. It's a long story. I'll tell you about it later." She stood and glanced at the man before looking at Starr. "Keep an eye on him for me. I'm going to change and see what I can find about the guardians on the net."

"I thought you knew all about the prophecy. Isn't that what you teach at that school of yours?"

"I'm familiar with lots of cultural mythologies, but that doesn't mean I remember the intricate details of each and every one. I want to make sure I have the facts straight, not confused with another one."

"You? Confused? I don't believe it."

"I appreciate the vote of confidence, but I'll feel better if I read up."

Aiyanna stepped from the room and headed up the stairs. At the top of the first set of steps, she turned on the landing, marked by a large glass window before she climbed the remaining ones. When she reached the top, she turned to the right and walked down the long hallway, her room the last one on the left. She stepped inside and closed the door. Drawing a deep breath, she released it with deliberate slowness, allowing herself a few moments to relive the events of the evening.

What would happen next?

Her hand rose to her neck where her fingertips encountered the residue of teeth marks left by Cameron's bite. She rushed to the bureau mirror and turned her neck. Four tiny white pinpricks marred her skin. Strange, she never healed that fast before, even as a witch.

She gave herself a mental nudge to get her butt in gear. This wasn't the time to waste precious minutes worrying about a few little scars. She changed out of her hunting clothes and into a relaxing pair of navy blue jeans and a T-shirt that read, "I'm with…" on the front, and "no one" on the back. A favorite of hers, she'd bought it after Harris, well, after he split.

She grimaced at her pun and left the room.

At the bottom of the steps, she peeked into the living room where Starr held vigil over their still unconscious visitor.

In the den, opposite the living area, she flicked on the table lamp. She sat at the small desk, pushed the buttons of the computer, and waited for it to boot up.

Searching her memories, she tried to recall what

she knew of the guardians. Products of Luna, the Goddess of the Moon, granted these men immortality and supernatural strength. In turn, they protected humanity from the half-breed by-products of the succubus Deidra Sidhe and her Fomorian lover, Ághmach.

She turned her attention to the computer now fully booted. Opening her browser, she typed her favorite mythology site in the address bar and waited for the home page to display. She used this site in her teaching, and, over the years, it proved to be more accurate than most on the web. Mythology could be a touchy subject.

She clicked on the link, Celtic Mythology, and watched as numerous entries appeared. Aiyanna scanned through the list until her eyes fixed on one: the Otherworld.

A domain of Celtic deities or supernatural beings, the Otherworld remains hidden from mortal eyes by magic. Dagda is an important god in Irish mythology. Irish tales depict him as the supreme god, a figure of immense power. Regarded High King of the Tuatha Dé Danann, the supernatural beings who inhabited the Otherworld bowed to his calling.

Time slipped away as she read legacies surrounding the Tuatha Dé Danann, their battles, their enemies, Ághmach, Deidra and finished with the creation of the Síoraí Guardians.

She leaned back in the chair, cringing at the loud squeak that emulated from the springs—nothing that a little bit of oil wouldn't cure. Stretching back, she interlaced her fingers behind her head.

Glimpsing the time on the table clock, she groaned at the realization she'd been reading for more than an hour.

What an exciting tale.

She spun the chair around and peered across

the hallway into the living room where her guardian visitor rested.

So, the next question was...

Which guardian lay out cold on her couch?

Chapter Five

Cameron opened his eyes. He squinted at the bright light that intensified the white walls of a room.

He sat up in one fluid motion, planting his feet on the floor. Bad move. Sharp pain shot through his skull, and he slumped against the back of the couch. He grabbed his head and groaned, massaging his temples with his palms.

After a few moments, the pain subsided, and he took the opportunity to glance around, his eyes narrowed.

A high arched ceiling made the room appear huge. Two outward bowed windows adorned the wall on each side behind the couch, each one covered by dark, burgundy drapes.

"Thank the gods," he muttered.

The draperies were closed.

He emitted a quick breath of relief to note the lamp on the table that brightened the room. Sun and Síoraí were a lethal combination. In fact, if the sun grazed his flesh, he'd be one large crispy critter.

Cameron glanced at the wall clock. The hands pointed to eleven-fifteen. Studying the sliver of light that seeped in between the curtains, he gauged the time of day to be early morning.

Basic furnishing garnished the room, nothing fancy, a couch, table, and a couple of wicker backed rocking chairs. A television sat in the corner, and shelves filled with books lined one wall. On the opposite side of the room, large French doors led to a hallway. Cameron stared through the opening hoping to catch a glimpse of someone or something.

He passed a hand over his eyes.

Where the hell was he?

Flashbacks of the parking lot and a cat woman brought a wry, twisted smile to his face, and he pushed himself forward.

Aiyanna must have brought him here after Dagda's god bolt struck him in the shoulder.

His eyes rolled upward, and he muttered a curse under his breath at the god who Cameron knew, at this moment, sat on his proverbial throne laughing his ass off.

Centuries ago, when he'd been informed of his destiny as a Síoraí, the magical powers the gods granted empowered him. After a few decades of training, Dagda accused him of being too cocky for his own good. Cameron laughed at the god and boasted that with this power no one would beat him down again.

Him and his big fucking mouth.

No one challenged a deity, especially not Dagda, and so came the god's pledge. Every time Cameron landed on his ass, Dagda promised to collect a reward of his choosing.

Cameron grimaced. This made number two, the first time a hundred years ago during a sparring match with one of the other guardians. The eldest, Devlin, had knocked him down, and Dagda had taken that opportunity to show Cameron the prize he would receive for his imperfection.

Each time, Dagda's *reward*, a god bolt, hurled Cameron floundering like a fish out of water, on the edge of a deep hole, where he waited for the healing darkness to claim him.

Guardians usually didn't experience pain in its extreme, but the shock of a god bolt was another story. Pure electrical currents, combined with the heat of fire did have the ability to drop a person, namely him, to his knees.

"It's about time you woke your lazy butt up."

Cameron's heart skipped. His gaze shot around the room, searching for the owner of the female voice. He didn't recognize it as Aiyanna's soft, rich tone. Much too high pitched. His gaze landed on a silky, longhaired white cat that watched him from the seat of the wicker chair on the opposite side of the room.

He stiffened and shot an annoyed look at the animal.

He hated cats.

"What? You've never seen a cat before?"

Once again, Cameron gaze scrolled the room. Who the hell spoke?

"Hey, over here."

Cameron followed the sound of the voice, his eyes resting on the cat whose paw waved through the air. He blinked in surprise and shook his head. "It's me...over here...see me? The cat on the chair. Hello."

Cameron blinked again. When he opened his eyes, the cat's paw continued flapping. He shot to his feet. "Ye have got to be fucking kidding me. A talking cat?"

In the next moment, Aiyanna entered the room carrying a tray. She must have noticed the stunned expression on his face, for she laughed. "I see you've met Starr."

"Starr?"

Aiyanna set the tray on the table, indicating the cat with a nod of her head. "The cat."

"Are ye sure it isna a shape shifter in disguise?"

Starr hissed and raised one paw, claws bared, and struck at the air in a threatening gesture. "Watch it buster, or I'll shift your shape."

Aiyanna giggled and shook her head. "Starr,

behave. Stop threatening our guest." To Cameron, she smiled and reassured, "I'm sure. Starr is more than just a cat."

"And how's that?"

Aiyanna hesitated before answering. "She's family."

****

Warmth rushed into Aiyanna's cheeks at the confusion on his face. How much did she dare tell him about Starr and her life?

Trust didn't come easy to her. At one time, she believed the old adage that good could be found in everyone, but experience taught her a painful lesson. To this day, she carried the scars.

Erring on the side of caution, she commented, "Starr is a big part of my life." She held her breath waiting for his reaction.

He shrugged. "To each their own, but *why* a talking cat? I doona get that."

She laughed.

"Most people wouldn't. Can I get you some coffee or, perhaps, something to eat?"

Cameron shook his head. "No thanks," he replied, in a dazed voice.

She studied his face. "Can I get you anything?"

"I'm fine." A smile ruffled his mouth.

Aiyanna poured herself a cup of black coffee. She inched backward and slid into the wicker-backed rocking chair, pulling her feet up beneath her. Wrapping her hands around the warmth of the mug, she brought the cup to her nose where she closed her eyes and inhaled the nutty fragrance.

Taking a sip of coffee, she settled the cup on the saucer. Glass touched glass with a soft *clink*. Her eyes met his over the rim. "Tell me, which one are you?"

"Pardon me? Which what?"

"Which guardian are you?"

His smile vanished, wiped away by astonishment. She bit her lip to throttle a grin when his eyes widened in concern.

"I doona understand what ye're talking about, lass."

"You don't need to act so surprised. I know what you are, Cameron. I just don't know which one." She broke into a wide, open smile and shrugged. "I don't think it's a hard question. Is it?"

He stared at her for a moment and then burst out laughing. "How did ye uncover my secret?"

"I have my ways," she said, with a smile before nodding to his chest. "I recognized the *Mark of Luna*, which, by the way, stopped me from killing you after you bit me."

He flinched as if she'd struck him. His brows pinched in pain, and a faint tinge of pink shadowed his cheeks. Was he blushing? "Aye, well, I'm sorry about that."

"Hmm, you should be. So, tell me, which magical city do you come from? Falias, Findias, Murias or Gorias?"

"Ye have been busy, havena ye, lass?"

"I have to know who I bring to my home. A woman can't be too safe."

"Findias."

"Ah, I see, then Uiscias trained you, and you carry the *Fragarach*."

Cameron stood, and walked over to the bookshelf. He ran a long finger across the spines of the books. "Well, aye, I suppose. Look, I doona think I should be talking to ye about this. It could put ye in danger."

Aiyanna raised her hands in a sign of surrender. "Okay, I understand. I'll try not to pry, but just so you know, you can trust me."

"Thank you. That goes both ways."

Aiyanna nodded, but in truth, she could be

considered the foremost expert on being a nosey body. "If you can't tell me about your life as a guardian, perhaps you can tell me what you're doing in Arlington?"

He turned to face her, raising an eyebrow.

"Oh come on," she muttered.

"Orders," he answered, in a grudging voice, pushing his hands deep into his pocket.

"By the gods?"

"Aye," he muttered.

She laughed to cover her frustration at his one-word answers. His replies weren't as forthcoming as she would have liked.

"For?" she prompted.

"For a while." He hesitated, his mouth thinning with displeasure. "I thought ye said ye wouldna pry."

"I'm not. I would like to get to know you a little bit. Where have you been staying?"

"Wherever I can find a place. Hey, what is this? Fifty questions?" She detected a hint of censure in his tone, yet refused to back down.

"What? That's not enough for you?" She laughed at his brief look of annoyance. "What happened to you at the warehouse? What hit you?"

He rolled his eyes. "Fifty one...two..."

"Well?"

"Dagda's god bolt."

Aiyanna's brows furrowed, and she took another sip. "A god bolt, huh? They must not like you very much."

Cameron smiled. "They like me fine enough. That strike was justified. I earned it."

"No one deserves that. You were bleeding all over the place."

He chuckled, spreading his arms wide. "No harm done. As you can see, I'm all better."

"Then why?"

"A lesson for being knocked on my arse, that's

all." Cameron held up a hand. "Enough. I've already told ye more than I should have. Yer turn now." After a moment, he asked, "Why were ye fighting a bunch of demons?"

"Looking for information."

"Ye already told me that, but what ye dinna tell me is what information ye expect to gain from a vampire?"

Aiyanna sat forward in the chair, setting her cup and saucer on the tray. Standing, she straightened her shoulders, cleared her throat, and replied, "I'm going to bed. It's been a long night."

"So, I'm no' going to get my answers."

She wrinkled her nose and shook her head. "Not right now." She picked up the tray and headed for the door. Over her shoulder, she said, "If you need a place to stay, this is a big house. There are three extra bedrooms upstairs. Take the hall to the right. Help yourself to any one of them."

Before she rounded the corner into the kitchen, he called to her, "Aiyanna—"

She turned to face him. "Yes?"

"Thank you. I appreciate everything ye've done for me, especially the no' killing me part."

The glow of his smile warmed her across the room.

She managed a small, tentative smile and nodded. "You're welcome," she said, in a soft voice. "Rest well."

Reflected light glimmered over his handsome face, and she forced herself leave the room. As she stepped into the hall, she felt his eyes bore into her back, and resisted the urge to turn around.

This man was toxic to her senses, and she wasn't going there. Not now anyway.

Chapter Six

The wind raged and howled, whipping the forest outside her prison into a frenzy of bending, cracking, and groaning trees.

Cheyenne Grey closed her eyes, listening to the sounds of the intense storm. Her stomach churned with a mixture of anxiety, frustration and fear.

Wherever she was being detained, lights and heat must not have been included in the rent. She'd been provided a ragged cot and a thin wool blanket, not much comfort in her seven-by-seven cooler. She rubbed her arms in an attempt to re-circulate the blood through her veins. The cold seeped through the mortar and settled under her skin and into her bones.

A solid wooden door and one small window, about two-by-two, lined the room constructed of four concrete white walls. The window, clouded by dirt and grime, was too small for her escape.

Since her confinement, she'd attempted to connect on a spiritual level with Aiyanna, but with no luck. She hadn't found a way around the black magic that circled her.

For a moment, lost in her reverie, her conscious thoughts focused on Anya, her sister, her twin, and her best friend. What would her life have been like without her?

An empty shell to be sure.

Reality struck like a blast of bitter bile rising in her throat, and she hurtled back to the moment.

She glanced toward the corner of the stone

building where a large gray rat with bright beady eyes sat in the shadows. It reminded Cheyenne of the sewer rats she'd seen when she and Aiyanna lived in the orphanage in New York.

Careful! She mentally cautioned. Closing her eyes, she forced herself to collect her wistful thoughts of a reunion with her sister.

When she managed to calm her racing heart, she opened her eyes wide and focused an unblinking stare on the oversized mouse. Its whiskers twitched as though taunting her, daring her to free her mind. She had no idea when the flea-ridden animal appeared in her cell, but it had been her companion for the past two days.

Red eyes watched her.

"I see you," she whispered, and then tossed a piece of chipped concrete at it.

The granite struck two inches in front of its long snout, but the rodent never budged.

Malevolence radiated from the rat. Her body tingled with unease, prickling a path from the top of her head to the tip of her toes. The animal, a shape shifter, had the ability to change its physical shape, which might explain how it arrived in the room. By transforming into a beetle or a fly, it could easily slip under the door or through a crack in the walls. Maintaining that size was impossible due to the size of its internal organs and the amount of body space required for survival. Why it chose a rat's body was anyone's guess.

Cheyenne shuddered. Nasty, filthy creatures, gross!

This creature boasted the talent of delving into a person's mind and had the ability of gathering information from their thoughts. Chills raced up her spine.

Out of spite, she turned her thoughts to Starr, the sisters' familiar. Over the years, the feline became much more than their teacher and protector. She was family. A loud squeak emulated from the rat as if it pictured the large Himalayan cat.

Cheyenne smiled at its reaction. As much as she hated these vermin, she wouldn't let anyone or anything intimidate her.

She'd show them.

She rose from the cot, whispering a chant to freeze the animal where it sat. In silence, she waited to see if the spell had any effect.

When it didn't shift, she took all of three steps in the small room. She reached the corner where the rat sat, bent down, and stretched out her hand as if to pet the creature. It didn't move when her fingers closed around the scuff of its neck.

With the animal in her grasp, she stopped reciting. Within seconds, the rat released a high-pitched cry. Its legs thrashed around, claws bared.

Cheyenne held her hand away from her body and chanted another spell. This one intended to keep the animal from shifting into its natural body. She didn't look at it. Keeping her expression unreadable, she stared at the door and whoever, or whatever, waited on the other side.

"Do you think I'm a fool? I can sense whatever you send my way and will crush all of you like this."

The rat squealed again and struggled in incensed fury. Its body whipped around with supernatural strength and agility.

She gasped when razor sharp talons connected with the tender flesh on the inside of her wrist. She refused to release her grip. Burning pain raced down her arms into her fingertips. A quick glance at the injury confirmed her suspicions. A river of blood spilled from the jagged tear, but that didn't matter.

Proving her point did.

She raised her other hand until it surrounded the rat's neck. Triumph rose in her. She squeezed until the creature grew limp in her grasp. Although it stopped struggling, fury blazed in its eyes.

Cheyenne twisted her hands around its neck until the bones snapped beneath the force.

She opened her hands and released the shape shifter. It dropped with a solid *thud* to the cement floor.

With a self-satisfied smirk, she brushed her hands together in nonchalance. "Just like taking out the trash," she murmured. Grimacing, she brushed her hand up and down her pants as if the motion would wash away the vulgarity of the act.

She glimpsed toward the door, keeping her features composed. "Do you want some of that? Bring it on, and I'll be happy to oblige."

When no one responded, she gritted her teeth, full of ruthless determination.

"Go to hell!"

Chapter Seven

Aiyanna wrapped her hands around a steaming mug of coffee and raised it to her nose. She inhaled, taking pleasure in the rich hazelnut fragrance that flooded her senses. Taking a sip, she welcomed the heat that coated her mouth and throat.

She glanced out the porch window.

An extraordinary scarlet cloud raged across the moon's pale face, and the sky turned a pastel crimson as if tinged by blood.

Aiyanna frowned at her tired reflection in the glass. Dark circles lined the skin beneath her eyes. She drew a deep breath, smothered by a strange, unwelcoming fear. According to the Wiccan almanac, the change in the moon's color could mean one of two things: signs of iniquity and offered as a warning to predict the arrival of evil *or* indications of the upcoming reaping of reward offered by the Harvest Moon.

Aiyanna discarded the idea of the latter. This couldn't be considered a blessing.

Deidra Sidhe represented a powerful force, more so than her greatest adversary, the Black Witch, and much of what Aiyanna believed was now questionable against this new threat.

She sighed and rubbed the back of her neck with a free hand, overcome with helplessness. Without Cameron's presence, she didn't think she would be able to face this danger.

Her mouth curved in an unconscious smile when she thought of the man who'd moved into her home.

Cameron MacLean, Síoraí Guardian, sexy man, proud and untouchable, had settled in well. Most evenings he'd greet her at the door when she got home from the university, but as soon as it grew dark outside, he'd make a quick exit.

Last night, she planned to go with him, but he refused to let her tag along.

She blew out a breath and glanced toward the maple trees that lined the property. Their multi-colored leaves danced to the tune of the soft breeze that filtered through the air.

Starr, where are you? If close, her familiar would sense her thoughts and come home. She brushed an agitated hand through her hair and shuddered. If something roamed amongst the trees, she wanted the cat home.

An uneasy feeling flowed through her, and her stomach twisted into a knot when Starr didn't respond. Aiyanna stepped into the drive and attempted to call out again. No answer.

Aiyanna marched from the yard, around the fence, and into the woods. That's when she picked up the faint sounds of a scuffle. The noises traveled closer to the house. Hissing and screeching followed by a pathetic mewl. An animal fought for its life somewhere in the wooded area.

Starr! It had to be her.

Aiyanna dropped her mug to the muddy ground, paying no attention to the splashes of hot liquid on her ankles. She dashed into the thicket of trees. She tore through the brush, shoving low-hanging branches from her path. At the top of a small knoll, she hesitated, her gaze searching. A twisty path led to the right, but instinct sent her along the ridge of the hill to the left.

Panic raged through her. She gasped. With each ragged breath, her chest heaved and burned. Waves of nausea threatened to erupt in a stream of vomit.

61

Her muscles tightened until they were about to burst, and her legs grew heavy. She couldn't lose Starr too.

Move! She urged her legs to go and forced herself to breathe, encouraging her feet to take a step and then another.

One last high-piercing wail echoed through the trees before all grew silent. No animal or bugs whispered their familiar lullaby.

Even the butterfly-sized Forest Fairies who twittered amongst the leaves hid from sight, maintaining the quiet stillness of the night.

Where were they?

How minuscule the Fairies were in size, yet their impact on Aiyanna's life enormous with their innocence. Some had laughing faces, others impish grins, and, once in a while, she'd run across one with a sour temperament, but they all came upon rays of sunlight or moonbeams to cheer her forlorn heart.

They added warmth to her life. Starr once told her that every creature existed for a reason. The Fairies' world remained serene and quiet because for them, the outside world of anguish and hatred ceased to be.

Had evil destroyed them?

An urgent need to find Starr and get home flooded over her. She closed her eyes and kept them shut. The forest spun. Beneath her feet, the ground writhed and swayed like the deck of a ship ravaged by storm.

Aiyanna muttered another summons for the cat and then prayed she would answer. Her eyes shot open at a soft brush against her pant leg. She glanced down to find Starr whirling in a frenzied circle. The feline rubbed against Aiyanna's legs, the fur at the back of her neck raised, fangs and claws revealed. Starr may have been weak, but she was pissed. She glared at the shadows of the trees behind her.

"Starr!" Aiyanna bent and picked Starr up. Curled in her arms, the cat trembled and cried like a lost kitten.

Aiyanna caressed Starr's neck and murmured reassuring words. Beneath her fingertips, a sticky wet substance coated the cat's fur. She pulled her hand away and held it up in front of her eyes. A dark red liquid dripped from her fingertips. Her heart dropped to the pit of her stomach, and she ran her hand with tender care over the cat. Deep cuts and lacerations covered the feline. She had to stop the bleeding, needed to get Starr warm before her familiar hemorrhaged or succumbed to shock.

Until that happened, she needed to keep the cat talking. "What happened, Starr?"

"Witch...powerful..."

"Where?"

"In the air, grass, trees, she is everywhere. I have never sensed such power before." The cat's voice grew weaker.

"More than a witch wanders these trees, Starr. We need to get home."

She swallowed hard, fighting back another wave of nausea when a pained cry escaped Starr. "Stay with me, Starr," she begged.

Shock yielded quickly to fury, and Aiyanna's lips thinned with anger. She held Starr cradled in her arms while the wind whined around her. The trees swayed against an unseen breeze.

Aiyanna's eyes narrowed, and she peered into the darkness. An insipid luminescence vapor drifted through the foliage toward them. She recited a strong spell of protection, praying it veiled them from whatever walked within the mist.

Her hopes crashed when the haze disappeared and reappeared less than ten feet in front of them. The tall figure of a woman with long black hair and a billowing black gown emerged, surrounded by a mystic glow that shimmered in the moonlight.

Aiyanna tightened her hold on Starr then eased up when the cat squealed in protest.

The bitter scent of death burned her nose.

The woman smiled. Two-inch fangs seeped from the corner of her mouth. She brought a hand up to brush her hair from her face. Blood coated long fingernails...Starr's blood.

Aiyanna watched the woman, sending her a scathing look. Correction, not woman, but vampire, and that thing blocked their passage back to the house.

When the creature's arms reached for her, Aiyanna backed away. Twigs snapped under her feet. Keeping her gaze fixed on the vampire, she took cautious steps back until her butt came to rest against a solid object, and she could go no further. She side-stepped the tree and crept backward.

Inundated by pulsations of pure evil that radiated from the apparition, a shiver of fear soared up Aiyanna's spine, the malevolence so tangible, she gasped. The power smothered her, sucking the breath from her lungs. Everything she'd read about Deidra rushed back to her. She held a great power, the murderess of babies and children...a great Vampryss, the first evil.

"So, we finally meet, Deidra Sidhe."

A brief glimmer of a smile crossed Deidra's ashen face. Her eyes flashed ruby red, and she nodded. "I see you've heard of me?"

"Indeed, I have."

With a satisfied smirk, Deidra nodded. "Then let us forget the formalities."

"That works for me. So, why don't you tell me where my sister is?"

"Tsk! Tsk!" The figure wavered in and out of reality.

"If you're not going to tell me, then get the hell out of my way!"

Deidra eyes brightened, as if pleased by Aiyanna's apparent show of bravery. Her lips curved. Aiyanna cringed at the sight of her fangs. "Why are you so anxious to be rid of me? We can help each other, you and I."

"I will *never* help you," Aiyanna declared. She held her head high and faced the apparition with fiery eyes. Her breath froze in the air before her.

"You will if you ever hope to see your sister again."

Aiyanna swallowed. A chill whispered over her skin, and she recoiled back another step.

Deidra grinned at the action. She brought up a vaporous hand to sweep black translucent hair from her face. Bottomless black holes glittered at Aiyanna from the faded figure of the woman.

"Help me, Aiyanna. Help me to free my beloved. I need your powers."

Aiyanna didn't comment aloud, but her mind shouted, *Like hell I will.*

As if she heard, the wraith solidified for one second. Her face emerged almost human in the moonlight, her countenance beautiful, eyes haunted. Long hair flowed to her waist blending with the long black silk gown.

Too weak to sustain her connection with Aiyanna on this spiritual plane, Deidra's visage faded only to reappear a moment later.

Starr grew motionless in her arms. Aiyanna's nerves tensed at the realization the animal needed immediate medical attention. Aiyanna made an effort to walk around the Vampryss, but Deidra maintained an easy pace beside her.

"I will not help you, Deidra," Aiyanna said, freezing to a standstill. Her teeth clenched, and she glanced at the Vampryss from the corner of her eye.

"I know what you are. How can you possibly think I'll help you after what you've done to my cat?"

The woman chuckled, the sound cruel and mocking. Her shoulders moved up in a lazy shrug, and her beauty melted to a hideousness that did not belong in this world.

Deidra's expression turned hard and resentful. "It is only a cat."

"She is more than a cat, as well you know."

"A familiar." She spat the words out as if the very utterance burned her tongue. "And by the looks of it, a weak one. I can conjure you up a legion of loyal, *strong*, servants, if that is your wish."

Deidra's ravaged face gazed at her in the pulsating light, wispy and inhuman. Blackened tree shadows danced behind her, framing her half-formed image.

"Monsters?" Aiyanna hissed. "You offer me servants that belong in hell. No thank you. I'll pass." Tired of playing games, Aiyanna seethed with mounting rage, her tone heavy with sarcasm. "What I want is for you to go away and leave me alone!"

"Look." Deidra pointed to an area between two tall pine trees.

Aiyanna turned and looked. Her heart thumped a gallop against her breast, and she choked back a cry, frightened, electrified.

Cheyenne stood along the hedgerow of the trees. Aiyanna almost gave into the urge to run to her before she realized the vision wasn't her sister. The pungent smell of body odor and wet dog identified the figure as shifter.

How dare they insult her with tricks?

Anger singed the corners of her control. She faced Deidra. "That is not my sister," she replied in a low voice, taut with anger.

One arm held an unconscious Starr, but she raised her other hand toward the creature and whispered the words of a relinquishing spell to send it away.

When she'd finished, she ordered, "Go back to hell where you belong!"

The shifter screamed and covered its face with its hands. Its form shifted and dissipated until a chalky sketch of only its body remained. Mere seconds later, the outline burst into flames. Red sparks sputtered into the air, disappearing until darkness remained.

Aiyanna swung around to face the witch who'd thought to trick her. "Where is my sister? Where is Cheyenne?"

Deidra smiled another wicked, evil smile. "Do you wish to go to her?"

"What I wish is for you to release her."

"That, I cannot do."

"Then you can join your friend over there, and go back to hell where you belong, I command it."

"Stupid witch! My powers grow stronger each day that passes. I can force you to obey me, by hurting those you care about." She nodded to Starr. "Like your cat. What would you do if I killed your sister?"

"You won't."

An eyebrow shot up in surprise at her assertion. "What makes you so certain?"

"If you kill Cheyenne, you won't be able to secure enough power to free Aghmach from the underworld." Aiyanna smiled at the deep frown that lined Deidra's forehead. "Admit it. You need both of us to achieve that."

"You will not be able to stop me," Deidra stated.

Pissed, Aiyanna's fury burned like boiling oil under her skin. She held her head high; eyes fixed on Deidra, and chanted one of the most potent spells she knew to subjugate evil spirits.

At first, it didn't appear as if the spell worked.

Deidra's apparition never wavered. In fact, her image solidified, drawing from Aiyanna's power.

After a few moments, Aiyanna's strength waned. Her voice shook and muscles ached with weariness. At the end of the incantation, Deidra laughed, standing tall and true before her.

Aiyanna held her breath and began again. Her legs buckled beneath her, and she fell to her knees.

Suddenly, from behind Aiyanna, a man's voice joined in the recantation. Aiyanna didn't take time to analyze the man's voice, nor did she care, grateful for the assistance.

An earsplitting screech resounded from Deidra's open mouth. Aiyanna grimaced at the bone-jarring echo but didn't break her chant. The Vampryss' image wavered, and Aiyanna drew on her inner strength to expound the tenor of her voice. The hideous face melted like wax on a candle, the eyes once again empty holes, and the figure turned to white bones. For a second, the skeleton faded in and out before crumpling into dust. The powder evaporated into nothingness.

Aiyanna collapsed, keeping her arms wrapped in a protective hold around Starr, weakened by the power of Deidra's resistance.

She lay on the ground for a couple of seconds gasping for breath. Strong arms surrounded her, and she glanced up into Cameron's handsome face.

His eyes sparkled with golden warmth. A tender smile lit up his face, and he helped her to her feet. "Ye're a strong witch." There was a slight tinge of wonder in his voice.

"Not strong enough. She'll be back." Aiyanna shook with exhaustion.

She leaned against him while he escorted her through the trees. It took almost an hour for them to reach the house. She hadn't realized she'd traveled so far in her search for Starr. As they traveled,

Aiyanna murmured a spell that would shield their location from evil.

Once inside the kitchen, Aiyanna reached out and shoved the door shut with her foot. She recited another spell to strengthen the invisibility protection spell already in place. She walked to the bistro table in the center of the room. With tender care, she lay Starr down. Exhausted, she caressed the top of Starr's head with gentle sweeps of her hand.

The sound of splintering glass echoed behind her. Startled, she jumped and spun around searching for the source. Her nerves tensed. With each crack, spider vein fractures marred the glass in the windows that lined the wall above the sink.

"Watch out!" Cameron shouted, at the same moment the glass imploded. He lunged toward her.

With a frightened cry, she flung her body over Starr, shielding the already injured animal. Flying shards of glass slashed through her clothing, tearing her skin. Cameron covered her body with his, protecting her, but the airborne glass left tiny cuts along her arms and shoulders.

Then silence.

Deidra's laughter rang out from the trees behind the house. The spell that Aiyanna placed around the house kept the Vampryss outside, but that didn't stop her from stirring up a bit of chaos.

"Are ye okay, lass?" Cameron asked coming up behind her.

Goose bumps materialized on her legs at the concern in his voice, and she trembled.

The cuts on her arms stung, but she nodded, gazing blurry-eyed at the shattered glass and wood littering the floor. "I'm fine. The bitch couldn't let me win this round, could she?" she asked, her gaze taking in the glass on the floor. "What a disaster," she whispered, shaking her head in exhaustion.

Cameron pressed a tender kiss on her forehead.

"Take care of Starr. I'll take care of this mess."

"I couldn't ask that of you. I'll tend to Starr and then clean up."

Cameron inclined his head toward the cat. "Go! She needs ye, and ye need to rest. Now, where's yer broom?"

"Are you sure?" At his nod, she whispered, "Thank you." With a tilt of her head, she indicated the door on the opposite side of the room. "In the pantry."

He walked across the room, opened the door and disappeared inside. A moment later, he reappeared, holding a broom and dustpan, one in each hand. He held them up in triumph. "My weapons of choice," he said, with a grin.

In spite of herself, she chuckled, shaking her head.

Aiyanna turned to the table where Starr lay. Shaky and dazed, she patted the cat's head. "You're a bloody mess. Worse than I am."

Starr opened her eyes and mewed pitifully, laying a trusting, bloody paw on her arm.

Behind her, the soft sweep of the bristled broom across the linoleum swished around the room, and she smiled. Cameron was hard at work.

Wiping tired tears from her face, Aiyanna stared at Starr's wounds before grabbing the lemon healing balm from the cabinet. She applied a liberal amount of ointment to the cuts, and then covered them with bandages.

She whispered a curative spell over the cat, so she would sleep and begin the healing process. She'd done her best and prayed it proved to be enough. After she took care of the cat, she cleaned up her own wounds and applied a bit of the salve to them. About to ask Cameron if he needed fixing up, she stopped at the sudden memory of the alleyway and his magical healing powers.

Instead, she turned to face him. "Thank you. I'm not sure how you came to be out there." She shook her head. "I guess it doesn't matter, but I owe you a debt of gratitude."

He stopped sweeping and glanced up. "Are ye sure ye're going to be all right, lass?" he asked, obvious concern in his voice. Leaning on the broom handle, his gaze, sharp and assessing, moved over her as if examining her himself.

She blinked, focusing her gaze on his face. "Yeah, I'm just exhausted."

"Before ye go, lass, I think it best if ye no' venture outside anymore. I doona know how she...they found ye, but if they discover the strength of yer witching powers—" He left the sentence hanging.

Aiyanna's lips curved how fast he changed direction from "*she*" to "*they*". It was obvious he didn't want her to know that Deidra lay behind the madness that ravaged her life. She'd let him keep his secret for now. "I'm afraid they are already aware of my capabilities."

He crossed the two feet between them in less than thirty seconds. He placed his hands on her shoulders in a gentle, yet possessive gesture. His golden eyes flashed, and his nose flared. "What? How in bloody fucking hell did they find out?"

She shook her head. "It doesn't matter, Cameron. Look, can we talk about this another time? I need to rest."

"But—"

"Another time. Good night," she insisted.

He must have recognized the desperation in her tone, for he nodded and replied, "Goodnight, then."

She cradled Starr against her and carried her up the stairs into her bedroom where she laid the cat on the bed. With her last bit of strength, Aiyanna wove a final enchantment spell to mend the broken windows downstairs.

She climbed into bed and tucked the cat into the crook of her arm. After burrowing into the warmth of her covers, Aiyanna eased into an unsettled sleep.

Chapter Eight

His long legs carried him up the steps two at a time. When he reached the landing that separated the set of stairs between the two floors, Cameron stopped and glimpsed out the bay window.

Set against a backdrop of sinister darkness, the sky mirrored a collage of red and black colors. A dense fog floated across the horizon. In his experience, these signs didn't bode well for the future, whether that meant mere hours or days. The malevolence surrounding this place spilled over him, twisting his gut into a knot.

His fear for Aiyanna's safety swelled. He hadn't realized how special she was until tonight. A black shiver ripped through him at the terrifying realization of how close he came to losing her.

Thank the gods he hadn't left to go hunting.

Given another ten minutes, he would have been gone. He'd been packing up his hunting gear when a strong awareness of evil slammed him between the shoulder blades. The bitter sensation engulfed the room and saturated the air. It seeped into his bones and ripped the breath from his lungs.

His instinct revved into overdrive, and immediate concern for Aiyanna filled him with urgency. He performed a hasty search of the house, banging doors open for a quick peek inside before he moved on. Each room, dark and empty, propelled his blood racing through his veins like a volcano on the verge of erupting.

In the kitchen, the back door swung open. He

rushed through the porch and outside. When he stepped onto the pavement of the drive, Aiyanna's fear reached out and struck him like a slap across his face.

Sixth sense led him racing through the forest until he located her. His stomach clenched at the sight of Aiyanna and Deidra Sidhe standing within five feet of each other.

By the gods!

He glanced toward Aiyanna just as she fell to her knees clutching Starr in her arms.

Eyes closed, her brows furrowed in concentration. Her lips moved, and he listened to her words. He recognized the ancient spell. His heart pounded, jolted by the realization that she attempted to battle the Vampryss alone.

As a guardian, he'd learned Deidra's apparition contained enough power to wipe out small communities. Here, in this dark isolation, Aiyanna held her ground against the powerful woman without even knowing what that bitch was capable of doing.

Deidra weakened under the potency of the spell, but it took its toll on the wee lass. Aiyanna's voice wavered, her shoulders drooped and her body shook with visible exhaustion.

He admired her courage and perseverance.

When he united his voice with hers, the electrifying surge of power that coursed through him sent ripples up his spine.

A star broke through the colors of the night sky drawing him back to the present. He exhaled. The night turned out to be informative to say the least. First, his discovery of the true strength and nature of Aiyanna's powers, followed by his own recognition of the intense protectiveness he carried for the lass left him reeling with fearful clarity and his heart thumping with a feeling he thought long dead.

When the windows exploded, his heart nearly hammered a hole out his chest at the thought she might get injured. He'd rushed across the room and protected her body with his.

After he sent her to bed, he decided to forego hunting for the night. He set about sweeping the floor but never had the opportunity to finish the job. The glass fragments shot into the air where they hovered, literally suspended in air. After a brief moment, the tiny shards shot outward locating their respective window where they merged and mended in their frames as though they'd never been broken.

Aye, even in her exhausted state, Aiyanna cleaned up the mess.

Cameron walked up the final set of steps and hesitated. Instead of taking the hall to the right, he turned left. He needed to check on her and make sure she rested.

Outside the room he assumed to be Aiyanna's, he pressed his ear to the door. He heard nothing inside. No movement, no stirring, and he concluded she'd fallen asleep.

He turned the knob and pushed the door open a crack to peek inside. Aiyanna lay on a full sized bed, the cat tucked close against her side. The deep rise and fall of her chest signified a sound sleep.

He closed the door with a soft click. She needed to rest and recoup her strength. And yet, Cameron found himself thinking of another need, his own need for the beautiful Cherokee woman who lay asleep on the other side of the door.

****

A hushed quiet descended over the grounds. Even the night animals didn't disturb the total, utter silence.

Henry Mason ambled through the cemetery. The light from his flashlight swept over the headstones. As a security guard at this place for thirty years, every night was always the same, dark and uneventful.

Tonight was different. Hard-pressed to explain why, something brought an ache to his ole bones. He snorted. Age probably played a role.

A shiver raced up his spine when the air around him plummeted to frigid temperatures, his breath a cloud of white mist. He shook his head in confusion. Odd weather for this time of year.

A tug at his pant leg sent his attention to the ground.

Panic rioted inside him.

He lowered the flashlight to his feet.

Nothing.

"What the blazes?" His question met a chilly black silence.

With the snap of a twig nearby, Henry whipped the light up and shined it into the trees. "Who's there?" he called out. His gaze followed the beam; his eyes squinted.

No answer.

Kids and their practical jokes. He grumbled at the notion.

The tug turned into a hard jerk, and once again, he glanced down.

"That's it. I'm out of here," the groundskeeper declared. Whether joke or not, the situation was too spooky for his tastes.

A cry rent the air, a howl, both human and bestial, unlike any sound he'd ever heard before.

He turned to leave the area, his movements stiff and awkward. He staggered through the maze of headstones, and when he reached the line of trees, he exhaled the breath he held. The guard post lay twenty yards ahead.

Just as he stepped onto the pavement of the sidewalk, a monstrous, furry, hundred and fifty pound animal jumped from the tree above him. It landed with a thud in his path.

Henry's heart palpated against his breastbone, and he stumbled five steps backward. In a voice rough with anxiety, he shouted, "What the hell?"

He stared into slanted scarlet eyes. The beast grunted, releasing a puff of air into Henry's face. He recoiled from the fetid odor of dead flesh that burned his nose and made his stomach roll. A quick assessment of the creature ruled out his first conclusion. Although covered with thick, rancid, black fur, no dog walked on its hind legs.

The creature curled its top lip, revealing two-inch incisors.

Henry faltered back another step, his eyes wide. His hands rose up to shield his face. "No!"

The beast trailed, enfolded Henry in its powerful arms, and squeezed the breath from his feeble body. Panic gripped him, and he kicked out a foot connecting with the animal's shin. It growled and fastened its claws into the tender flesh of his back. Henry groaned at the stinging pain. Drawing him closer, the creature opened its jaws, ready to clamp down on his head.

Adrenalin-enhanced fear rushed over him, and Henry whipped his head sideways. A shredding sound filled the air. Pain shot through his head stealing his breath. A wave of nausea coiled in the pit of his stomach.

The animal stepped away, releasing him.

Henry dropped to the ground, holding his head. He gagged in reflex at the sight of his ear dangling from the corner of the creature's mouth.

Ruby eyes flashed burgundy. It spit the wrinkled piece of skin and cartilage into the air. Holding out a furry paw, complete with one-and-a-half-inch claws, it caught the torn appendage. Its gaze fixed on Henry's face when it popped the piece of meat between its lips, chewing and chomping with boisterous pleasure. Henry gagged at the blood cascading down its chin.

"No!" Henry howled. Blood flowed down his neck and soaked the collar of his jacket.

The creature smiled.

Henry cringed at the pieces of flesh, his flesh, dangling from between its teeth. Weak from loss of blood, he maintained eye contact on the animal. Warm liquid seeped through his fingers and poured down his arm.

A bone-chilling chuckle echoed behind him, and he glanced toward the darkness.

"I don't know who's there, but if this is your...your...animal, you're going to pay for what it's done to me," he said, struggling to stand.

No sooner had he regained his balance when his legs were wrenched out from beneath him. His hip smashed against a nearby headstone, and the sound of bones cracking rent the air, accompanied by his shriek of agony.

Despite the pain, Henry rolled onto his stomach. Something or someone dragged him into the recesses of a nearby catacomb. His fingers dug into the dirt. He groaned when one of his fingernails caught a rock and split.

"No," he gasped, panting in terror.

He clawed at the ground attempting to stop. His hip throbbed and fingers burned, but he twisted one leg free and turned on his side to see what held him. His ankle hovered a good foot off the ground, but his eyes met darkness. He kicked out. The sole of his shoe connected with a solid, yet invisible object.

"Dear Lord," he cried.

The heavy concrete doors of a burial chamber opened, and something yanked him inside.

Henry screamed as he shot like a cannonball across the concrete floor. He hit the wall with a resounding *thud*. Stunned by the impact, he lay motionless.

After a moment, he lifted his chin and glimpsed glowing red eyes less than two feet in front of him. They gleamed redder and brighter. Suddenly, the candles on the wall scones flared with fire. Light swamped the crypt.

A beautiful woman stood before him. Her long black hair hung to a slender, well-proportioned waist.

When she smiled, Henry gasped. A long, pointed tongue came out to caress full ruby lips. He opened his mouth to scream, but the shout died in his throat when she pulled him up from the ground and against her body. Fangs exposed, she lowered her head.

An excruciating pain flared in his neck. A warm stickiness bubbled against the chilled air and coated his skin. He swayed, and would have fallen if not for her arms around his waist.

He opened his mouth to beg, but only a gurgle escaped. When he lowered his eyes, he saw blood, his blood. Gallons of it coated his shoes and splattered the concrete slab. His body weakened, growing limp. And then, relaxing warmth seared through his cold body.

He no longer hurt and gave into blessed oblivion.

Chapter Nine

Sizzling heat scorched the surface of Aiyanna's body. Fire surged through her veins until her blood boiled and threatened to erupt in a stream of blistering lava.

Her heart hammered an erratic tempo.

A warm body lay beside her; its presence stirred sensations she thought buried a long time ago.

But who?

And then the answer came on a soft whisper. "Aiyanna."

Cameron's breath brushed her ear. Sexual electricity fashioned goose bumps that tingled up her spine.

He leaned away, but stared into her eyes, his face inches from hers.

By the moonlight that filtered through the window, Aiyanna saw a smoldering flame in his eyes. The heat of his body coursed over her, beginning at her toes and spreading to the tip of her head where her scalp prickled in response. His essence, the sheer magnitude of his virility seared across her skin.

Cameron's mouth caressed the flesh beneath her chin, his lips hot against her skin.

He cradled her head in one hand, and his thumb traced her jaw. His touch light, butterfly strokes skimmed her flesh.

She turned her head, parted her lips and met him. His mouth covered hers, taking her with savage intensity.

Her eyes snapped open when he shifted, moving

away. She reached for him, clutched his shoulders and pulled him back to her.

He returned to her. He drew her bottom lip into his mouth, suckled for a moment before his mouth trailed the length of her neck to the sensitive skin beneath her ear. One hand sunk in her hair. His other cupped her breast. Beneath her bra, her nipple puckered in response.

He moved away again. This time, his hands gripped her wrists. With a gentle tug, he pulled her arms up, pinning them above her head. He loomed over her, eyes gleaming ominous gold. He held her wrists in one hand while his other explored her body with slow, sensuous strokes. One finger began a slow descent from her cheek, down her neck, across the perky nipple of her breast, and over her stomach where he traced a tender path on her inner thigh.

Her back arched at his touch, begging him to delve further into her nether region.

In the darkness, the only thing that mattered was her body's response to the man whose hands petted and tickled, teased and aroused her.

His mouth moved across her cheek. Her lips burned in the aftermath of his fiery possession.

And then, his hands moved away, her body driven against the mattress by the welcome weight of his body. The power of his desire rolled over her, captivating her. So intense, his passion mesmerized her, his closeness like a drug that lulled her to euphoria.

"No!" a voice shrieked.

Aiyanna jerked at the razor-sharp reprimand. Cameron was ripped from her arms, and an icy burst of air cascaded over her like a bucket of cold water.

Aiyanna's eyes flashed open, and she jolted upward.

She blinked in surprise at the realization she was in her room, in her bed, cold and alone.

Victoria Noxon

And yet, Cameron's scent of sandalwood and musk lingered in the air and on her flesh.

"What the hell is going on around here?"

****

Cameron's eyes shot open, and he sat upright in bed, the air around him electrified.

Explosive currents of desire raced through him. His heart thumped in rapid threads against his chest and throbbed in his ears. Images of their entwined bodies flooded him. He recalled the smoldering passion that raged between them. Even now, the desire on her face haunted him. The expression of want, need, and, finally, the acceptance in her eyes, fired his blood.

Sprawled naked on the bed, he sat up, resting his head against the headboard. He stared up at the rich, dark wood of the bedroom's ceiling, his mind afire with a thousand thoughts that made sleep impossible. Here, in Aiyanna's house, he had a room and a comfortable bed, but what he ached for the most was to be inside her.

Bewildered, Cameron hesitated. A chill ran up his spine at the terrifying realization that he had been in her bed and in her arms. He grimaced...virtual reality in another realm, but it would have sealed the deal on this plane. They would have consummated their union if not for the unseen energy that tore them apart.

The ear-splitting shriek came from a different place, outside Aiyanna's bedroom. It stretched across space with enough power to rip them apart. Whoever it was didn't want him to fuse their union. The evil had vanished, but the residual malevolent vibrations dampened the atmosphere.

The episode was more than a mere mirage. Even now, Aiyanna's scent lingered on his skin. He closed his eyes and inhaled the soft jasmine fragrance that belonged to her.

The question barely crossed his mind before the answer followed. His eyes shot open. The bond! His connection with Aiyanna.

Bloody Hell!

He bit her. The moment his teeth pierced her flesh, they united as one. Their worlds were intertwined, and she was as much a part of his life as he was of hers.

And then another thought blind-sided him, and he drew a quick sharp breath. Optimism cascaded over him. His body pulsed with new life.

Could it work?

Was it possible?

Why not?

It wouldn't be the first time a guardian got involved, fell in love, and married a mortal.

A year past, the Vampryss escaped her prison in Michigan. Of course, the guardians fought her, but if it hadn't have been for one wee spiritualist, they probably would have lost. Elizabeth Forrester, spiritualist turned Princess of the Light, now Elizabeth O'Callaghan, wife to the second eldest guardian, Fallon saved their asses.

It's funny to think of them now. For centuries, the gods considered destroying Fallon. With a history of recklessness and contempt for the gods' edicts, Fallon boasted a reputation as the *rebel guardian*. But then he met Lizzie and changed.

He fought hard against the union he created with her, but in the end, Fallon accepted love again. He became a different man who lived up to the expectations of the Síoraí Legacy.

Fallon and Liz got married. The elder embraced his destiny and accepted his place in the circle.

No longer condemned to walk at night, Fallon retained his guardian powers, ate regular food, and even fathered a child. The last Cameron heard of the couple, Lizzie expected their first child in a few months.

Aiyanna, a powerful white witch, and himself, a guardian...now wouldn't that make a potent combination?

Cameron's body tingled with exhilaration. Aye, they would, a voice whispered in his head. He fought but failed to control swirling emotions of excitement, anticipation, and apprehension.

He stiffened at the unexpected vulnerability that ripped through him. Only one woman touched his soul, spurred his emotions the way Aiyanna did, but that woman was dead because of him.

Full of evil and danger, his world was no place for Aiyanna. And if he failed her like he failed Sarah, he would never forgive himself.

He pushed himself to the edge of the bed and swung his legs over. Reaching for his cell phone on the bedside table, he punched the auto dial button that would ring Fallon's number.

He needed advice.

"Hello," a sleepy voice answered after the fifth ring.

"Hey, Lizzie, is Fallon there?"

"Cameron, is that you?"

"Aye, 'tis me. I'm sorry to be bothering ye so late, but I really need to speak to Fallon."

"What the bloody hell do ye think ye're doing calling at two o'clock in the morning?" Fallon's angry voice blared through the earpiece.

Cameron winced and held the phone away from his ear.

His jaw tensed in deep frustration. He needed answers, and he needed them now. "How do ye release a mate from a blood bond?" he asked, in a tight voice.

Silence.

"Fallon? Are ye there?"

"I'm here." The anger had drained from Fallon's

tone, and Cameron heard the other man's deep exhale through the phone. "If ye're asking, I'm thinking ye've chosen."

"Aye."

"Is she a strong woman?"

Cameron heaved a sigh. "She's a verra powerful witch."

A low satisfied grunt echoed in his ear. "Then ye have chosen well."

"Fallon, what if I doona want a mate?"

Fallon chuckled. "Ye doona have a choice. Ye've made yer selection."

"No' yet. No' in that way."

Fallon released a long, audible breath. "Give it time, lad. Ye wilna be able to avoid the attraction."

"Tell me how to release her?"

"Ye canna," Fallon replied, with quiet emphasis.

"There has to be a way," Cameron insisted.

"There isna, Cameron. Trust me. I've been in yer shoes. I tried everything to sever the tie. The only way to break a Síoraí bond is for one of the mates to die before the union is consummated. Have ye made love to her?"

"Nay."

"Are ye willing to kill her before yer desire overpowers yer senses?"

"I wilna kill the lass," Cameron asserted, masking his inner turmoil with deceptive calm.

"Then, I say again, ye've chosen well."

A solution not forthcoming to his current personal dilemma, Cameron changed the subject to the one that curdled his insides. "Deidra Sidhe is here in Arlington."

"What?" Fallon's voice hardened. Cameron imagined the man sitting straight up in bed.

"She's been attracted to the lass. I think she's after Aiyanna's powers."

"Are the gods aware of yer situation?"

"I'm sure they are. They sent me to the area a month or so ago. There must be a reason why they havena called the rest of ye in."

"What about yer lass? Are ye able to protect her? Do ye need us there?"

Cameron smirked at Fallon's rambling but kept his tone neutral. "So far, I've been able to handle it. I appreciate yer offer, but I think it best for ye to wait."

A deep exhale ricocheted through the phone. "Will do, but if ye need us, call. We'll come running."

"Thanks. Now how about ye? Is all well with ye? Lizzie and the babe?"

"Aye, Lizzie's bonny. She's getting as big as a house. *Ouch!* And just as cranky."

Cameron pictured Fallon's feisty wife slapping the elder upside the head.

"I'm sorry I woke ye, Fallon. Tell Lizzie the same. Thanks for yer help."

Just as Cameron was about to hang up, Fallon's voice echoed through the earpiece. "Hey, kid."

"Aye?"

"All isna what it seems. Our lives were destined. Doona forget that."

With those final words ringing in his ear, Cameron closed his phone.

What the hell had he done?

Chapter Ten

The sky, overcast with dark clouds, emphasized the dreary afternoon. A chilly breeze blew across the parking lot from the east, driving a light sprinkle of rain into her face.

Aiyanna zipped up the front of her rain jacket and pulled her collar against her neck. She cursed herself for leaving her umbrella in the car this morning, but the cool, fresh air soothed her after a long day at the university.

Taking long strides, she hurried through the rows of parked cars to her own.

While her students took their unit exams, her gaze remained ever watchful on the hands of the clock. The seconds ticked by in slow motion, her thoughts centered on her personal situation. An urgency to locate her sister swamped her, and by the end of the day, Aiyanna came to a decision.

She would take a much-needed vacation. With the disappearance of Cheyenne and the appearance of a Síoraí Guardian in her home, she needed to focus all of her attention in those areas.

Dean Hastings pitched a fit over the short notice but granted her request for time off. She had three weeks to get her life in order.

When Aiyanna left for work this morning, Cameron still slept. She'd instructed Starr to observe their guest's actions. The cat snarled her displeasure, but after a bit of coaxing agreed. Perhaps, with news of her upcoming vacation, Starr's mood would improve.

A blast of cold air swept over her, and she shivered. Her body prickled and crawled with unease.

She glanced around the area, searching for its source, but the only other occupants of the parking lot were Tim Morrow's wife, Jane, and three-year-old daughter huddled beneath a large yellow umbrella. Jane's face was a mixture of humor and frustration. Her eyes focused on the grape lollipop stuck to her white jacket. She pulled the candy off with a visible grimace. A pale purple mark stained the material.

Aiyanna smiled. Tim was sure to catch hell for that treat.

She shrugged and rushed to her car.

****

Jack Stannard ducked behind the wheel of his SUV and watched the dark-haired woman cross the parking lot.

Much like her sister, Aiyanna Grey was quite beautiful. He began following her yesterday, waiting for the opportunity to snatch her. At first, he'd been tempted to keep her for himself but decided he'd benefit more by passing her over to Deidra Sidhe. The occasion to seize her hadn't yet presented itself, but it wouldn't be long before he brought this white witch to Deidra. The Vampryss would feel obligated to reward him the immortality he sought. As a human, none of the customary taboos that affected vampires applied to him.

She pulled out of the lot. He put the car into drive and pursued. When she pulled into the driveway behind a large two-storied house, he cursed and ran a frazzled hand through his hair.

He knew better than to attempt to capture her in her own backyard. That would be suicidal.

Damn it!

Maybe tomorrow.

****

At the kitchen table, Aiyanna nursed a tuna salad sandwich and cup of tomato soup. She slurped a teaspoon of soup and swirled the spoon around the bowl. Hypnotized, she watched the liquid ripple in reaction.

When she arrived home earlier, Starr informed her that she hadn't seen Cameron all day. She thought that a bit strange. No one could sleep all day, could they?

Aiyanna slipped upstairs to peek into his room.

He'd pulled the heavy drapes across the window committing the room to total darkness. The only light to soften the sinister blackness filtered in from the hallway behind her.

Aiyanna tiptoed inside and stopped beside the bed to stare at him. He lay on his stomach, looking handsome and peaceful. A wild strand of golden hair curled across his forehead, and Aiyanna stilled the temptation to brush it away.

His right hand hung over the side of the bed. Her gaze traveled up his arm to the nakedness of his broad shoulder. Moving down his back, she noted the comforter draped across his middle. A flash of desire rushed over her at the sight of his muscular thigh, corded and tight. Was he naked beneath the blanket?

Aiyanna's heart skipped a beat when he rolled onto his back. The comforter shifted granting her a full frontal. Her eyes widened, and she drew an electrified breath. Oooh, what a man!

With forced calm, she took a step backward then another until she reached the door. Outside, in the hallway, she closed the door with a hushed click. She dropped back against the wall. Her heart hammered in her ears, and a delicious shudder heated her body.

Oh my!

Drawing a deep breath, she headed back downstairs to clean up the kitchen after her dinner.

****

Her hands slipped into the sudsy water.

A loud cough ricocheted in the room, and she glanced over her shoulder toward the doorway. Cameron leaned against the doorframe wearing no more than a pair of tight jeans. Her breath quickened, and her cheeks became warm as she visualized what lay beneath those jeans.

His brawny arms folded over his powerfully built bare chest. The tingling in her stomach matured to a flaming fire of desire between her thighs.

Oh crap!

She turned away from the sight and closed her eyes against the vision of being crushed in his strong embrace.

After a moment, she grabbed the dishtowel from the counter, dried her hands, and then she faced him.

He gave her body a raking gaze. His stare was bold and assessing before capturing her eyes with his. Light smoldered in his gold-flecked eyes.

Did he read the desire in her eyes?

Heat flared into her cheeks, and she attempted a smile. "I wondered if you were going to wake up today."

He ran a hand through his tousled hair. "Aye, well, that's my nature. I sleep during the day and spend most of the night-time hours hunting."

"Are you sure you're not a—?" She stopped, but not before the implication was understood.

His lips curved crookedly, and he nodded. "I'm sure. Back ass-ward, if ye ask me, but that's how the gods played it."

Aiyanna's eyes widened, and she rushed across the room. In the process, her thigh knocked the table. Unable to squelch her astonishment, she asked, "Are you telling me the gods fashioned their guardians after *vampires*?"

He nodded, a boyish grin on his face. "If ye wish to view it that way, but we're no' vampires, love. We doona kill innocent people nor do we drink their blood. I canna walk in sunlight, but neither can they. Our prime directive, the reason we exist is to protect humans. We imitate vampires. We're given all the characteristics to behave as they do."

She snorted. "Why the hell would you want to do that?"

"To kill them."

"Oh," Aiyanna stuttered, and raised her hand to her neck. "Is that why you bit me? Another fashion?"

Cameron grimaced. "That's another story. One we'll need to discuss soon, but no' now."

"I'm not going to change into some hideous, grotesque monster, am I?"

His mouth quirked with humor. "No' tonight, leastwise." He turned, about to leave the room, when she remembered her manners and called out.

"Hey, do you want something to eat?"

He turned, smiled, and winked. "I doona eat food, but if ye're offering another delicacy, I might be persuaded." He chuckled when heat rushed into her cheeks, and her face flushed with what she knew to be a pretty shade of pink.

For a moment, he studied her intently, his eyes humorous and tender before he replied with sincerity. "Thanks anyways. Would it be okay if I took a quick shower? I have to go out." He winked. "I have my own toiletries." At her raised eyebrow, he chuckled. "Special soap."

His scent, rich and sexy, filled her nose. A special soap did that? Bullshit! Did he have a woman? A secret love? She held a hand to her throat, surprised at the sudden tension that gripped her neck. Would he see her tonight? Did this woman hunt with him? Her shoulders knitted into two painful knots.

Instead, she lowered her eyes and kept her voice neutral when she answered, "Sure, you know where to find the shower. Towels and washcloths are in the cabinet beside the sink."

"Thanks," he replied, before he rounded the corner into the hallway and disappeared from sight.

Visions of their bedroom play replayed in her thoughts. She hadn't mentioned it, and neither had he, so she kept her silence.

A few minutes later, the old pipes rattled and shook the walls. That was the thing about old houses; corroded pipes and hollow air ducts left no doubt what others did in other areas of the building. Sound traveled, and in this case, it was the hum of rushing water through the rusty conduits in the wall.

She imagined his gorgeous body, muscular arms and chest lathered with suds, soapy, wet, and her hand sliding with little effort across his muscular shoulders down his back to his tight...

The water stopped, and she envisioned him stepping from the tub, droplets of water coating his body.

She giggled, shook her head and released a deep breath, startled by the wicked thoughts that flashed through her mind. What the hell was wrong with her? Under her breath, she muttered to herself, "Stupid woman."

"Did ye say something?" She jumped when Cameron's voice echoed from the doorway. Her head shot up, eyes wide at the sight of him standing in the doorway, bare-chested, a T-shirt slung over his shoulder. Water dripped from his hair across his forehead.

A faint light twinkled in the depths of his golden eyes, his smile as intimate as a kiss. "Sorry, I dinna mean to startle ye."

"Did you need something else?" Aiyanna asked, her voice raspy.

"Aye, I wanted to make sure I could come back in the morning?"

What? He couldn't stay with his woman friend?

She bit her tongue and shrugged. "Sure, why not? Where else are you going to go?"

"Thanks." His head tilted to the side, eyes dark with emotion. "Are ye okay, lass?"

She cleared her throat and turned away, so he wouldn't see stains of scarlet flare into her cheeks. "I'm fine. Why do you ask?"

"Because ye look a bit flustered."

She shivered at the brush of his chest against her back. Damn, he moved fast. He pressed a soft kiss to her cheek. The minty smell of toothpaste filtered into her nose.

"I'll see ye in the morning, lass."

And then he disappeared. His fresh, masculine scent lingered behind.

Hunting? Smelling so damn nice?

A pit knotted her stomach at the tumble of confused feelings assailed her...anger, jealousy, and then disappointment.

Cameron MacLean exuded rare, masculine charm, a charisma that hypnotized her. Her heart swelled with tenderness.

What did that mean?

Oh crap!

Chapter Eleven

Aiyanna finished up the dishes and headed up the stairs.

In her room, she flopped on the bed. Her hands settled behind her head, her gaze fixed on the ceiling.

Images of Cameron's naked body filled her vision and merged with the high arches in the room. A brief shiver rippled across her flesh at the glimpse of his strong, golden body. She fantasized sliding her hands over him, running over the beefy tendons in his neck, across his shoulders and chest, and down past his muscular stomach. Her heart beat in rapid succession; her pulse skittered at an alarming tempo. The air around her sizzled with electricity.

Passion rose in her like the hottest fire and clouded her ability to think.

Stop it! She admonished herself and forced herself to focus on something other than uncensored thoughts of lust. Cameron MacLean projected an energy and power that undeniably attracted her, but now was not the time to let her sexual frustrations consume her.

Her sister needed her. And with that thought in mind, she focused her thoughts on Cheyenne.

Where did Deidra hold her? And find the privacy no one would infringe upon? The vampires she'd hunted to date possessed no knowledge of the Vampryss' whereabouts. Or if they did, Deidra's hold was so powerful they chose to die at her hands than divulge their leader's location.

She'd attempted every spell she knew, except the one used to contact the children of the Great Mother. That spell, more potent than any other, gave her the heebie-jeebies. The notion of pestering dead people who possessed enough power to destroy her in a flash...she shuddered...no great motivation there.

She faltered with indecision. Her sister was worth it, wasn't she?

"It couldn't hurt," she murmured.

She jumped up from the bed and dashed to the armoire in the corner of the room where she whipped open the door. Scanning the contents, she grabbed enough candles, potions, and oils to fill her arms.

She marched to the center of the floor, positioned her precious cargo on the braided oval rug, and sat cross-legged in front of her goods. From under the bed, she tugged out the altar Cheyenne gave her last year on their birthday. Handmade, the altar's solid oak top had been sanded down to a smooth and glossy finish. A hand-carved, intricate design decorated the sides.

She placed one candle in the center of the podium and surrounded it with greenery. In the center of the flat surface, she set her bottle of evocation oil containing a concoction of frankincense and copal, resins myrrh and other scents such as white sandalwood, lavender and mastic, all known for their magical powers to open communication lines. To the side of the oil, she placed a vase of dried sunflowers and a razor-sharp knife on the level surface.

Aiyanna lit the lavender incense, drawing the essence into her lungs, and spoke, her tone soft and inviting, "*Pure and holy, fair offspring of the Great Mother, I call to you. Your presence speaks of sunlit days and dewy flowers, and your smiles fill my heart with joy and unending love. I beg of you. Please hear my call."*

She opened her eyes and lit the candle, her voice soft, yet commanding in the silence of the room, *"In a world beset with malevolence, you seek to unify the species of this planet, whether man or animal. You grant the blessings of companionship and loving friendship upon each child of the Great Mother. And so, in my need, I call upon your tender hearts and ask for guidance."*

"You have brought into my life the one I call sister. She is trustworthy, honest, and kind, one who understands my spirit as I understand hers."

She grabbed a handful of wildflowers and scattered the petals around the candle.

"Holy children, she has been taken from me. I beg of you to help bring her back into my life. Into the great Web of Life, please send your power. Purpose, thought, and magic flow. The pathway has opened. May all that is good flow to me and lead me to her. Please stretch out your hands and guide me. Blessed be."

Aiyanna waited for the visions of her sister to materialize behind closed eyelids. When nothing appeared, Aiyanna chanted again. She gulped hard. Hot tears of frustration slid down her cheeks.

A soft click followed by a blast of air signified the presence of another person in the room. She opened her eyes and swiped at the moisture that soaked her cheeks. Cameron, legs crossed, sat Indian style on the floor in front of her. A swath of wavy blondish hair fell casually on his forehead.

The scent of sandalwood infused her nostrils and lingered in the room.

"I thought you'd left," she blurted, her tone fragile and shaky.

With a lop-sided grin, he shrugged. "I did. I forgot something and had to come back to retrieve it." He held her gaze. A probing query came into his face, and he nodded toward her magic charms. "What's with the spell?"

The rich timbre of his voice sent shivers spiraling down her spine. "Nothing."

"There has to be a reason ye're calling to the bairns of the Great Mother."

Her eyes widened in surprise, "How do you...?"

"There's a lot ye doona know about me." He gave her a conspiratorial wink. "Now, what gives?" his soft voice urged.

She shook her head. "It doesn't matter. It's not working anyways."

She leaned forward on her knees and would have risen, but Cameron's hand stretched over the altar and gripped hers. With a tender tug, he drew her downward. "Aiyanna, I canna begin to understand what turmoil ye suffer if ye doona tell me. I can help."

"How can you?"

Across the altar, their hands remained connected. His grip tightened. "Trust me. Let me help. Together, with our powers combined, we may be strong enough to reach out and find the answers ye seek."

He closed his eyes and recited the same words Aiyanna had spoken moments ago. She joined in. Their voices echoed through the room.

Cheyenne's reflection, although faint, flashed behind Aiyanna's closed lids.

It was working. She trembled with excitement.

Her sister sat on a rust-coated cot in a small room with barely enough space to stand. Her head rested on knees pulled up beneath her.

Using only her mind, Aiyanna's thoughts rushed forward. "Cheyenne, are you okay?"

Cheyenne's head jerked upward. "Anya? I don't understand. How is this possible?" She tucked a wayward strand of dark hair behind her ear and made a slight gesture with her right hand, as if pushing the question aside. She glanced to the door. "It doesn't matter. You've got to be careful. She's looking for you," she said, in a hushed tone.

"Do you know why?"

"She hopes to unite our powers, to make her stronger. If she succeeds, Anya, we will both die."

Manifesting her human form, Aiyanna stepped into the room and sat beside her sister. She drew strength from her presence and wrapped her arms around Cheyenne in comfort. "We won't let that happen."

Cheyenne rested her head on Aiyanna's shoulder. "Fight her, Anya, for both of us. Every day, she takes a little more of my powers, strips them away piece by piece. I've stopped fighting because when I struggle, I lose more of myself," she said, in a voice that seemed to come from a long way off.

"You've got to hold on."

"I should have sensed her that night. I should have—" Cheyenne's voice broke, and she leaned back to look into Aiyanna's face. "I'm sorry. I failed us."

"What are you talking about? You didn't fail anyone."

"I don't even know where I am, Anya. Take me with you now," Cheyenne begged.

Aiyanna caressed her sister's hair and murmured, "I'm sorry, sis, I can't. My physical body lies on the other side of the portal. Yours is here, but don't worry. I will find you."

Words stuck in her throat, and Aiyanna caught her bottom lip between her teeth. They were powerful witches, yet Deidra was much stronger. To gain the power of the both sisters would make her even more powerful. And yet, the evil bitch was draining her sister of the willpower to endure. Aiyanna feared Cheyenne's mind would become feeble, and she would surrender to death just to escape the torture.

As much as she wanted to tell Cheyenne of Cameron, to reassure her they weren't alone in this, she couldn't. Not yet.

Instead, she asked, "Do you remember what Starr taught us? The first thing she told us when she arrived on our doorstep? To always keep a little spark of magic hidden."

Cheyenne smiled. Tears filled the corners of her eyes. "I remember. I have it, Anya. It's what I hold on to when it gets bad." She spoke in a suffocated whisper, her voice faint.

"Good girl. I'll see you soon in real time, and then, we'll get you the hell out of this place, and home, where you belong."

"Have you seen her?"

Aiyanna nodded, swallowed hard, lifted her chin and met her sister's gaze. "Yeah, Shy, I've seen her and felt her power. She's wicked. Pure evil." Her finger traced the bruise lining her sister's jaw. She clenched her mouth. Her jaw tightened at the anger that bubbled up inside her and threatened to erupt. "I'm so sorry she's done this to you."

"It's not your fault, Anya."

"I'm going to destroy her, tear her apart."

All of a sudden, the air inside the cell changed. The temperature dropped ten degrees, and a bitter wind whipped through the small area. An unseen force ripped Cheyenne from her arms, slamming her against the wall. Cheyenne groaned.

Aiyanna jumped up from the bed, her gaze sweeping the room.

An immortal force spanned the area. It wrapped dark tentacles around Aiyanna. She fought for freedom but failed, wheezing for breath. Her sides ached, stomach cramped, and blood thumped at both temples.

Cheyenne's gasp echoed behind her.

Aiyanna tried to leave but couldn't, not until she could breathe again. Not until she could blink without this sensation of intense panic.

Wrenched from the cot, she catapulted through the air to an area enshrouded with blackness. A chill circled her, and the darkness closed in, but she fought the invisible assault. When her limbs weakened, she peered over her shoulder and saw terror and helplessness on Cheyenne's face.

Deidra's apparition appeared in the room. Red electrical currents shot from her fingertips. The scarlet bolts closed around Aiyanna's arms, midsection and squeezed, suffocating her.

"*No!* Leave her alone," Cheyenne demanded, in a distant voice.

Pride swept over Aiyanna at her sister's strength and passion.

The woman laughed in a malicious, mocking tone. "Come and get her, witch."

Deidra's expression taunted, and when Cheyenne jumped up from the cot, the Vampryss released one hand and shot an electrical, half-powered pink bolt toward her. It struck Cheyenne in the chest. Her body jerked once before she collapsed on the cot in spasmodic writhing.

After a moment, Deidra's attention and power returned to Aiyanna. "I knew it wouldn't be long before you came to her aid. Patience is not one of my strong attributes, but it has paid off nicely this time." Her lips twisted in a cynical smile.

Like a yo-yo, the lightning bolt recoiled, drawing Aiyanna toward the apparition of the Vampryss. A meager second before they connected, Deidra materialized into her physical existence.

"Help me!" she called out, using her mind and hoped Cameron heard her cry.

Aiyanna's inner spirit weakened. She gave a mental shout for her powers, but they were spent, leaving her defenseless to prevent Deidra from tearing her soul from her body.

What was happening to her?

A sudden jolt wrenched her to a stop. Power radiated from nowhere, yet flared everywhere. Another presence reached for her.

Cameron!

His power crackled through Aiyanna's body like heat lightning, and a luminous glow radiated from the surface of her skin similar to diamonds in the sunshine.

White magic exploded from her fingers in bolts of flashing multi-colored lights that intertwined with Deidra's red currents. The combination proved explosive and spun them around in a whirlwind.

The ground beneath them opened and created a powerful suction that beckoned. Just as Aiyanna descended into the black hole, a white light appeared and ripped her from Deidra's grip. The energy held her steady while the earth fissure sucked Deidra inside and resealed with an ear-shattering *crack*.

The force settled Aiyanna's spirit with gentle care to the ground.

She turned to Cheyenne and smiled with reassurance. Lifting her hand to her lips, Aiyanna blew her sister a kiss.

"I'll be back. Be ready."

Chapter Twelve

Aiyanna's eyes shot open, and she drew a deep, ragged breath. A flash of wild grief rippled through her at the memory of the terror she'd witnessed on Cheyenne's face. She bit her lip until it throbbed, and her throat ached with defeat. Tears trembled on her eyelids.

Over the tip of the candle's flame, she studied Cameron's face. Aiyanna sensed his spiritual essence had not yet returned from the other plane. The fire's glow bestowed a lethal blaze in his golden eyes that reminded her of a tiger, untamed and deadly.

His eyes cleared, and he focused on her face.

She managed a small, tentative smile. "Thank you, again," she murmured.

His eyes twinkled in the soft lighting, and an easy grin played at the corner of his lips. "Ye're welcome, again."

His expression changed and became almost somber. He inclined his head in a deep gesture, his eyes sharp and tolerant as if he waited for her to explain.

She opened her mouth to speak but clamped her lips closed. Did she dare tell him the story of her sister? After everything he'd done for her, didn't he deserve the truth?

She bent her head and studied her hands.

"Talk to me," he started, and then hesitated.

His hand stretched across the altar to catch her chin with his thumb and forefinger. He lifted until her eyes met his. "Anya."

In stunned surprise, she shook her head. She set a hand on the floor and pushed herself to her feet. Her legs wobbled beneath her weight.

Cameron vaulted from the floor and wrapped his arms around her to steady her.

"Maybe ye should sit down, lass."

She glanced into his face and blinked. Her vision doubled, and then tripled. "I think that might be a...good...idea." With each word, her voice grew fainter than the last.

In a flash, he swung her up against his solid chest. The scent of sandalwood and musk permeated her senses.

He carried her to the bed where he laid her on top of the quilt. Her eyes flickered open at the absence of his warmth. He stood above her, his body stiff, features drawn, and lips tight. A vein pulsed in his neck, and she thought she heard him make a noise. A groan, perhaps?

She reached out and caught his hand in hers. "Cameron. Don't leave me. Please."

He settled beside her on the edge of the bed and caressed her cheek, leaning toward her. "Ye're safe, love. I'll be here. I promise. We'll talk later," he whispered in her ear.

Aiyanna nuzzled her cheek against his palm. Comforted in the knowledge he would remain by her side, her eyelids grew heavy, and she slipped into the dream world that summoned.

After all, she trusted him to be a man of his word.

****

Huddled beneath the thin wool blanket, Cheyenne shivered at the arctic air that settled in the room. The concrete blocks lining the room acted as an insulator to maintain the freezing, damp temperatures.

Exhausted, her eyelids lowered. Her head

bobbed against her chest. When her chin made the connection, she jerked upward, her eyes widening.

If she gave into sleep, she feared she'd succumb to hypothermia. Already, the cold numbed her fingers and toes. The chill that ravaged her on the outside would seep through her skin to attack her internal organs until they shut down, one by one.

A key turned in the lock. She glanced toward the entryway. The handle twisted, and the door swung open. The metal casing scraped against the frame until it slammed against the wall with a loud *bang*. The thump resounded in the room like a judge's gavel moments after passing sentence.

Her stomach twisted in a mass of bitter bile.

She struggled to her feet and stood on the cot. Unable to maintain her balance on frozen toes, she leaned against the wall. She placed a hand over her heart, but it proved impossible to steady her erratic pulse. She struggled to take a deep breath, then another, slower, deeper. Her legs were as shaky as wet noodles, and her knees threatened to buckle if she dared to take one solitary step.

A blast of stagnant air filtered into the room. Cheyenne gagged and coughed. Her throat tightened.

The man in the open doorway glared at her, his expression filled with cold fury. His wintry gaze pierced hers. Cheyenne's skin crawled with painful pricking sensations, almost as if sharp shivers of glass were being driven through her in slow, painful degrees.

Aiyanna's face hovered in her mind, and the pain dulled to an ache. The nausea faded, and she took a single step forward but maintained a hand solidly fixed on the wall behind her.

Her jailor paused in the doorway. His head almost reached the top of the doorframe. He held a candle lantern, which he hoisted above his head to shed light into the room. Cheyenne found it unusual a vampire chose to be close to fire until his scent drifted up her nose. He carried the human scent. The man searched the room, his face, hard and cold.

"Where the hell would I go?" she asked in a tight, low voice through gritted teeth. Even her teeth ached from their incessant chattering from the cold. Her jaw clenched, and the lump reappeared in her throat when his gaze flashed back to her, glowing of crimson fire. The sight shocked Cheyenne until she realized this man must be possessed by one of Deidra's minions, for they were not the eyes of a human.

She pressed tighter against the wall when he stepped into the small room and strolled toward her. He captured her by the arm, yanked her off the cot, and dragged her from the cell into the narrow corridor.

Cheyenne's heart thudded against her breast like a monstrous gong. Petrified, she breathed in shallow, quick gasps, until her mouth grew so dry her tongue stuck to her teeth and her vision blurred.

Oh god, she didn't want to die.

The scent of fall roses filled the air and merged with the mellow fragrances of sweet late autumn grass and shrubbery. The velvet black of the night sky twinkled with stars.

She glanced around. Her body shook with disbelief.

A cemetery?

What the hell?

She didn't care. She gulped in the fresh air as if starved for breath. The night breeze caressed her cheek and curled over her skin. She shivered with pleasure, enjoying its warmth.

It calmed her, and her lips curved into a serene smile.

She returned to reality, fully aware of her

surroundings.

Her mind filled with bitter thoughts.

How cruel to give her a brief taste of freedom before they ripped her to shreds.

Chapter Thirteen

He promised to stay with her, and Cameron MacLean always kept his word.

Perched on a chair beside the bed, he held her hand. His thumb caressed her palm while his gaze swept over her face. He inhaled deep breaths, his nerves tensed at the ashen color of Aiyanna's cheeks and her ice-cold skin.

He glanced at his wristwatch, alarmed at how much time had passed. It had been more than three hours since Aiyanna's astrophysical projection, and she still hadn't stirred.

By the gods! She should have awakened by now. The longer she remained unconscious, the stronger his fears grew. His gut clenched, churning with absolute horror. What if she never woke? What if Deidra damaged her mind? Her spirit? What if—?

He fought against a rising panic that created a bitter combination of acid and bile in his stomach. The mixture rose in his throat and threatened to asphyxiate him.

"Damn it!" he cursed. His chest tightened, and he searched her face, willing her to waken.

During the spell, Aiyanna's body rose from her position on the floor, suspended in mid-air. A moment later, the familiar banishment spell spilled from her lips and reverberated through the room. Without hesitation, he closed his eyes and advanced into her trance to link his voice and powers to hers.

Now, he jumped to his feet, paced the room, and ran his hands through his hair in agitation. What the hell had he been thinking? What possessed him to help her? He flexed his fingers taut until the palms of his hands burned.

Deidra Sidhe was a powerful force and should never be taken lightly. Experience educated the Síoraí to that fact, but only the gods understood the extent of the poisons the bitch was capable of infusing in Aiyanna while in her control.

This was his fucking fault! All of it.

He shouldn't have helped Aiyanna. By aiding her, he'd done the one act he swore never to do to another. In his eyes the ultimate betrayal. He put her in danger and almost got her killed. He should have entered the realm with her or, better yet, refused to let her go.

He'd possessed no foresight to predict their spell would lead her into the arms of the vampire bitch, and yet, even though he lacked the knowledge, it was no excuse. He failed Aiyanna, just as he had Sarah. The revelation delivered a well-sounded punch to his self-worth, reinforcing his resolution not to let his emotions for the beautiful, young Cherokee deter him from his path.

He couldn't, *no,* he wouldn't risk her life.

In hindsight, Cameron wished he'd taken the opportunity to glance toward the woman, to find out who was so important that Aiyanna felt compelled to risk her life, but there hadn't been enough time. Getting Aiyanna out of there had been his main focus.

"What have you done to her?" Starr's high-pitched voice resounded in the room.

He swung around. Starr stood in the open doorway. Cameron met the cat's gaze, felt the animal's disdain like a slap across the face. She sprinted into the room and pounced on the bed where she walked the length of Aiyanna's body toward her face.

With her white, fluffy paw, the cat patted her friend's face. "Anya? Anya? Do you hear me? Wake up!"

"And ye think slapping her like that will bring her around. By god's teeth, cat, leave her be. She'll be fine." He hoped.

Starr's gaze met his, her yellow cat eyes sharp and critical. "Says you!" she said, in a nasty tone, flashing him a look of contempt.

His eyes narrowed, and his face grew hot. His stomach and shoulders knotted and stiffened with a sudden flush of rage. He sat in the chair beside the bed and leaned forward. Through clenched teeth, he gritted, "Look, cat, Aiyanna says ye're family, but if ye canna control yer tantrums, then leave. If no', I'm going to throw ye out of this room on that furry arse of yers."

"You and what army?" the cat muttered the question under her breath.

"Doona push me."

Starr hissed and spat, brandishing her pointed, sharp claws at him. "I told Aiyanna you were going to be nothing but trouble. I told her, but she's always been too stubborn to listen to what I say."

The cat lowered her paws, shook her head and dropped to her belly. Ignoring him, her eyes fixed on Aiyanna.

Concern for Aiyanna flared in Starr's eyes, and self-incrimination flooded over him. He reigned in his anger and drew a deep breath. "I'm sorry, Starr."

"Humph!"

"I wilna let anything happen to her. I promise ye I'll take care of her."

Starr grimaced and grunted. She lifted her gaze to his. "I've been trying to do that for years." As if seeing the sincerity in his expression, the cat smiled crookedly. "I can see you believe what you say, and I wish you much luck and success."

A soft groan resonated from the bed, and Cameron and Starr spun around at the same time.

Aiyanna's eyelids fluttered open.

"Thank the gods," he mumbled, smoothing the hair from her face. Despite his resolve, his hand caressed her cheek in an affectionate motion.

"Are ye feeling better?" he asked, gathering his thoughts. He held her gaze and probed her eyes, searching for the truth. They glittered like chocolate gemstones, set wide beneath heavy brows. "What happened to you, Anya?"

Aiyanna sat up, settling against the headboard. She stretched out a reassuring hand to caress the top of the cat's head. "It's okay. I'm fine, Starr."

"But what happened to you?" The cat leaned closer. "What did he do to you?" she asked in a whisper.

Aiyanna giggled then grimaced. Her eyes fixed on Cameron when she answered, "He saved my life." Glancing at Starr, she asked, "Would you give us a few moments, please? I'll explain everything to you later."

Starr made a slight *tsking* sound before she left the room.

"Do ye feel all right, lass? Can I get ye anything?"

Her mouth curved into a glimmer of a smile that transformed her face to an angelic vision of sheer glowing beauty. Everything about this woman, from her bronzed skin to the raven hair spread out across the pillow, amazed him. He loved her lips, how full they were, how ripe.

"She's alive."

"I assume ye speak of the woman?" His forehead pinched. "Aye, she still lives, but ye almost got yerself killed. Is she worth yer life?"

Aiyanna's eyes misted. He recognized distrust in their depths before she dropped long, thick lashes to hide her internal struggles. She rolled to the opposite side of the bed and sat on the edge.

After a moment, she pushed herself to her feet, keeping the palm of one hand on the mattress until she regained her balance.

Sensing her need to put distance between them, he clamped his lips together and remained silent.

His gaze followed her steps. She paced across the room, swung around and strolled back the other way. She never looked his way. And yet, he noted her set face and stern mouth. Her hands clenched into fists at her sides.

"Aiyanna?" he called, his voice calm, yet tinged with an authority that brought her to a standstill.

When she lifted her eyes to his, a quiver touched her smooth, marble-like lips.

"Doona do that."

"Do what?" she asked, in a weak and unsteady murmur.

"Doona shut me out. I want to help."

Tears spilled down her cheeks. She swung around, her back to him.

He strode up behind her and wrapped his arms around her shoulders. "Trust me, lass."

"Cameron," she whispered his name, shook her head and stepped out of his arms. With hands that trembled, she swiped the moisture from her face.

He went silent, but only for a second. She stiffened when his hands rested on her shoulders and turned her to face him. Tears sparkled on her lashes, and he pulled her into his arms. His chin rested on top of her head. "Please."

"I do not trust easily," she mumbled, in a broken whisper.

"A fact I've discovered about ye." He leaned back and stared into her face. "If ye but give me a chance, I can try to help."

Aiyanna opened her mouth. Her body shivered

111

against him. Her lips parted on a soft exhale. Forgetting his recent vow, he lowered his head and placed his mouth over hers. She tasted like paradise. When her tongue met his, Aiyanna moaned. He didn't know how he would ever be able to let her go.

With a groan, he pulled his mouth away. His forehead dropped and rested against hers. "As much as I desire ye, lass, I wilna take ye when yer in this state of mind. No' in this way, Aiyanna."

He softened his grip but didn't let her go. Not yet.

An inexplicable look of hurt crossed her face before she released a quick rush of air. "Don't you think I know what type of mood I'm in?"

Cameron chuckled at her cheekiness and stepped away from temptation. "Trust me, lass. Now isna the time. We need to talk first." Conscious of Aiyanna's uncertain gaze, he winked. "What do ye say? Talk then maybe, we'll see what happens."

He stared into her beautiful face and struggled with his decision to let her go.

He had an oath to honor.

Didn't he?

Chapter Fourteen

The tenderness in his expression startled her.

After a moment of indecision, she nodded and muttered, "Okay then."

Turning, she strolled to the opposite side of the room. She ran her hands along her arms, massaging away the arctic breeze that slithered across her flesh.

Keeping her features composed, she turned back to him. "I'm not sure where to begin."

"Why don't ye start with the woman? Who is she?"

"That woman is my sister, Cheyenne, and yes, she is worth my life. I've been searching for her since she disappeared a few weeks ago."

"Disappeared? What happened?"

"Cheyenne is an executive for a large advertising agency downtown. She travels a lot for her job and just got back into town after being in Chicago for the past month. I received a call from her at the university. A ritual she always did, to let me know she was back. As I was talking to her, I heard a sound like splintering wood followed by a loud crash. Before the phone went dead, she screamed." She drew an agonized breath. Tears spilled from her eyes and down her cheeks. "I rushed home, but by the time I got here, she was gone."

"And ye think vampires were involved with her disappearance?"

Thrown by the question, she hesitated. Her mind whirled. "Huh?"

"On the night we met…the night ye fought the vampires at the warehouse, ye told me ye hunted them when ye searched for information, but ye wouldna share what kind of information ye sought. It was about yer sister?"

She nodded. "Here, Cheyenne and I found a peaceful existence. There was never a need for the protection spells I use now. No one's ever bothered us until that night." Her voice cracked. She cleared her throat and continued, "I believe vampires broke into our home and took her."

"What makes ye so certain, lass?"

"I caught a whiff of their stench in the room. It took everything I had not to throw up, and I found traces of vampire ash." Her eyes sought his, and she continued, "Cheyenne fought them, killed some, but they still took her."

She noted his set face and clamped mouth. He gave her a brief nod. "It makes sense, but what do ye think a wee lass like yerself can do to find yer sister?"

"I hope to locate the one who isn't loyal."

"What does loyalty have to do with this?"

"She has vampires, werewolves, even shape shifters under her control. And then, she's commandeered the help of humans who are too weak to stand up to her. They're all afraid of her."

He stiffened. "Her? Then ye know who holds yer sister?"

"In the beginning, I didn't, but then you arrived, and the pieces all came together. You know who it is, too, don't you?"

Now for the moment of clarity, would he, Cameron MacLean, Síoraí Guardian, protector of mankind, tell her the truth?

His gaze turned dark and unfathomable.

With relentless determination, she pressed, "Its Deidra Sidhe isn't it?"

She eyed him with a calculating expression. His brows rose, and his mouth spread into a thin-lipped smile.

Fury almost choked her when he remained silent. She grabbed a brass candlestick holder from the dresser. "Do *not* play games with me, Cameron," she warned, and stormed across the room, the weapon held high as if to strike. "I am not in the mood."

His smile vanished, wiped away by astonishment.

In a defensive action, he held his hands up in front of him. "Okay! Okay! Ye win, lass. Put that thing down, and we'll talk."

She lowered it at her side. "Now talk," she demanded, in a soft voice.

He eyed the object clutched in her hands and shook his head. With a wave of his hand, he added, "No' with that in yer hand, lass. Put it down."

A quick jerk of her wrist sent the object flying to the bed where it bounced twice on the mattress before it stilled. When her gaze met his, a smile trembled over her lips. "Satisfied?"

"Humph!" He grunted, but gazed at her with a bland half smile.

"Well?" she badgered.

"How do ye know of Deidra Sidhe?"

"I'm a witch, or have ye forgotten?"

"I havena forgotten. And aye, she's in Arlington. Do ye have an idea what might have drawn her here?"

Aiyanna grunted and spread her arms wide. "Hello!"

At Aiyanna's obvious insinuation, comprehension filled his expression. His brows drew together in an angry frown, and a muscle quivered in his jaw. "Bloody hell!"

With a quirk of an eyebrow, she asked, "Figured

it out, did ya?"

"She wants yer powers."

"I believe so. After all, a white witches' power is supreme over most." She watched his expression for a reaction to the news she was not just an ordinary witch.

He smiled. "I'm no' a dim-witted man, Anya. I know only a white witch is capable of the things I've seen ye do. But what I still doona fathom is why ye? Even a witch as powerful as ye canna help accomplish the feat she's set out to do."

"And what feat is that?"

Cameron nodded. "She seeks enough power to release her bastard lover, Ághmach, from his prison in the underworld."

"Thank you."

Cameron's head shot up in surprise at the sincerity in her voice. "For what?"

"For your honesty."

"Ye already know much about Deidra, but I doona think it is enough. Ye need to understand what ye're up against. She's powerful, and she's evil. I doona want to see ye get injured."

"What about Cheyenne?"

"Is the lass a witch as well?"

Aiyanna nodded. "I don't think Deidra will harm her. Not until she has me."

"Are yer sister's powers as great as yers?"

"She's a white witch too, which makes her just as powerful. Imagine the power Deidra would gain from two white witches. All she has to do is string us up, spill our blood and comingle our powers."

"It wilna be that easy, lass. The only way Deidra can tap into yer combined powers is if she bridged the fissure that naturally exists between witches. Sisters or no', that wilna be an easy task to accomplish, even for a powerful bitch like her."

Aiyanna's stomach knotted. He didn't

understand. She had to make him understand.

She gripped a hold of his hand and squeezed. "Cameron, Deidra doesn't have to bridge the powers between me and Cheyenne. We're already connected. We shared the same womb for nine months."

Cameron's face paled. "Twins?"

Aiyanna nodded. "Identical."

She watched the play of emotions on his face as he realized the magnitude of the situation. If Deidra tapped into the sisters' combined powers, they would not be able to stop her.

His expression darkened with an unreadable emotion when he stared into her face and demanded, "Tell me about yer family."

"Why?"

"Please," he begged, drawing her toward the bed where they sat. He gripped her hands in his. "I want to understand the relationship ye share with yer sister."

"We're very close. We were born witches like my mother and our grandmother before her. The gifts and skills we possess have been passed from one generation to another with no split in the powers. We each received equal share, equal strength and skills. Both of us have the power to heal and the power to foresee the future. We have limited control over the weather, and we can shift from our human shapes to an animal, although Cheyenne never quite mastered the skill. My animal is eagle, and Cheyenne's is fox. Our ancestors were witches or warlocks, sworn to help humanity. According to the memoirs we received when our powers blossomed, the members of our family have always believed in a merciful God and have never worshipped Satan. We originated from the old religion before it split into Dualism."

"Dualism?"

"It's a creed that holds to the existence of two

sides of God. White witches believe in the good side. God is stronger. He bestowed our powers upon us. The Diabolic are black witches. They believe that, the evil side, Satan, is stronger."

"What happened to the rest of yer family?"

"They're gone. Our parents were killed when we were very young. Cheyenne and I grew up in the state's foster care system."

"How did ye learn of yer heritage?"

"Starr."

"Starr?" His brows rose. "The cat?"

Aiyanna giggled. "With all your knowledge of the paranormal world, I'm surprised you've never heard of familiars. No matter what form they take, a familiar helps their witch with different types of magic and helps direct manipulations of natural energies contained in stones, herbs, and astrology, even the four elements. Starr has taught us all of this."

He shrugged, his lips curved into a lop-sided grin. "I've heard of them but never seen one before. 'Tis no' normal to see a talking cat." His lips quirked into the beginning of a smile, and then he raised an eyebrow. "Do ye mean to tell me that a familiar can take the form of a talking beetle?"

She giggled. "Familiars form an invisible bond to their humans. Most people I know would stomp on a bug, so no, they wouldn't choose a beetle."

He shook his head in utter disbelief. "Still, it all seems unnatural to me."

"You see a cat. I see family. Starr came to us when we turned eighteen. About that time, things around us were a bit bizarre. Cheyenne and I didn't understand, and, like you, add a talking cat to the mix, well, let's just say it was a difficult time. We adjusted. Starr showed us the memoirs and taught us how to stay alive. We keep a low profile and help people from behind the scenes. We can do no more than that. The hardest part is watching."

"Watching?"

"The religious groups who preach—"

"Do ye speak of the cults?" When she nodded, he continued, "Are ye telling me the animal and human sacrifices, the sadistic mumbo jumbo that's plastered across the television and the front pages of newspapers are the bad side of witchcraft?"

"The dark side," she corrected. "You'd be surprised how many people still practice black magic. Those people are evil and follow the Old Religion's beliefs. They worship Satan and his legions. They are sick people who want attention, people who've given witchcraft a bad name. True witches are healers not killers." Her fist clenched at her side. "Most people don't see the difference. If we use our powers to hurt, we pay dearly for it."

"And who punishes ye?"

"Just as you answer to your gods, witches answer to our covens."

"And who are they?"

She shrugged. "I've never had the pleasure, which is a good thing."

"How so?"

"I haven't done anything that's drawn unwanted attention to myself or my exploits." Her face turned thoughtful. "But once, I—" She stopped mid-sentence, shook her head, and granted him a crooked smile. "Never mind, it's not important.

"It must have been if ye thought to catch the holy hell for it."

Aiyanna laughed at his colorful phrase. "Holy hell, huh?"

"Aye, tell me what happened?"

She turned and walked to the window where she pushed aside the curtains to peer outside. "I trusted someone I shouldn't have." She swiveled around in slow motion. "I almost got both of us killed."

"But ye dinna."

She shook her head. "It's in the past and best left there."

"Tell me."

"I can't."

"Canna or wilna?"

"Does it matter?" she asked, her eyes locked onto his face. "Hey, look, I trusted someone once. Big mistake. End of story. I learned never to grant anyone unconditional trust. It gives them too much power over your emotions, especially your common sense. Makes you do stupid things."

All the anger, terror and guilt she held inside her spilled into the words. When he stepped forward and wrapped his arms around her, her body shook with the memory.

Her next words came on a broken whisper. "He was so handsome, gentle, and kind. I loved him so much. I trusted him." She hesitated, took a step back and eyed him with a critical squint. "And then I killed him."

****

He witnessed the stark terror of remembrance in eyes overshadowed by an ashen face.

Another man? His gut knotted, and his fists clenched. The bastard dared hurt her! By instinct his arms tightened around her.

Cameron's heart sank when she stepped away. Motionless, he recognized that Aiyanna needed time. She did something everyone does on impulse and without control. She fell in love and trusted someone with her heart.

Beautiful, passionate, brave Aiyanna. The thought provoked a smile, but hard on its heels came the desperate need to banish her fear, build up her courage, and make her believe in love again.

"Aiyanna, I canna begin to understand what that man put ye through, but I know ye. Loving someone doesna come with ease. Ye followed yer heart, and ye're still here. Ye beat him," Cameron said, closing his arms around her again.

She held herself stiff then softened. Her body melted against his. A faint sob tore from her.

"Did I? Funny, in a sense, I think he won. I suffer from horrific nightmares. One minute, I'm tied to a stake, and the flames rise up around me. I feel their heat, and, oh god, my skin burns." She shuddered. "I smell my smoldering flesh. Then I'm hung from a tree, and the rope tightens around my throat. I can't breathe." Her hand rose to her neck, her eyes glazed as if reliving the dream.

And for a moment, the flames licked at him. His body blazed in fire, and his throat tightened.

Images of Sarah's body and his daughters flashed in his mind, but he pushed them away. Not the time for self-pity.

"Doona do this to yerself," he said, his tone fierce. He lowered his head and stilled her trembling mouth with his own, devouring the softness of hers.

The gentle massage sent currents of desire through him, and he forced himself to pull away. His gaze roamed over her face, and he searched for the soul imprisoned in self-inflicted, suffocating darkness. Aiyanna Grey was afraid to live, afraid to love. A brief flash of regret filled him as he realized he wanted her to feel again, wanted her to live again, with him.

Her body relaxed against his, and she rested her head against his chest.

"Who are you, Cameron MacLean?" The words rushed out on a husky whisper. "Tell me who you are and why I feel so safe in your arms."

Cameron's thumb tipped her chin up. He lowered his head. First, he kissed the tip of her nose then her cheek, and finally, his lips skimmed the corner of her mouth. "I'm just a man, lass."

The caress of her velvety soft lips against his mouth set his body on fire.

Stop this!

Now!

****

His feather-light kiss robbed her of breath. Aiyanna couldn't think of anything other than the need that grew inside. She wanted this man for her very own.

And then, she was cold. The chill spread goose bumps along her spine. Her eyelids flicked open to discover Cameron no longer in the room.

She was alone.

She raised a hand to her mouth. Her lips burned and tingled in the aftermath of his fiery possession.

Had he simply vanished? How did he do that? Where had he gone?

A quick glimpse toward the window informed her that the sun had gone down. Even if she went looking for him, instinct warned her that she wouldn't find him inside the house.

She released a deep sigh of regret and sank back to the edge of the bed as a mirage of emotions bombarded her. Her hand moved to her throat, and she gasped for breath. Confusion raced through her.

What was wrong with her? Why didn't he want her? She shuddered, drawing air into her lungs. She settled her head in her palms and forced herself to calm down.

Suddenly, anger replaced her uncertainty. The fierce emotion swelled to a feverish pitch that drove away her depression. *Damn him!*

Even as emotional exhaustion claimed her, she grabbed her nightclothes from the bedpost and headed for the bathroom. A nice, cool shower before bed might help her sleep.

Obviously, that was the only thing she was getting tonight.

Chapter Fifteen

Darkness...a black inkiness encircled Aiyanna. Worse, an overpowering evil flooded the area and smothered her with malice.

She sat immobile on a hard wooden surface, her legs crossed, helpless to do anything except watch a man stroll from the shadows.

And then the clouds dissipated to free the skies. The moon and stars appeared and lit up her surroundings. She stole a quick glance around the area and recognized the scenery of Fort Ethan Allen Park on North Stafford Street.

How the hell had she gotten here?

The grounds were empty, and a sigh of relief left her lips. Whatever the evil, no innocence would be lost.

Aiyanna tilted her head and glanced toward the man. Dressed in black, he blended with the gloomy background of shadows behind him. Her eyebrows rose in awe of his size. Well over six feet tall, the span between his shoulders was at least two feet wide. His stance spoke of power and strength. If she were to stand beside the broad expanse of his chest, she would appear a toy doll by comparison.

A glass object flashed bright in his hands. She craned her neck forward to focus on the orb and view its contents, but it emitted such a blinding light, she could do no more than squint.

Who was this man? Her gaze returned to his face, his features grave. Hollow cheeks, a hooked nose, and a chin so sharply defined, he defied beauty.

This man should have been chiseled in stone, a sculpture destined to grace the parks for the pigeons.

Shoulder-length black hair swayed behind him in a breeze. Dark eyes flashed red and black like the hazard light in front of a firehouse, giving him a dangerous, predatory appearance. Of course, this look could only be enhanced by the definitive aura of raw power that radiated from him.

Who was he?

What did he want from her?

"Magnificent, isn't he?"

At the sound of Deidra's voice, Aiyanna jumped and swung around to the woman standing behind her. Horror gripped her stomach to find the Vampryss less than two feet from her.

Deidra smiled, nodding toward the man. Aiyanna's gaze whipped back to watch him, eyes wide.

Àghmach!

Fear and anger knotted inside her.

Had he escaped? But how?

He set the glass object on the ground and knelt on one knee. His gaze moved over her, his look filled with hatred. From the shadows, his minions entered one by one to form a single-file circle around him and the glowing sphere. They wore brown robes that hung to the ground. The material covered their faces, but the stench of death rolled off them.

A rush of adrenalin poured through her. She flew off the park bench and exploded in their midst like an avenging angel. She slammed one of the robed creatures against the stone wall. His shrill bellow rent the air before he burst apart in a puff of gray ash.

Another underling left the circle and attacked. His cowl slid from his head revealing red eyes and large fangs, identifying him as a vampire. She grabbed a broken tree limb, swung it with the force of ten men and slammed a protruding pointed limb into the bloodsucker's chest. Its image wavered a moment and then faded into a column of black smoke that spiraled into the sky and blended with the darkness.

She spun to face Ághmach and Deidra but froze. The glass object transformed into Cheyenne's still figure.

Ághmach smiled. He raised a knife and lowered it in slow degrees. When its descent halted at Cheyenne's blood-streaked cheek, Aiyanna stretched a hand toward her sister and screamed, "No!"

"One move, witch, and your sister will die." He issued the threat in a hoarse guttural order full of arrogance and intense hatred. Ághmach wrinkled his nose in disgust. "You reek."

Apparently, her white magic smelled as bad to him as his black magic did to her.

In the next instant, hoping to draw his attention from Cheyenne, she released her smart-assed nature and asked, "You mean to tell me I don't smell pretty?"

It didn't work. A moment later he raised a hand over her twin. A bright light emulated from Cheyenne's body. With his other hand, he pulled an object from the light and stood, raising his hands above his head. His hands discharged a radiance that circled above him with dizzying speed. Suddenly, a bolt of lightning broke free and shot outward. As if drawn by a magnet, it reversed course and struck Ághmach in the chest.

He dropped to both knees, his body convulsed and flesh smoked. A gray mist surrounded him, obliterating him from her sight. When it settled, Aiyanna's eyes widened in astonishment.

The man wasn't dead.

He remained on his knees, his body the color of charcoal. He tossed his head back and laughed in ecstatic hilarity. His laughter died on a sharp note, his gaze fixed on hers. He opened his hands to release what he'd extracted from the light.

The object dropped and landed on top of Cheyenne.

Panic and pain ripped through her at Cheyenne's wide, staring expression.

A cold block of ice took up residence in Aiyanna's stomach. Now, she understood the meaning of the glass object he'd held in his hands. It held her sister's magic. Cheyenne's soul.

No! No! No! How could this be? She shook her head to erase the vision. This couldn't be happening. A dream, a haunting, Cheyenne was alive. She had to be.

She couldn't ease the unnerving panic, grief or the sense of loss that struck every nerve, every cord in her body.

For certain, this entire situation, whether nightmare or reality didn't alter her perception of the man, or beast, standing before her. When she'd first seen him, he looked harsh and deadly, uncompromising. Now, he looked cruel, maniacal, and inhuman with narrowed eyes that delved into her soul.

As she stared into his face, she perceived the evil that uncoiled inside him. Unmitigated fear enveloped her, and she forced her way toward consciousness in an effort to escape.

Aiyanna's eyes circled the rest of the gathering. They lowered the cowls over their heads. Ashen-colored flesh; blue veined skins marred the bodies of the vampires who surrounded Ághmach. She also noted several humans among the crowd, their eyes wide, their faces distorted with blood lust.

Aiyanna grimaced. As Deidra's army grew, the world's chance of survival diminished.

God help us!

Ághmach's image faded. "Aiyanna, you cannot escape me. I will find you, and when I do, I'll steal your powers as I have taken your sister's."

Terror shot through her at the warning. His voice was soft, a caress, but it held the most menacing sound she ever heard.

He hadn't given her a warning.

He made her a promise.

****

Aiyanna bolted upright in bed.

Her hair clung to her face, and sweat ran down the length of her spine. She trembled.

"Just a dream!" she muttered, clutching the covers in a tight fist. With her other hand, she thrust her fingers through her tangled hair, trying to ease the remnants of her fear, but even the painful tug against her scalp had no effect against the terror in her heart.

"It had to be a dream," she whispered again. "If it wasn't, then Ághmach has returned."

She shook her head, not daring to believe the scenario her vision presented.

Sneaky bitch! It had to be an apparition, an image conjured by Deidra to make her believe Ághmach killed Cheyenne. When grief over the loss of her sister consumed her, the door to her realm would open and lie unprotected against the Vampryss' attack.

Her sister still lived, but time was running out.

Aiyanna needed to find her fast.

Chapter Sixteen

Aiyanna rested her hands on the desk. With a quick heave, she pushed herself backward. The chair's legs chafed across the hardwood floor with a shrill squeal. She cringed. The sound pierced her eardrums, creating a cluster of goose pimples at the base of her spine.

Exhausted, her eyes burned. She'd been staring at the computer screen for more than an hour, surfing for information on the Camarilla's imprisoned ruler and his succubus. Other than the traditional myths and legends, she uncovered nothing new.

Her nerves stretched tight and threatened to snap. She leaned back against the chair and brushed her hands over her face.

After a disturbed night of soul-searching, Aiyanna decided not to tell Cameron of her vivid dream—a decision based on Cameron's seemingly over-protective nature. Just the other day, the man had the nerve to demand she stay in the confines of the house for her safety.

Although she appreciated his position, she didn't agree and refused to obey his dictate. She couldn't remain housebound. The silence and loneliness would drive her crazy.

A smile tipped her lips when the exchange replayed in her mind.

"Ye're no' to go beyond the boundaries of this house. Do ye understand?" His voice firm, final, as if to say he expected her to calmly accept his command with no argument.

She disappointed him. His condescending tone grated on her nerves, and she eyed him with a decisive look. "Stop speaking to me as if I'm a child," she ordered, setting her chin in a stubborn line.

His mouth tightened, but she continued, "I hate to break the news to you, Cameron, but you are *not* my lord, master or even my father. I realize eating is not a prerequisite of your survival, but in my case, I'm human, and it's a basic need."

As if grasping the truth of her words, his expression grew serious. "I'll do the shopping at the twenty-four hour grocery mart on the opposite side of town," he offered.

Although she wanted to laugh, she forced remote dignity into her voice and asked, "When was the last time you visited a grocery store?"

He hesitated, and Aiyanna could almost see his mind work in an attempt to come up with a sound argument in response to her question. She didn't allow him time to contrive a half-assed scenario that might work for him but not for her. "I didn't think so. I'll do my own shopping, thank you very much."

For the next ten minutes, he'd done everything from threatening, consoling, even begging, to make her change her mind.

In the end, she won; however, the small victory had been overshadowed by the promise that her outings occurred during daylight hours. She would go to the store, return home, and never, ever go out at night.

And so, off to the supermarket she went for the first time in a week. Exhilaration at her newfound freedom swept over her but was soon overshadowed when she left the market. No sooner had she passed through the automatic doors into the fresh air than goose bumps crawled up her spine, and she was overwhelmed by an eerie sensation of being watched.

Her gaze gave the parking lot a once over, but seeing no one, she exhaled a deep sigh. Still unnerved, she rushed through the rows of parked cars until she reached her own where she threw her bags in the backseat and jumped behind the wheel.

She sat for a moment and gazed over the lot. Empty. Aiyanna drew a deep breath, put the keys in the ignition and mentally berated herself for her wild imagination.

But the sensation didn't end there. The feeling continued to nag her all the way home.

The flash of the computer screen caught Aiyanna's attention and drew her back to the moment. Cameron represented a safety net for humanity, but that was only a classification. It didn't speak of the man. He kept his life before immortality a well-guarded secret. She knew nothing about him, where he came from, his age, or parents, those general topics covered on a first date.

She scooted her chair forward and settled her hands on the keyboard. Her fingers flew across the keys, and she typed her Internet search engine in the URL bar of the browser. After a moment, the page opened, and she typed *Cameron MacLean* in her web seek assistant.

There were more than 1,000 links related to Cameron MacLean. Her gaze scanned each one until one caught her attention, and she gasped aloud. The summary read *Scottish born man, Cameron MacLean, kills his Irish wife and two daughters.*

She blinked and shook her head. *Impossible!* Cameron would never hurt another human being, let alone kill his own wife and children.

A new page opened. An aged black and white picture loaded onto the screen. The historian must have scanned the image into a computer. The picture had been sketched with charcoal, and the parchment appeared torn and yellowed against the white backdrop of the browser page.

She clicked on the likeness to enlarge it and leaned into the screen for a closer look.

Aiyanna gasped at the man whose likeness resembled Cameron. His arm rested across the shoulders of a petite woman about eight months pregnant. On his hip rested a smiling, chubby, little girl. His arm wrapped protectively around the child's waist.

In her heart, she knew the man whose face stared at her from the screen was *her* Cameron MacLean.

Her breath caught in her throat at the stab of jealousy that sent her blood pounding an irregular pace through her veins. This was a side of Cameron she'd never seen.

At one time, he'd been happy.

Brushing aside the thoughts, she read the caption. *Cameron MacLean, his wife, Sarah, and their daughter, Keara at a local fair, 1749 AD.*

She scanned the article.

Scottish born, Cameron MacLean, met and married Sarah in Ireland. The picture depicts happier times of him with his wife and daughter. In 1750 AD, it is believed he murdered his wife and two daughters, ages 4 years and 8 months. He disappeared, his death never recorded.

"My family was verra beautiful."

Her heart jumped. Her nerves tensed, and a thrill of frightened anticipation touched her spine.

With a twist of her foot, she swiveled around in the chair. Cameron leaned against the doorframe, his gaze absorbed by the image on the computer screen. Tears glinted in the depths of his honey gold eyes.

"I'm sorry."

His mouth spread into a thin-lipped smile before his gaze riveted from the screen to her. "What are ye sorry for?"

"For the loss of your family."

He focused on the picture one more time before he ran long fingers through his hair. "It happened a long time ago."

"Would you like me to print the picture for you?"

His shoulders sagged. Aiyanna saw the sadness in his expression. Shaking his head, he said, "No need. I havena forgotten them." He nodded toward the computer screen. "That was sketched at the local fair before Zaira's birth. She was born less than a month later."

"What happened to them?"

He shrugged. "I'm no' certain." Raw hurt glittered in his eyes. "I dinna do what they say I did. I dinna kill them." His voice broke. "I would never—"

"I know."

"I'd gone to Dublin that morning. A trip I made once a month for supplies and other necessities. I dinna get home till late. The house was so quiet. I checked on the girls and..."

He closed his eyes and swallowed hard. She rose to her feet, walked over to him, and brought her hand up to his arm. "You don't have to tell me. I know you didn't hurt them."

He opened his eyes. "'Tis ok, lass. It is all but a memory."

"That may be so, but I see it's still very painful for you."

His mouth spread into a thin-lipped smile. "Aye, well, the vision has stayed with me throughout the years. I found my daughters butchered in their beds and my wife gone."

"Oh my God!" Aiyanna murmured. Her voice faded in the hushed stillness that engulfed the room.

"I prayed to Him, too, but He dinna listen. I rushed off through the forest searching for my sweet Sarah. In the wee hours of the morn, I found her hung from a tree. She'd been beaten, her pretty face bruised and swollen. A rope tied around her neck like a—" he couldn't go on, his voice cracked with pain. He stepped back and leaned against the wall. His arms crossed over his chest. Closing his eyes, he thumped his head against the plaster.

"A witch." Aiyanna finished for him, her voice shakier than she would have liked.

He opened his eyes and nodded. "Aye, like a witch."

Tears formed on her lashes, and she leaned toward him. Stark realization swept over her. He blamed himself for the death of his family.

She reached out a hand and stroked his arm in reassurance. "It's not your fault. People who believe we are to be feared have cursed witches. I'm so sorry you experienced that cruelty."

His brows dipped into a frown. "Donna say that. Ye have naught to be sorry for. It was fated." He spoke with cool authority.

Aiyanna lifted her hand and caressed his cheek. "And do you believe in fate?"

Cameron covered her hand and drew it to his lips where he pressed a soft kiss to her palm. Her body tingled from the contact.

"Fate? I doona know if such a thing exists, but I believe in destiny."

"Aren't they the same thing?"

His eyes were hooded, and his brows drew together in an agonized expression. "Mayhap."

"I don't understand."

One corner of his mouth pulled into a slight smile. "No one controls fate. It is predetermined by the higher powers, but I have to believe I control my destiny. The road I take will be forged by my own hands, and by mine alone."

"I am glad that road has led you here."

His mouth curved with tenderness. "Are ye?"

"Yes."

An inexplicable look of withdrawal came over his face, and he took a step back. "I shouldna be here, lass."

"Why do ye say that?"

He shrugged. His face went grim, his expression tight with strain. "I almost dinna survive my family's deaths. I wanted their murderers dead and vowed to destroy them."

"What happened?"

"Uiscias happened. As I knelt before my wife's body, she helped me understand my grief and encouraged me to use the heartache, let it fuel my anger, so I could channel it in preparation for this battle against evil. If I dinna, misery would have ruled my life. It is because of her, I held onto my sanity."

"But you're not crazy, and neither am I." She stepped toward him. Her hands buried in the thickness of his hair. Her breasts pressed against his chest, propelled involuntarily by a slender, delicate thread of passion that formed between them.

"Aiyanna?"

"Kiss me, Cameron."

Large hands cupped her face, and his thumbs caressed her bottom lip. The air around them sizzled with eroticism.

Cameron exuded an inhuman sexual attraction, a lure Aiyanna had never experienced before.

Cameron took possession of her lips in a masterful kiss that made her head spin. Her body melted against him.

She moaned at the minty taste of his lips on hers. His tongue swept into her mouth. He pulled her against his hard body and into his strong arms. Running his hands down her back, he clenched the fabric of her blouse in his fists.

His muscles flexed around her. A raw, manly

scent of sandalwood invaded her senses. Her body burned with desire when he hardened against her stomach.

He took a step back but brushed his thumb across her now inflamed lips. His eyes, warm and tender, stirred her insides.

"Kiss me again," she whispered, an instant before she leaned toward him and kissed him, his cheek and mouth.

He gripped her forearms and held her away. Closing his eyes, he rested his forehead against hers. "Stop, Anya!"

Taking a deep, unsteady breath, she stepped away. Aiyanna read the passion in his eyes. She wavered, trying to come to grips with his rejection.

She shrugged to hide her confusion. "I don't understand. I thought you wanted me."

He tilted his head upward and closed his eyes. He swallowed hard. When he glanced back at her, his lips curved into a grim smile. "I do want ye, lass. More than ye can possibly know."

He shook his head as if denying himself the very thing he wanted. "Please understand. As much as I want ye, I canna. Every day when I close my eyes, I see the lifeless bodies of my wife and daughters behind my lids. I wasna there to save them. And for over two hundred years, my life has been fraught with danger. I wilna take a chance with yer life. I couldna live with the knowledge I was responsible for yer injury or death."

"You need to get it through your thick skull you weren't responsible for their deaths. You didn't kill your wife or your daughters, nor would you be responsible if something happened to me. I'm a big girl and do not need your protection."

"I'm sorry, lass, I wilna."

With those words, he turned and left the room without giving her any chance to reply.

Chapter Seventeen

Aiyanna rolled over and hugged the pillow to her chest. She should crawl from bed and start her day but couldn't get past the melancholy that wrapped around her like an extra layer of skin.

As a competent witch, she sensed the magical nuances that transpired through her world. She didn't have to see them; their essence strong, suffocating. Malevolence touched her skin and chilled her to the bone.

Pieces of her old beliefs slipped away, replaced by a new outlook that proved difficult to define. She'd changed, altered in some way and not only in her physical abilities as a human. Her magical spirit had become sensitized to her mood, and it was hard to distinguish one from the other.

In this process of self-awareness, she gained a special ability that brought her more in tune to other people. She sensed their emotions, happiness and fears. These sensations were better than the chary, lightless, perpetual darkness she'd witnessed in the past.

At first, she assumed her physical symptoms were signs of the onset of illness. She didn't want to move, and when she did, her body, lethargic and frail, refused to obey her commands.

But when she swelled to a feverish pitch of desire, in desperate need of release, she'd been forced to rethink her theory of contracting the flu. She tingled. The sensation originated in her shoulders, traveled across her back, continued onward until it paused and radiated between her legs. Her stomach grew hot and tight; her nerve endings strained for a man's touch, Cameron's touch.

Without a doubt, no flu bug afflicted her, sex not to be confused with illness.

Since their kiss, Cameron kept his distance. He stayed close to the house, but not to her.

Was he really afraid of her or for her as he claimed? She didn't know what strange notions went through his thick skull.

A floorboard creaked followed by a high-pitched whistle.

Aiyanna pushed herself into an upright position. The bed comforter slid from her shoulders. The room turned frigid, bitter cold. Arctic air stroked her flesh; fingers of ice slid up her backbone.

Wide-eyed, she stared at the corner of the room. A light the size of a tennis ball appeared and fluttered in the shadows. It grew larger and brighter.

The bedroom door whipped open and slammed against the wall.

"Aiyanna, are ye okay? I felt a surge—" Cameron stopped midstride, his attention drawn to the sphere of bright light. It drifted four feet from the ground. "What the hell is that?" His voice, crisp and clear, broke through her stupor.

Aiyanna shook her head, her gaze transfixed on the image. The bed dipped beside her, and Cameron's hand gripped her arm. The action drew her gaze from the vortex.

"Aiyanna!"

She leaned into him, rested her hand on his arm, and tilted her face toward his.

"What is it?" he asked a second time. Golden eyes, full of question, locked with hers.

"I've never seen one before, but I believe it's a gateway," she replied in a whisper.

His gaze darted to the light in stunned surprise. "To where?"

A trap, a temptation to draw her from the protection of her home, Aiyanna snuggled closer against Cameron. Instinct warned her she would need him, especially if this passage led to her sister.

"To another plane," she whispered. "Whatever happens, don't let go. No matter what I do, or what I say, promise me."

"Go in there? I wilna allow it," he assured in a deep, controlled voice. His arms tightened protectively around her.

A chilly black silence surrounded them, and a cold knot formed in her stomach. The muscles of his forearm hardened beneath her hand.

And then pain, a sharp biting pain exploded in her head, and she winced at the vise grip that wrapped around her chest. The handles constricted and squeezed the breath from her lungs. She moaned and clutched her upper body, doubling over.

"Camer—" she gasped. A hand closed around her throat and choked off her cry. Her teeth chattered, and her body trembled.

He must have heard the pain echo in her cry and pulled her into his embrace. His nearness comforted her. As the agony subsided, a shadowy, shapeless form revealed itself just inside the doorway.

Aiyanna blinked, picturing a large man dressed in black. His demonic eyes gleamed, fixed on them in curious disdain. A cloak, blacker than midnight, flowed behind him swaying in an unseen breeze.

Light from the hall filtered through the open bedroom door and lit up the features of the creature. His face portrayed an expression of sinister unearthliness. Could this be Satan? Or perhaps Àghmach endeavored to use his scare tactics on her again?

The shape distorted and transformed, first, to a blob of oblivion before it molded into another form, that of a dark-haired woman, Deidra, her face ashen, eyes a black cavern, empty and bleak. The woman's arms reached out to them, but she couldn't cross the barrier that separated their world from hers.

"It's Deidra," Aiyanna choked, scooting closer to Cameron.

And then, Deidra turned sideways and pointed at an object just inside the opening of the vortex.

Aiyanna gasped and shot from Cameron's arms. "*No!*" Ice spread through her veins.

Cheyenne hung on a cross. Blood poured from a wound on her head. Her arms and legs were nailed to the wooden column. Stakes pierced her palms and feet.

Cameron wrapped his arms around her, held her tight. "That isna yer sister, Anya," he murmured, his voice urgent.

Aiyanna shuddered at the agony her sister must have suffered when they hammered the wooden pegs into her body.

"*You don't know that!*" Aiyanna screamed, and struggled to escape Cameron's arms. The need to save her sister overshadowed all else.

"Bloody Hell, Aiyanna! Stop fighting me! Deidra canna pass through the doorway between her world and ours. She isna strong enough to cross the boundary of yer protection spell. If ye go into her world, ye wilna be able to come back. No' this way."

"But Cheyenne. Do you see what they're doing to her?" Her right hand rested on his chest, gripping the fabric of his T-shirt in a tight fist.

"Aiyanna, I doona believe that's yer sister, but if it is, Deidra wilna kill her. Doona forget. She needs her."

Aiyanna struggled against his embrace. "Let me go! Please, Cameron! I have to help her."

Cameron's arms tightened. His hands massaged her arm in a circular motion, offering his reassurances.

He kept his promise.

****

As much as he understood and appreciated her need to help her sister, Cameron refused to release her. She would, without hesitation, rush across the boundary separating the two worlds and become lost to him.

"Nay, I wilna let ye go," he stated again, his voice hard and unyielding.

Aiyanna ceased her struggles and dropped her head against his chest, but not before he saw her grief-stricken expression. His heart broke for her, but he wouldn't take a chance with her life.

"I'm sorry," he murmured, against the top of her head.

In the next instant, she swallowed hard, lifted her chin, and boldly met his gaze. Through gritted teeth, she demanded, "Let me go! Now!"

"Nay!"

With a loud shriek that resonated in the room, Deidra dashed into the vortex toward her wounded sister. When she reached Cheyenne's side, she cast an evil smile over her shoulder.

Deidra's eyes never wavered. If it weren't for the self-satisfied grin on her face, she would appear almost bored. She crooked a finger toward Aiyanna angling the bony appendage in a 'come hither' gesture. When Aiyanna didn't, she raised her hands in the air, her face twisted with disgust.

Just as quickly as it appeared, the doorway closed.

Cameron released her.

"I have to help her," Aiyanna whispered. Tears glistened on her pale, heart-shaped face, and she collapsed against him.

"We will find her, lass, but it has to be on our terms, no' that bitch's."

She bent her head and studied her hands. "Thank you."

"For what?" he asked, and tilted her chin, so she couldn't avoid his eyes.

"For not letting go. I knew—"

He pressed a kiss to her forehead. "Ye're welcome, lass."

Cameron drew her against him and rested his chin on top of her head, overcome by helplessness. Aiyanna's sister, if that was her sister, appeared in rough shape and faded fast.

They didn't have much time.

The muscle in his jaw clenched, and he fought to conceal his anger. Aiyanna needed his reassurance, not his rage.

A memory of the experience ricocheted through his head.

What had he observed? Maybe there had been a clue that would tell him where they imprisoned her. His eyes widened. *That's it*!

"Aiyanna, what did ye notice about Cheyenne?"

"She was hurt."

He nodded and sighed heavily. Of course, that would be the only thing she'd notice. "What else?"

Aiyanna pulled out of his arms to gaze into his face.

She bit her lip, her eyes thoughtful. She appeared to flounder in the agonizing maelstrom of memories. "What...what do ye mean?"

"Aiyanna, Cheyenne hung from a cross. *Think!* Where would ye find a cross as large as that one?"

The heavy lashes that shadowed her cheeks flew up as if the shock of discovery just hit her full force like a slap across the face. With a quick intake of breath, she muttered, "Oh my God! Why didn't I see that before? A cemetery?" Hope-filled eyes met his.

"Do you think it's possible?"

"I'd say 'tis a good place to start."

"Which one?" Aiyanna rushed to the edge of the bed where she draped her legs over the edge and reached for her slippers.

"Where do ye think ye're going?" Cameron asked in a terse tone.

"To check it out."

Cameron stood and rushed up to block her from leaving. "I doona think so." She opened her mouth to speak, but he pushed her back on the bed. "Ye're no' going anywhere, lass. Ye will lie down and get some rest."

"Cameron!"

"I said nay. Ye havena felt well the last couple of days, have ye?"

"How did—?"

He studied her for a moment before he replied, "I've seen the way ye've been acting. Ye doona have the usual fire in ye."

Her eyes widened in alarm. "Do you know why I've been feeling this way?"

"I have my suspicions."

"Then tell me."

"I canna. No' yet." He leaned over her and gave her a kiss on the forehead. "Rest."

Chapter Eighteen

A thunderous *thump* downstairs startled Aiyanna awake. Her eyes whipped open, and she gasped, drawing in quick breaths. For a few moments, she strained to listen for further sounds, but her ears met silence.

She managed a choking laugh, flopped back on the pillow and glanced at the bedside table where the bright red numbers of her alarm clock illuminated the darkness.

2:01.

Damn! She'd only fallen asleep an hour ago. She sat up, grabbed her pillow, and beat it with both hands. Satisfied with its softness, she lay down and closed her eyes.

The door opened. The hinges squeaked, and a soft glow pushed its way through the slight opening to cast a streak of light across the room. It disappeared a moment later when the door closed. Footsteps soft, yet solid ambled toward her.

Aiyanna, tense under the sheets, pretended to be asleep.

The footsteps ceased at the side of the bed.

And then she smelled him, his scent, sandalwood, leather, and all man.

Cameron.

The floorboards creaked beneath his feet when he turned and walked away. She cracked her eyes open a slit and peeked. He strolled to the corner of the room and sat in the antique rocking chair. His head bent forward, forehead to hands. He drew a deep breath and exhaled before he tipped his head back against the chair and crossed his arms over his chest.

Aiyanna should be angry with him for coming into her room uninvited. Instead, his nearness comforted her, and an incredible safe sensation swept over her.

Within moments, she drifted back to sleep.

****

Lee Stark staggered across the vacant side street to the all night coffee house for his *after-drunk* black coffee. As he neared his target, the familiar coffee flavors of French vanilla and mocha wafted across the light wind to invade his nostrils, and he sucked in a deep invigorating breath. He tripped and cursed at his stubbed toe but managed to stay on his feet.

In front of the shop, he pressed his forehead to the window glass. The place was empty except for a waitress and the busboy that cleaned the tables.

A tap on his shoulder drew him away from the vision.

Who the hell?

He shoved himself away from the window with both hands, turned, and lurched forward. He would have fallen if someone hadn't been there to catch him.

"Thank you," he murmured. He thrust himself away from the person who'd saved him from, most likely, a broken face.

"You're welcome."

Lee spun at the soft, enticing voice. He gasped at the beautiful woman who stood there. An ebony black gown draped her hourglass figure. Long ink-colored hair flowed down to her waist and blended with the flare of her dress. Her slender hands bore inch long nails, which she lifted to sweep loose tendrils of curls from her face.

Exquisite.

And then she smiled, presenting him with the picture of two-inch long incisors protruding from those full red lips. The image sent Lee stumbling three steps backward. His eyes widened, and a knot formed in the pit of his stomach.

"What the fuck are you?" he gasped.

The vision shrugged. "A woman." She laughed a soft, short giggle before she said, "And you are my meal."

Lee opened his mouth to scream, but she raised her clawed hand upward and slashed down before the sound escaped. The fingernail punctured his larynx, slid from his throat, and down his chest, where it sliced through his shirt and into his flesh. A pop exploded; then warm moisture flowed, followed by excruciating pain, as the cool air chilled his organs.

He swayed on his feet and clutched at the innards that spilled from his body. The sticky warmth of his blood hissed and bubbled between his fingers.

With another carving tear, his shirt and skin separated from the other side of his body. He lowered his gaze to see a combination of blood and intestines splash on his shoes. Blood splattered the sidewalk vibrant red.

He opened his mouth but gurgled, and a stream of blood spewed from his mouth.

His body fell forward, and the pavement rushed up to meet him. Funny, the one thought that came to mind...so much for that broken face.

And then, the throbbing pain subsided. The chilled temperature no longer mattered.

Warmth radiated across his skin before he remembered no more.

****

Light filtered into the room, sneaking through

the crack that separated the drapes.

Aiyanna stirred, fought to lift her lashes. She stretched and managed to split her eyes open, only to squint against the bright light. Moaning, she burrowed beneath the bed covers and whipped the comforter over her, tucking it beneath her chin.

She was so tired, far too tired to climb out of bed. An inner voice encouraged her to go back to sleep and return to the wonderful dreams she'd just left.

"Ye can never go back."

A gentle massage of electric desire immersed her at the sound of Cameron's accented, sexy tone. She rose from her prone position in one fluid motion. Her emotions whirled and skidded when she discovered Cameron in the chair he'd occupied the evening before.

Had he been there all night? How did he know what she'd been thinking?

"Aye, I've been here all night. For the second question, I have the ability to hear yer thoughts, lass."

Her eyes widened. Did he know of her dreams?

He chuckled. "I know only what ye feel when ye're awake. Dreams are private and meant for the dreamer alone."

"But how?" Aiyanna wrapped her arms around her knees.

"In time, ye will be able to do the same."

"You mean I'll be able to read people's minds?" At his raised eyebrows, she said, "Cool."

He laughed and shook his head. "Sorry to disappoint ye, lass. Ye wilna be able to read everyone's mind. Only mine."

"I don't understand."

"Aiyanna, our lives have been entangled by an unbreakable bond," he said with quiet emphasis. His left eyebrow rose a fraction. "Our thoughts, our powers will become one. Remember when I asked ye if ye've been feeling out of sorts?"

"Yeah, and you told me we'd talk about it. Is this the talk?"

He chuckled. "I guess ye can call it that."

"Okay, so fill me in. I'm all ears."

"I feel it as well."

"You've been feeling crappy too, huh?"

His mouth quirked, and he lifted one brow. "Nay, I wouldna say it that way." He paused as if searching for the right words. "Different. I've been different. It's hard to explain, but our connection has taken our relationship to a higher level."

"Relationship? Higher level? Geez, sort of sounds like marriage."

"Well—"

"You're kidding, right?" she asked, in a voice full of disbelief. Her heart jolted, and her pulse pounded.

An inexplicable look of withdrawal came over his face. "Would being married to me be so bad? Am I that terrible?"

A faint tremor of uncertainty touched his voice, and she recognized it as the need for acceptance. No, it wouldn't be bad being married to him, but...

"But what?" His tone was thick and unsteady, almost resigned.

"Would you stop doing that?" she asked, with exasperation.

His lips twisted. "Sorry, this is new to me too."

"How did this happen?" Even as she asked the questions, she already knew. She lifted her hand to her neck where he'd bitten her. "In the alley, when you—"

She stopped when he nodded.

"Ohmigod!" Aiyanna whipped off the covers, slid to the edge of the bed and jumped to the floor. "What are we going to do?"

"Sweet Jesu!"

Surprised by the tone of astonishment in his voice, Aiyanna spun around.

What the hell was the matter with him?

He stood still, his breathing ragged. His eyes traveled over her body. When his eyes met her, explosive currents of desire raced through her veins at the smoldering flame of need in his eyes.

"Put some clothes on. Please!" he choked, in a husky tone.

She glanced down and froze. "Oh. My. God," she muttered each syllable slow, steady and pronounced. She shot a look to his face. Her cheeks warmed under the heat of his wide-eyed stare.

Only a thin mini nightgown covered her body. Beneath the sheer material, no undergarments blocked his view of every curve, every detail...every...everything!

"My sentiments exactly," Cameron's voice choked back a groan.

Not waiting for her reply, he rushed from the room as if the hells of fire licked his heels.

The door shut with a resounding thud behind him.

Chapter Nineteen

Cheyenne struggled to stay awake.

She sank to the cot and clutched the thin blanket to her chest. Weak from loss of blood, her teeth chattered, and her insides trembled. Icy tentacles leached into every pore of her skin.

They always came for her when she dozed off. They'd whip her from the cot, half-asleep, for some demonic ritual. Whatever drugs they used on her erased her memories. The last time this happened, she woke with deep slashes coating her arms and legs, and a huge gash split the side of her forehead. Even the palms of her hands and the insteps of her feet hurt.

Someone please help me!

The shuffle of footsteps sounded in the hallway. She caught her breath when they stopped outside her door. Her heart beat a furious tempo against her breast, and her body shook at the fearful images that assailed her. Sounds of insistent chattering gushed in from the hallway and battered her eardrums.

Her chest threatened to burst. She swallowed, shoving back the tears that threatened to fall, and squared her shoulders, refusing to cower before her enemy. Her stomach churned, but she held her back ramrod straight, glaring at the entryway with burning, disapproving eyes.

The door swung open and slammed against the wall with a *bang* that reverberated in the enclosed area.

To her surprise, the faded vision of a woman stood in the open doorway. Her face held a self-satisfied smile, and yet Cheyenne recognized flashing contempt in her eyes.

"Yer sister is proving to be quite a challenge."

Cheyenne's laugh held a bitter edge. "It would appear she is the better of us. Aiyanna will not walk idly into your arms."

"Are strangers more important to her than you?"

"Innocent strangers," Cheyenne corrected.

"From what I have seen in this world, there is nothing innocent about your race. You wage wars against neighbors; steal and rob each other's possessions. How can you say your people are blameless?"

Cheyenne lifted her chin and met Deidra's gaze straight on. "We all have our flaws, but in your case, I believe they call it insanity."

Deidra's eyes flashed a spark of crimson. "Insanity? Maybe I am insane, but I shall win my war against the gods when I beat down the pathetic creatures of this world. The gods have taken everything from me, and I intend to get it back and make them suffer in the process."

"Gods? You're joking, aren't you?"

The woman shook her head.

Cheyenne snorted. "Who are you? If you wage a war against gods, why do you need Aiyanna or me? Our magic doesn't have the power to defeat them."

"I am surprised your sister did not tell you who I am."

"Must be you're not very important, for she didn't say a word." Another nice jab.

Her eyes flashed. "*I am Deidra Sidhe.*"

Cheyenne's stomach knotted. What little blood remained in her veins drained from her body. Frozen fingers reached in, gripped her heart and squeezed. This could not be happening. Could it? She remembered the stories Aiyanna told her about the evil Vampryss. The woman was a murderess, a child killer, the destroyer of entire cities and villages, but that was a myth. Wasn't it? Deidra Sidhe had been imprisoned by the Gods of the Tuatha Dé Danann, but her escape had already been prophesized.

Why the hell had it been *this* future?

At the smug look on the woman's face, she muttered, "Un-friggin-believable!"

Deidra snorted. "Ah, I see you have heard of me. So you know that your *God* cannot help you anymore than the Tuatha Dé Danann can help the pitiful race of humans in this time."

She swallowed hard. "What do you want from us?"

"Immeasurable power resides in the soul of a white witch. I have two within my grasp. That magic combined with my own will make me unstoppable."

"You have only one," Cheyenne corrected. She lifted her arms and displayed the numerous cuts and lacerations that marred her skin. "And, at this rate, I find it questionable whether I'll live to see you through your deviant plan. Draining blood does that to humans, or didn't you know?"

Once again, Deidra grinned. One of her hands flailed through the air in indifference. "I take enough to keep you docile."

"Docile?" Her eyebrows shot up in surprise. "You're a regular jokester, aren't you?"

Deidra's visage changed, hardened, the expression on her face one of undeniable malice. An electrifying shudder reverberated through Cheyenne when Deidra took a solitary step toward her.

"I never joke."

To prove her point, a satanic smile spread across Deidra's face, and she brandished a finger at Cheyenne.

Cheyenne shrieked in unbridled agony.

Thousands of needles pricked her flesh, jabbed over and over into the tender areas of her body.

Tears sprung to her eyes.

Deidra laughed at her pain. The bitch enjoyed her struggle to recapture her composure.

Starr insisted both girls memorize the *modus operandi*, the formulae designed to lay evil spirits to rest. Somehow, she drew power from her inner soul. Even though her voice vibrated, her tenor remained strong when she recited the ancient spell.

The Vampryss stepped closer, and Cheyenne raised her hands to shield her face. Blood dripped down her arms. Her head throbbed with pain.

She took a deep breath punctuated with several even gasps and forced herself to settle down. The bitch needed her to live, but she also needed Anya to achieve the power she sought.

Cheyenne lowered her hands, stood, and faced the woman, forcing her lips to part in a curved, stiff smile. "I won't give in to you."

Deidra's eyes flashed, and she raised a long, bony finger pointing at Cheyenne.

Cheyenne gasped for air. Her throat tightened, the airway pinched as if a hand wrapped around it, squeezing her life away. Her feet left the bed. She clawed at her neck trying to break the invisible grip. Gulping for air, her breath wheezed in and out of her lungs.

Deidra lowered her hand, releasing her hold on Cheyenne.

She fell to floor with a thud, moaning at the piercing pain that lanced up her legs. She inhaled, each breath a struggle that burned her throat and lungs.

The throbbing pain eased to a dull thud.

She grimaced and struggled to sit up, scooting back across the concrete floor until her back came to rest against the cold metal frame of the cot. Without taking her eyes from Deidra, she pulled herself onto the sagging mattress. The rustic springs squeaked in response to her weight.

"When will you learn it is useless to fight me?" the woman asked, her voice, though low, was condescending.

"Never," Cheyenne spoke, in a tremulous whisper. She folded her arms across her chest and leaned against the wall, averting her face from the Vampryss. A curtain of black hair fell over her cheeks, shielding her expression. There was no way she would allow Deidra to gloat over her fear.

"Then you shall have a lifetime of agony to look forward to."

Cheyenne jumped when the door slammed shut. Twisting her head, she glanced around the small room.

Empty. She breathed a soft sigh of relief. She'd survived a new ordeal at the hands of her captors.

Lord, she hated this place, and, even more so, those who kept her in this cage.

Staring at the dark ceiling, a shudder coursed through her. Could things get any worse?

She doubted it, but, then again, she'd been wrong before.

Chapter Twenty

Cameron would be pissed to discover Aiyanna blatantly disobeyed his orders and left the protection of the house.

"Too friggin' bad," she muttered. *He'll get over it.*

Not quite dusk, the fiery colors of the sun faded in the distance, leaving in its wake a bright caramel-colored sky. She gloried in the serenity of the day as it transitioned into night.

She strolled amongst the haven of oaks, staying close to the fence with line of sight to the house. When she decided to take this little stroll, the atmospheric vibes were stable, exceptional in fact. No evil lurked in the vicinity.

Tired of being cramped up inside all day, she needed fresh air. Cabin fever threatened to smother her. With so much extra time to think, her nerves stretched to the limit.

A twitter nearby caught her ears, and she stopped beside a row of pine trees. She spun around. Out of the corner of her eye, she spied bright, glowing white lights. They fluttered in and out of the gloom that linked the trees, as if to test the safety of the forest.

A flutter of air brushed against her cheek, the soft touch of a Fairy.

"Hello, my little angels," she called.

Forest Fairies flitted around Aiyanna's head. "Magic moves across the lands this eve. Be safe, dearest Anya," they whispered in her ear.

And then, the Fairies vanished. They rushed

into the green prickly branches of the pines. Their soft twittering receded and left the grounds frozen in silence. Aiyanna looked into the forest to see what alarmed them, but, with the exception of her, the woodland echoed with emptiness.

But then, another presence, perhaps more than one, brushed past her. The air chilled. The temperature turned glacial, almost hostile. A rush of frozen air touched her cheek.

Strange moans and grunts sounded deep in the woods.

What the hell was going on around here?

The answer came to her like a concrete block smashed between her eyes, and she cursed, *"Damn it!"*

The Summer Solstice. No wonder she'd felt strong and unstoppable when she'd left the house.

The Summer Solstice represented a time of fulfillment when gods and goddesses united, and people manifested great changes in their lives. The spirit world, magic, and the supernatural were also at its strongest. Spirits never unbound of their restraints were given freedom one night a year—this night, and she'd just intruded on their playground.

Aiyanna shifted on her feet and hurried in the direction of the house.

Halfway to her destination, cries of help echoed, and then her name whispered through the trees. Aiyanna stilled and turned to the darkening woods.

A woman's beseeching blood-chilling scream of fear sent a tingle of alarm crawling up her spine. She glanced into sweeping branches flickering in the breeze beneath the silver moonlight. The female voice pleaded for mercy. Her tone, stifled and unnatural, ended on a low, tortured sob.

Aiyanna held her breath and listened.

Sounds of galloping horses, their thundering hooves pounded the ground, followed by bloodthirsty shouts and jeers, drew closer. The clatter blasted around her, the noise so loud, it nearly burst Aiyanna's eardrums. She clasped her hands over her ears in an attempt to ease the pressure building inside her head.

Her heart squeezed at the anguished cries that circled her. The woman's fear was so genuine, it filled her with terror.

A gust of wind whipped the leaves into a swirling mass ensued by a loud *thud*. Mud splattered from the ground. The gooey muck splashed her jacket, and hefty gobs landed in her hair. Moisture lined her cheek, and she raised a hand to wipe it away only to discover not water, but sludge smeared her cheek.

The episode appeared real and transpired around her. A horse's warm flank rushed past. The lingering scent of wood chips, dust, and hay combined with the animal and the sweaty stench of its riders.

Aiyanna's stomach churned with nausea.

But she didn't see anything.

Phantoms and spirits.

In ghastly fascination, she listened. The woman pleaded and groaned on the ground behind her.

Aiyanna's heart pounded with every cry of the woman's agony. She spun in circles, sweeping the ground with her gaze and then with her hands, but there was nothing she could do to aid the poor woman.

Hit with the realization that this happened in the past, Aiyanna exhaled and stood.

Still, the racket climaxed then faded into the vibrating dusk before returning strong and vibrant. Instinct sent Aiyanna to her knees moments before an object whizzed past her head. The air rippled sweeping her hair into her face. She brushed it away, her eyes wide and staring.

A few seconds later, the woman's final dying scream faded, replaced by the shouts of the horsemen.

Aiyanna's insides quivered at the unearthly sounds. She couldn't escape them.

She clamped her eyes shut and chanted. The ancient spell would light the corridor leading into the next world, and grant these lost spirits freedom from the in-between realm of life and death.

Filled with anxiety, Aiyanna opened her eyes and continued her mantra until she achieved silence. No noise radiated from the dark, hushed forest.

Fighting to control her jangling nerves, she turned toward the house but hesitated when the wispy figure of a woman emerged from the trees. It paused, bathed in the cerulean light of the moon.

Her vision faltered, and her brows knitted together at the sight of a tiny, auburn-haired woman strolling from the trees toward her.

Aiyanna's eyes widened, and her mouth dropped open in stunned disbelief at the luminescent picture. Her heart thudded in shock at the vision of Cameron's wife standing in front of her.

His *dead* wife!

"Sarah?" Aiyanna asked, in a stilted tone.

"Aye." Sarah's eyes were pools of pain. Tears quivered on her eyelids and glistened on her pale cheeks.

"Why are you here?"

A heart-wrenching moan answered her question.

Aiyanna tensed; her body vibrated in fear. Her breath caught in her lungs.

Frigid water lapped hungrily at her feet trying to suck her into its murky depths. A strong force surrounded her, pulling her down.

She glanced toward the ground. Sheer black panic swept over her, and she gasped. Six inches of watery mud coated her feet. The sludge traveled above her ankles, moving up her legs at an increasing speed. It was as if she stood in a bed of quicksand. She twisted her body, trying to free herself.

What was happening?

And then, the muddy mess evaporated. An electrifying shudder reverberated through her, and her body jerked free.

Stumbling back a step, she swallowed hard, squared her shoulders, and lifted her gaze to Sarah.

Sarah's mouth moved. Her arms stretched toward Aiyanna.

"Aiyanna, ye must help him find peace," she begged over the untamed wind that whipped around them.

Aiyanna masked her inner turmoil with a deceptive calm. "Who?"

A secretive smile softened Sarah's lips. "Cameron."

Aiyanna heart jumped. "I don't understand," she stuttered. "How can I help him?"

"Ye must teach him to love again."

Aiyanna wavered, trying to comprehend what she heard. "What are you saying? How can I—?"

"Ye have already claimed his heart as he has yers."

"I do n—" Aiyanna's denial faded. A person could not lie to a ghost, but did she love Cameron? Or was it just a burning desire for his body?

The vision smiled, as if reading her thoughts. "It is love. Cameron believes it is his nature to fail those he loves. He wilna let his heart speak until he has released the guilt he holds so close." Raw hurt glittered in her eyes. "My time with him has ended. Yers has yet to begin. He dinna cause my death, nor is he responsible for the death of his wee bairns. It was our destiny. His mind understands why it was necessary, but his heart refuses to accept it."

Aiyanna frowned in confusion. "Why tell me? Why don't you tell him?"

"I canna." Sarah glanced from side to side as though looking for something or someone. "I shouldna be here," she whispered, catching Aiyanna's gaze. "Know this, love isna a sentiment to be spoken. It must be shown, experienced. Caress his heart with the strength of emotion ye have for him. Let him feel yer love." Sarah held her hand to her heart. "Just as I feel yer love for him now."

"I'm not sure I understand."

The woman's anguish and helplessness filtered across the small space that separated them.

"What can I do?" Aiyanna asked.

Sarah smiled. A glazed look of despair spread over her face. "Hold him close. Love him." She flickered then faded.

"No, wait!" Aiyanna stretched out a hand to the mist, but Cameron's wife had already disappeared.

Aiyanna turned on her heels and rushed through the trees. Her ankles ached, and her legs were weak. Panting, her lungs burned from the exertion.

She entered the kitchen to discover the house empty except of course, for her ever-faithful companion, Starr who lay curled up in the living room.

In her room, she stripped out of her muddy clothes, slipped on her robe and headed for the bathroom where she took a quick shower.

Downstairs, she kicked the thermostat up to seventy-five degrees and curled in one of the rocking chairs wrapped in a fleece blanket. She shuddered at the chilliness of her skin.

Starr jumped onto her lap, and Aiyanna smiled. No words were spoken; none were necessary. Starr always seemed to know when she needed a comforting hand. The warmth of the feline's body nestled against her calmed her, and she raised a hand to stroke the top of Starr's furry head.

Preoccupied by the evening's events, Aiyanna gazed at the floor plagued by ceaseless, inward questions.

Sarah MacLean died centuries ago. Why had she come back? Now? After all this time?

It was obvious that the woman loved her husband and worried about him, but why didn't she get in touch with him? Tell him her concerns? Why her? Had Sarah been tormented over Cameron's guilt all these years?

Aiyanna released the breath she held. She didn't know the answers to those questions and probably never would, but there was something Aiyanna could do for Sarah's spirit. In a soft tone, she recited words of the final resting spell and prayed it would grant Sarah's soul peace.

She slumped back against the chair, exhausted, and closed her eyes. Once again, she had expended too much magic for one day.

In less than ten minutes, she dozed off, with Starr cuddled protectively in her lap.

Chapter Twenty-One

With her wings stretched wide, Aiyanna soared across the sky. She never felt so free or at peace as she did in these moments. The glow of a cloud vapor appeared before her. The haze parted like the Red Sea when she entered. A cool mist brushed her feathers and remained with her until she exited the other side.

A flicker of light on the ground drew her attention. She flew down to investigate, landing in a large oak tree overlooking a group of vampires. There were too many to count. Arlington was rich in cult activity. Most of the time it was harmless, but tonight she decided to stick around and watch.

Dark-robed figures circled a burning fire, chanting a call to evil spell. A fog settled on the grass and curled around their feet. Her eagle vision allowed her to see through the thick murkiness. The foul stench of wickedness in the area overpowered her senses. Aiyanna should have found them by their stink alone.

An eerie sparkle flooded the vicinity, a faint flicker of light, but she couldn't locate its source. It was more than just the fog shimmering against the moonlight, but what was it? She leapt to a lower limb, taking her closer to the gathering. A thrill of frightened anticipation ruffled her tail feathers.

Cheyenne's motionless body lay in the arms of a figure that emerged from the shadows of the trees. Enshrouded by a black robe, the shape strolled toward the crowd.

Aiyanna jumped down to another limb for an even closer look. With her concentration on the activities below, her talons missed their mark. She lurched forward and almost lost her balance. Her wings twittered until she regained her footing.

She exhaled a quick breath of relief and turned her attention back to Cheyenne and the one who carried her.

The ashen-skinned, blue-veined, six-foot, lanky bloodsucker crossed the distance of the grounds to a makeshift altar that consisted of a flat slab of rock. Concrete bricks that had been ripped from the wall by the front gate supported each corner.

When he stood before the stone, he released Cheyenne's body, nodding when she landed on the smooth surface with a thud. Lifeless, her head slumped to the side. The figure then bent to light two black candles and place them at the foot of the altar.

After kneeling, he raised his hands, palms outward, and sang in a high-pitched voice.

The reciting figure's voice rose faster and higher until it reached a crescendo and ended on an abrupt note.

After a moment's silence the tall figure rose and turned to a shadowy outline that joined the group. They spoke to each other, their words gibberish to Aiyanna's ears. And then the recent joiner spun away from the group and disappeared into the trees.

The cult leader turned back to Cheyenne. He lifted his head, and the shade slipped back. Aiyanna glimpsed his shadowed face. He was only a man. He must be the high priest of this cult, no doubt, by the superior way he acted. He began his chant again, low this time, a soft mellow tone.

Perched on the branch, Aiyanna watched the activities below. In the distance, a glimmer of red light grew in size. As it drew closer, the assembly's chant increased in strength and loudness.

The circle congregated around Cheyenne, grunting and hissing a feverish chant.

The light progressed closer to the group, and Aiyanna watched Deidra materialize from the center of the red fog. The cult leader turned and handed her the knife, using his hand as a platter.

Aiyanna's gaze shot to Cheyenne before moving to Deidra who now held the sharpened blade. The Vampryss raised the serrated, long-bladed dagger above her head, preparing to strike Cheyenne in the center of the chest.

Anger raged through Aiyanna, and she leaned forward, prepared to drop from the branch and retake human form. Uneasiness swept over her, and she hesitated. Curiosity pulled her to examine Deidra.

Deidra always appeared as a creature of beauty, but tonight Aiyanna saw a different side of her. A hardened expression of callousness and repulsion resided on her face, certainly not the meager malevolent quality Aiyanna witnessed before.

As if she heard Aiyanna's thoughts, Deidra's lips curved into a semblance of a grin.

In the next instant, the Vampryss glanced in her direction. Their eyes met across the distance. Her smile widened. Her hands dropped, and she plunged the knife into Cheyenne's chest.

No!

Aiyanna screamed and jolted upright.

Starr hissed in surprise and jumped from Aiyanna's lap.

"Aiyanna, are you all right?"

Aiyanna rubbed her eyes and shook her head. "Yeah, I'm fine. It was just a bad dream."

Or was it? She gasped, panting in terror.

"What did you see?" Starr asked in a voice rough with unease.

Chapter Twenty-Two

Carrie Whittaker stepped through the doorway of Frederick Hall into the rain. She tugged the hood of her jacket over her head. A few droplets of rain slid down her face and spilled into her eyes. She blinked and adjusted the tweed material.

If her favorite teacher, Ms. Grey, hadn't decided to take a vacation, she wouldn't have to traipse around in this weather just to go to the library. What possessed Ms. Grey to go on leave less than three months after the start of classes? Carrie shook her head, baffled. It made no sense.

And now, Mr. Zimmer, the substitute, assigned a three-page report on the ancient Aztec Gods. If it weren't for this report due tomorrow, she'd be at the dorm, sucking down a few more beers while watching her favorite sitcoms on television.

Granted, she'd waited until the last day, but that was her prerogative, wasn't it?

Water poured from the skies. Within seconds, the pelting rain soaked through her coat into her sweater. The dampness settled against her skin, and she shuddered.

She rushed across the grounds to the concrete sidewalk. Her sneakers, slick from the grass, hit the path and slid out from beneath her. With a gasp, her hands shot out to catch the ground before her legs split in opposite directions.

"Shit!" Soaked, she stood and stretched the ache from her limbs.

Toward the end of the lawn, water roared along

the gutter and splashed over her boots. The shortcut, an alleyway between Welch and Safford Halls, loomed ahead. She staggered into the passage. Rain showered off the eaves of the buildings like a waterfall and splashed over her.

By the time she'd reached the other side of the passage, her teeth chattered, and her limbs quivered from the cold. Her anger boiled inside, ready to explode.

Wait until she saw Ms. Grey. She planned to let the teacher know the inconvenience her impromptu vacation caused.

Now, through the park, twenty yards over the grass and between the trees, she'd be home free. She shivered. Yeah right! The swaying branches would spray the rain over her again.

She entered the trees where the wind picked up in velocity, sending her spiraling backward. *What the fuck?* She drew a deep breath before each step, her hands wrapped around a tree for support. She traveled a few steps then stopped to rest before she continued. For the next five minutes, she struggled against a strong wind. She ducked her head and pulled her hat over her head, pushing forward.

She stopped and leaned against the base of a large tree. A chill spiraled up her back. Someone was watching her.

She glanced over her shoulder, expecting to see a group of fraternity boys. The boys of Safford liked to pull stupid-assed pranks on people.

No one.

What the hell?

The cold seeped into her bones and made her joints ache. She breathed a sigh when the wind eased up a bit making her travels a bit easier. Damn, she needed to get to the library just to get warm.

She picked up the pace to a near sprint, the

feeling of being watched persistent. To hell with them; they could play their stupid shit on someone else. She didn't have time.

Out of the corner of her eye, something moved...something other than the wind brushing against the leaves. She staggered to a stop and glanced back in the direction she'd traveled. A lamppost blurred against the side-swept rain.

Nothing.

She shook her head. Damn imagination!

Spinning around, the beating rain picked up in intensity. She stooped over and covered her face against the onslaught, but the cold breeze snaked around and brushed her cheeks.

A loud shriek, similar to the jaguar she'd seen on the television earlier, swelled from the trees. It echoed above the cascading rain.

She whipped around.

"Is someone there?" she shouted. "Whoever the hell's out there, this isn't funny. Knock it the fuck off!"

And then it appeared. A black mass stepped from its camouflaged position in the bushes. Its feet scuffled against the wet leaves. Covered with mud, it stood over six feet tall, broad across its midsection. A putrid smell lingered and floated across the breeze. She covered her nose. Her stomach shifted, nauseated.

Its eyes were a hellish red color.

She suppressed a gasp. The enormous, grotesque beast took shape. Pointed ears, a large snout, the animal, covered in long silver-black fur, strolled toward her on two feet. Fangs, sharp and pointed, seeped from the corners of a twisted mouth.

She closed her eyes. Her heart pounded against her breast.

Even in her alcohol-enhanced hallucinations Carrie had never seen anything like this. Not the type of horror any mind conjured.

So this must be real.

She took a step backward, twisted her body and ran. She stumbled through the trees, her legs weighted down by the mud that caked the soles of her sneakers.

Her lungs burned. The muscles in her thighs threatened to knot. Despite the cool air, sweat formed on her face. Her vision clouded.

As she bounded through the rust-colored leaves, the foliage kicked up around her. Footsteps trailed her, and then a maniacal laugh rang out bellowing through the trees. Its footsteps crunched down in the damp leaves in rapid succession and left no doubt it gained on her.

She tried to run faster, but she was too far out of shape, her legs too weak from the added weight of sludge.

She spilled through some brush and skidded across a blanket of leaves. Gripping a hold of a sapling, she spun to the right, jogged over a dead log and headed toward a cluster of oak trees. She'd almost made it when the animal caught a hold of her coat.

Like an animated film, her feet continued to move for several steps before she realized she wasn't standing on solid ground. Suspended in air, her movements proved worthless.

Mother Fucker!

She gazed over her shoulder into the fiery eyes of the creature. Hatred and bestial fury flashed in their depths.

She screamed. It yanked backward on her jacket and pulled her to its razor sharp teeth. For an instant, her feet touched on the ground, and she struggled but couldn't get a foothold on the slick carpet of leaves. She attempted to close her eyes, but they were frozen open, gaping at the disgusting, deformed face.

Pulling back her foot, she brought it forward in a swift jerking motion, connecting with the creature's furry gut. It grunted, and with a swift flick of its wrist, tossed her through the air. Her insides turned and twisted. She landed with a thud against the trunk of an oak tree. The agony of the collision brought a cry to her lips.

Stunned, she lay motionless. Her fingers touched a jagged-edged object, and she wrapped her hand around the precious weapon.

Terrified, she stumbled to her knees, the rock clutched in her hand. She pushed herself to her feet but held the rock behind her back. The creature snarled.

Her hand tightened around the small boulder. She waited until the animal stepped toward her. When it came within reach, Carrie hurled the rock at his head with all the force her hundred pounds could muster.

It didn't even attempt to dodge the rock. The mini-boulder struck the animal's right cheek. Its head jerked to one side. When it turned back to face her, its eyes flashed crimson. It growled in anger and took two steps toward her but stopped when a loud whistle ripped through the air.

"Learned your lesson did ya?" she taunted. "You're messing with the wrong girl."

"No, you are."

Carrie stiffened; her eyes widened at the soft voice that echoed behind her.

She whimpered and turned with deliberate slowness.

A beautiful woman with long, flowing black hair emerged from the shadows. Her eyes flashed toward the beast, and she nodded, "Thank you, my pet. I've got it from here."

Carrie's gaze whipped to the creature that

backed into the darkness, disappearing from sight.

"Thank you," Carrie wheezed. "I thought it was going to kill me."

The woman smiled and displayed inch-long fangs as eyeteeth. Fear twisted inside Carrie.

"My tracker, Samuel."

"Pardon me?"

"You carry the scent of someone I desire."

Carrie's brows pinched, and she took a step back. "What? I don't know what you're talking about." She shook her head, turned and started to walk away. Over her shoulder, she said, "Thank you again for saving me, but I've got to go."

And then, the woman faded, only to reappear a moment later less than two feet in front of her, blocking her path. She cocked her head at an angle.

Red eyes flashed.

Carrie leapt back. Before she could twist and run, the woman's hand wrapped around her. Claws dug into her flesh, piercing the skin. She whimpered, panting in terror.

Fear settled in Carrie's stomach. Bile rose in her throat. She shut her eyes.

A hand settled beneath her chin, jerking her head sideways. Pain pierced her throat, and liquid seeped from the wound, spilling down her neck.

Her strangled scream rang out through the trees but was overshadowed by the rain.

Then the forest went silent.

Chapter Twenty-Three

Aiyanna tightened the sash of her bathrobe around her waist and entered the kitchen. The day's newspaper sat in the center of the table.

The headline smeared on the top of the front page caught her attention. *University student murdered on campus.* Her stomach knotted.

She charged across the room and whisked the paper up in shaky hands. Tears filled her eyes at the gray and white image of Carrie Whittaker.

She scanned the article.

Reported missing yesterday by roommates, the mangled body of university student, Carrie Whittaker, was discovered by a woman jogger in the trees at the north end of campus.

The investigation is scheduled to continue throughout the day. Authorities are not releasing any information regarding her death; however, unconfirmed reports indicate she died as a result of an animal attack.

She gasped, dropping into the chair with a *thump* in stunned anguish. Her hands clenched, folding the paper into a crumbled, wrinkled mess before releasing her hold. The paper fluttered to the table.

She closed her eyes, swallowed hard and choked on a cry. Not Carrie. A picture of the bubbly, blonde teenager swept behind her closed eyelids.

Her hands covered her face, and she yielded to compulsive sobs that shook her body.

After a moment, she became conscious of

another presence in the room, recognizing Cameron's crisp, clean, masculine scent.

His hands dropped to her shoulders, and he gave her a squeeze meant to console. He released a long, audible breath. "What is it, lass? What's the matter?" he asked, in a low, husky tone.

His mellow baritone, edged with concern, calmed her.

She hiccupped and jumped to her feet. Her finger tapped the front page of the paper in a series of rapid blows. His gaze followed, his brows drawn. He leaned over her and read.

"Look what the bitch did, Cameron. Carrie never did a thing to her. Why?" she demanded in a high-pitched voice, only to end in a whispered, "I don't understand why."

"I take it ye knew the girl," he asked, his gaze returned to her face.

"Carrie was one of my students."

He nodded and dropped the paper. "An acquaintance. Perhaps she carried yer scent. Something as wee as a pencil can leave yer essence on a person."

"But why this? Why kill her?"

"Pain and sorrow have a way of opening up a person's senses. In doing this to Carrie, Deidra hopes yer grief will grant her access to yer psyche. Ye need to discover a way to control yer pain, lass, or channel it in another direction so she canna use it against ye."

"Carrie didn't deserve this."

"No one does, lass." He shook his head. "There's no justification in that kind of death, but ye have to combine yer pain with yer powers. It may no' seem so now, but ye will be stronger because of it. I promise ye." He drew her into his arms. His chin rested on the top of her head. He caressed her back in slow, circular motions.

His nearness hurled her emotions from the hurt and anger she experienced over Carrie's death...to a subject that overran her conscious thought a lot over the past few weeks...their spiritual connection.

With this newfound awareness, Aiyanna didn't know what to feel, what to expect or do.

A guardian's mate.

Her, Aiyanna Grey, who would have figured?

She'd done a bit of research on her current situation and learned some interesting facts about their "matrimonial state."

What she couldn't understand was why Cameron didn't tell her all the details.

"Tell ye what?" his velvet soft voice whispered in her ear. His warm breath brushed her cheek, creating a surge of goose bumps on her legs.

"Nothing." Maybe he didn't know.

"Know what?" he asked, his tone smooth but insistent.

"Nothing," she replied absently before pulling away. She picked the dishcloth up from the table and draped it over the oven door handle.

In the real world, Cameron MacLean was dead. More than two hundred and fifty years dead to be exact, but she felt him, his passions, his desires, and the warmth of his body. To her, he lived, and she wouldn't have it any other way.

"Thank ye." This time, sensuality laced his words and captivated her. She remained motionless. A flash of heat raced like a fever across her skin. Turning, she took a deep breath and pasted on a smile, betraying nothing of her annoyance that he read her mind. "Would you stop—" Her words caught in her throat when she found her nose against the broad contours of his chest.

Oh Lord, he was hot...and sexy...and hot. Even his scent intoxicated her and sent explosive currents curling her toes.

Sweet heavens, she wanted him. Desire rose in her, scorching and undeniable.

Aiyanna hadn't been this close to him in almost two days, two long, excruciating days. She harbored no doubt that he ignored her on purpose, and yet now, in this moment, nothing mattered except the two of them.

She glanced up from beneath her lashes. His gaze raked boldly over her. When his eyes returned to her face, fire smoldered in their golden depths.

Did he reach for her?

Or had she been the one to stretch out her hands for him?

The bond that connected them drew them into each other's arms. In one fluid motion, he wrapped his arms around her and pulled her against him.

Cameron's trembling hand brushed across her cheek. Aiyanna saw the tremor and realized how close he came to losing his control.

Undaunted, silky reassurance coursed through her.

****

He should leave, now, before things got out of control. Even as his mind argued with his body, the fresh, captivating scent of apple blossoms filled his senses. His gaze fell to the creamy expanse of her neck.

He ached to make passionate love to her. He needed to stop. It, *this*, wasn't fair to Aiyanna.

But no longer could he deny the fact that he wanted to see passion flare in those chocolate-colored eyes, to feel her tremble for him, her muscles clenching around him when she reached her release.

The magnetism that built between them since the first day they met took control. Powerless, Cameron couldn't resist her lure.

She stood on tiptoes, tilted her face and leaned toward him. "Please," she whispered. Her hot breath seared his ear.

Her lips trailed across his cheek. He closed his eyes and enjoyed the tantalizing sensation. And then, she touched her lips to his in a kiss as tender and light as a summer breeze.

Her tentative, uncertain touch sent a shock wave through him. "Aiyanna, we shouldna. Ye need—" His voice husky, little more than a growl against her lips. Words trapped in his throat, his rationale moments behind. He leaned away and opened his eyes, needing to see the expression on her face.

"You. I need you, Cameron," she said, and moved against him. Her breasts, nipples erect, brushed his chest.

Her invitation was a challenge, hard to resist, and he hauled her against him. His mouth moved over hers, and he devoured her lips in a passionate kiss.

Raising his mouth from her, he gazed into her eyes. "Ye doona understand what will happen. What ye will become." He fought an inner battle, his inner demon.

Aiyanna tilted her head and gazed up at him. A saucy smile curved her full lips. "I do."

Cameron's heart jolted, and his pulse quickened. She accepted him, all that he was and all he was meant to be. She'd uttered the two words that would bind them together for a hundred lifetimes.

Was he worthy of her?

Two simple words, but their meaning held the power of the ages, the marriage vow said out of context. Centuries of pain washed away, replaced by the realization of love and happiness.

Did he dare allow himself the luxury?

At a loss, Cameron hesitated. In the past, he'd fought many wars. Even when the fight lasted all day, he endured the battles and rejoiced in his victory. Never had he been faced with the struggle he had now. All his honorable intentions were in danger of dissolving away with just her touch.

His gaze traveled over her. Desire flashed in the depths of her cocoa eyes. At the base of her throat a pulse throbbed and swelled as though her heart had risen from its usual place.

When she reached up to caress his cheek, he faltered closer to the edge of the cliff he'd always feared tottering over. He didn't know what lay at the bottom of the chasm: happiness or sorrow. He'd lived through both, and if he were to look deep into his heart, he knew he wouldn't survive any more misery.

"This moment belongs to us," she whispered. Her gaze moved over his face as if memorizing him. "It's not about your past, my past, not about the future. Right now, it's you and me, here, just the two of us. Make love to me, Cameron. Please."

Magic words. She'd uttered the words to break his last thread of sanity.

He swept her, weightless, into his arms. Reclaiming her lips, he crushed her to him, his kiss more demanding this time.

Instinct led him through the kitchen and up the stairs to her room, all without breaking the contact. At her door, Aiyanna reached for the knob and turned it.

Cameron strolled inside and released her legs, his arms wrapped around her torso. Her lower body slid the length of his in a soft caress.

Stepping from his arms, Aiyanna gripped the front of his shirt in her fists and pulled him toward her. She took a few small paces backward toward the bed, drawing him with her. Her actions, firm and persuasive, invited more despite the infinite gentleness in her touch.

She stopped and pressed her palms against his

chest in an action meant to halt his advance. Her eyes glowed with a savage inner fire. She retreated a pace. His heart thudded a violent beat when she raised her hands to her shoulders and tugged the robe from her body.

His breath caught. The fluffy fabric fell away, and she stood before him covered in the thin, white gown he'd seen her in before. He loved that gown, for it was little more than a hindrance, and she looked so sensually sexy in it.

One step and he stood before her. He wound his fingers through her onyx hair and took her mouth hard. She met the plunge of his tongue, clinging to him. There was no hesitation in her, only a need that matched his.

His hands traveled and skimmed each side of her body, across her hips to her buttocks where he tenderly gripped her cheeks in his hands and pulled her against him. He wanted her to feel his need.

He clenched the material of her gown and drew it upward to bare her skin to the waist. Without releasing his hold on the white silk, he stepped away.

Aiyanna raised her arms, and he slipped the thin material the remainder of the way over her head.

He groaned.

"Ye're beautiful, lass," he remarked, in a voice hoarse with desire.

She smiled. Her hand reached for his tee. As she tugged it out the waistband of his jeans, her palms brushed against his skin.

Cameron raised his arms and allowed her to remove his shirt. Just as the material clutched tight to his upper arms, she stopped. Her hands held the tee and his arms in place. Blinded by the cover, he heard her soft giggle moments before her lips touched his bare chest. He groaned in sweet agony when her hot, wet mouth moved over flesh, spreading tiny kisses across his skin.

"Aiyanna," he murmured, when she nipped at the now hardened buds. An explosion of fiery sensations raced through him and fired his blood.

After a few moments of sheer, blissful torture, he brought his hands forward where he grabbed the material of his shirt. With a quick yank, he pulled it over his head.

He faced her yet took a step away. When she followed, he held up a hand to halt her. His gaze remained locked on hers as he reached for the button of his pants. With a flick of his wrist, he released the closure and slid the zipper down. His fingers slid into the waistband of his jeans. He caught his briefs and lowered them and his jeans to the floor.

He kicked them to the side of the room.

With exquisite harmony, Aiyanna and he moved into each other's arms. Their lips met in a passionate kiss.

He explored the soft hollows of her back with his palms, marveling at the silkiness of her skin.

His blood boiled when she buried her face against the corded muscles of his chest. Her trembling limbs clung to him. His fingers traced a path across the silken skin of her thigh, sliding into the nest of curls that shielded her womanhood.

Hot moisture coated his fingertips. He groaned aloud.

So much for taking it slow, he thought, as they tumbled across the bed. He came down hard above her, but she didn't seem to notice. She clasped a hand around him and guided him to her warmth.

Forcing her lips open with his thrusting tongue, he sheathed himself in a single plunge. The pleasure of her velvety passage surrounded him, pure and explosive. He stilled, allowing her a moment to adjust to his size before he thrust hard and fast.

Aiyanna moaned beneath him; her hips arched and matched him stroke for stroke. A fine sheen of perspiration dewed her skin. She grasped his hips and pulled him closer, lifting her legs higher, taking him deep inside. Her fingernails burrowed into his thighs, and her body tensed before her breath rushed out as a long, surrendering gasp. When she reached the pinnacle of release, her muscles clenched, released, and tightened around him again.

Cameron could no longer control the force she'd unleashed in him. He groaned. His climax erupted without warning, savage in its intensity.

Stunned, he slumped against her, hardly believing the force of his orgasm. He had never taken a woman like that in all his life, but then he'd never known one who was so explosively responsive.

No one compared to Aiyanna.

****

Cameron rolled to his side, pulling her with him. Aiyanna snuggled against him, resting her head on his shoulder. She traced a path over his chest with her fingertips. He covered her hand with his own, giving it a brief squeeze before he held it against him.

Aiyanna had dreamed of him for so many nights, erotic, passionate dreams of untamed sex and heights of pleasure she never believe existed.

Wow, was she ever wrong.

The moment his lips crushed hers, his mouth hot and full of fire, she was lost. They melded together, two halves of the same whole, devouring each other with fire and electricity.

A story, committed to memory as a nine-year-old child, rushed to the forefront of her thoughts. In one of their many foster homes, she overheard the caregivers talking. They didn't know she hid beneath the stairs, listening in awe. They claimed that when people found true love, the earth moved at the moment of their joining.

She smiled at the vow she made never fall in love if it meant a quake would follow. But tonight, when Cameron wrapped his arms around her, a curious rippling cascaded over her.

It felt right.

Together, they felt right.

Was that what the two ladies meant?

Cameron pulled her closer and fit her body tight against his.

Aiyanna turned in his arms. She leaned over his chest, cradled her chin in her palms, and studied his handsome face. His eyes were closed. The moonlight filtered through the curtains and glimmered over his features like beams of radiance, and she fought a battle of personal restraint. He needed his rest.

"I'm not asleep."

Aiyanna blinked twice and took a sharp breath. His lips hadn't moved, but how had she been able to hear his voice?

"Cameron," she spoke in a suffocated whisper.

He opened golden eyes. They met hers, and he offered her a sudden, arresting smile.

"Aye, lass. I no longer have to speak the words aloud for ye to hear me." His calm voice matched his steady gaze.

"Are you telling me that we are truly joined?"

Cameron's eyes shadowed a hint of sadness, which, in the next heartbeat, he masked. "Aye. In my world, we are one."

"You forget your world is now mine."

"Aye, but I fear ye will regret it in time."

She shifted, holding herself up on one elbow. With her other hand, she traced a lazy finger over his chest. "Cameron, you have shown me a world of hunger and passion. How could I ever come to regret that?" She broke into a wide, open smile. "But we will have to keep out of each other's minds. That is a bit unnerving, don't you think?"

"Aiyanna, there is more to my world than that and well ye know it." His palm slid down her hair, his breath warm on her face. "And aye, I promise no' to infringe on yer thoughts, but know this, if I feel ye might be in danger, there will be no debate. Understood?"

Aiyanna smiled, nodded and pressed a gentle kiss to his chest. "For tonight, my handsome prince, there is only the two of us...here...alone. I can think of other things to do besides talk."

A delicious shutter heated her body at the look of undisguised desire in his eyes. He wrapped his arms around her and rolled her onto her back. She squealed in surprise but giggled when she looked up into his smiling face.

"Do I scare ye, lass?"

Aiyanna sensed a deeper meaning to his question and draped her arms across his broad shoulders. "No, Cameron, I'm not afraid of you, and I'm not afraid of the future."

"Ye should be."

She shrugged. "Perhaps, but I'm not feeling it at the moment."

"Why no' now?"

"Simple. Ever since I met you, I feel protected."

He smiled. His lips hovered over her mouth before dropping to hers. His kiss was slow, leisurely, as though he were pleased with her answer.

She pushed him away and laughed.

"What?" he asked, his brows drawn in uncertainty.

"Oh, I just thought you might like to know you'll be safe with me, too."

He chuckled. "Is that a fact?"

"But of course."

His expressive face changed and grew solemn. Before he could speak, she covered his lips with one finger and shook her head. "Shhh! Please, don't say anything. Just for tonight, can't we leave that world outside this room?"

Aiyanna wrapped her fingers through his hair and pulled his lips to hers. Before his lips touched hers, she whispered, "Just the two of us. Show me there's something worth fighting for. Please."

****

He did his best, at great length and repeatedly throughout the night.

Even he forgot what waited for them outside the walls, but when Aiyanna curled against him with a satisfied murmur and drifted off to sleep, he remembered Sarah, his girls, and their brutal deaths.

Had he sentenced Aiyanna to the same fate? He'd never forgive himself if that were the case.

Cameron glanced down at her, drinking in the sight of her. From the top of her raven-colored head to the bottom of her delicate feet, she radiated perfection. Her limbs were slender, her waist a deep indentation above the chalice of her hips. Her breasts filled his hands, her nipples perfect, made for his mouth, and above all else, she exuded beauty inside as well.

Aiyanna Grey was everything he desired in a woman, and more than he had known could exist.

He gathered her close and pulled the covers over them.

"I've never asked anything of ye before, always doing what needed to be done. Now I ask but one thing of ye...please keep her safe," he whispered, pressing a soft kiss to her forehead. His arm tightened around her, drawing her close, and he closed his eyes.

Night wrapped around the house and shut out the world giving the lovers a little more time.

Chapter Twenty-Four

Light brightened the darkness behind Cameron's eyelids, urging him to stir from sleep. He fought the radiance, reluctant to awaken and leave the dream that felt entirely too real. The fantasy of making love to Aiyanna, her body pressed to his, was too incredible a sensation to give up.

He plunged back to earth at the warmth of a body snuggled against his back. An arm draped over his shoulder. Well-defined bare breasts with hard nipples rose and fell next to his naked skin. Aiyanna's apple fragrance invaded his nose, and his eyes popped open.

How could he have let this happen? A stab of guilt buried deep in his chest like a hot poker at the realization of what they'd done. He'd taken advantage of her while she was in a fragile state over Carrie's death and cemented her role in his life. He'd finalized their union, drawn her into his world even when he vowed not to.

His blood soared at the memory of their night together, the pleasure of their lovemaking pure and explosive. With her fiery passion, Aiyanna Grey left a burning imprint on his heart—one he'd unlikely ever find again.

She shifted and inched closer, if that were possible. Her muffled moan, followed by a soft purr struck him as the most soothing sounds he ever heard. Her hand slid over his hip and caressed a path across his abdomen, up his ribs where it came to rest on his chest.

His sight, still blurry from sleep, searched the room. Through the heavy blue drapes covering the bedroom window, slivers of sunlight peeked.

Regardless of Aiyanna's soothing touch, painful memories of his past ambushed him. He'd lived without the sun in his life for two hundred and fifty years. It had been a long time since he'd seen a sunrise or felt the warmth radiate across his skin.

As he often did, he closed his eyes and imagined the sky flooded with pale pink light on a glorious Irish morning. A lump formed in his throat at the memory of the home he'd shared with Sarah. Aye, the lands were beautiful, yet beneath her exterior, treachery ran rampant.

When he lost his family, Cameron took his rightful place among the guardians. This was his destiny. The gods taught him, training him in the skills of battle, but they never made him forget. He missed the sweet sounds of his children's laughter, his wife's arms wrapped around him, and rainbows after a rough storm.

He lost so much.

Last night, Aiyanna gave him a taste of what he yearned for the most. Love.

Aiyanna fascinated him as no other woman, aside from Sarah, ever had. As a guardian, he chose random lovers, secure in the knowledge he'd never see them again. No one trespassed across the rough barrier he'd constructed around his heart, the rod-iron gateway impenetrable.

For centuries, he existed, content with one-night stands. Wanton women who wanted nothing more from him than the few hours of pleasure he offered. He'd placate them with minimal conversation and then screw them over and over. Often, three times in one night, but in the end, they went their separate ways. Most of the time, he hadn't bothered to ask them their name, the information unnecessary.

But now, that changed. Every detail about the woman he chose as his life mate was significant and vital to his well-being. The transformation, however unwelcome, brought a glow to his heart.

He couldn't count how long it had been since he shared a real laugh with a woman, a lover.

Aiyanna made him laugh.

She made him crazy.

Most of all, she made him burn.

She stumbled into his world and flipped it upside down. She touched the emotions he'd buried with his family and jumpstarted his heart. Alive again, and for a man more than two-hundred-fifty-years-old, that could be considered quite an achievement.

Like a small child on Christmas morning, overloaded with new sights and smells, his senses flooded with anticipation to see what the packages under the tree held.

What did the future hold for them?

He rolled onto his back, pulled her head to his shoulder and gazed down into her face.

Aiyanna Grey sparkled of beauty, intelligence and sweetness.

The corner of his mouth twisted into a slight grin. No. Sweet wasn't the best word to describe Aiyanna Grey. She had a tart mouth when provoked, could be a wee bit bitchy at times and carried herself with undeniable determination. Despite all of that, she exuded true gentleness.

He sighed and tucked an errant curl behind her ear. She caught his hand and pressed her lips to his palm.

Her eyes opened, smoky chocolate eyes filled with contentment. A small smile of enchantment touched her lips.

"If only we could stay like this forever," she said. Her voice filled with longing reminded Cameron of a young girl's innocent desire, a woman's eternal dream, "but I know—"

"Hush." He dropped a light kiss to her forehead. "There'll be plenty of time for that later."

With the tip of her finger, she traced the tattoo of a willow tree on his shoulder. In the background, the bright light of the moon billowed through the limbs. "I love this tattoo. Does it carry special meaning to the Síoraí?"

With a glance at his shoulder, he shrugged. "They're Celtic symbols of protection, power and longevity, the mumbo jumbo of the ancients. I'm surprised ye're no' familiar with them, what with yer teachings and such."

"It would appear the ancients didn't believe in disclosing all their secrets. Minor details are often left unwritten."

"Perhaps they believed it best that way."

She shot him a wistful glance from beneath her lashes but said nothing more. He gathered her against him and pulled the covers over them both before he settled back against the pillow.

His eyes fixed on the ceiling.

Time, he simply needed to find enough of it— moment upon moment—then watch it pile up and create a wall to protect them from the world and its madness.

Sleep whispered at the edges of his consciousness. Before slumber overtook him, a bitter memory emerged and burned in the back of his mind. He visualized his beloved Sarah hanging from a tree, an empty shell of the vibrant woman she'd been, and his wee daughters, no longer the happy, giggling girls that brought so much happiness to his life.

Damn it to hell.

A flicker of apprehension coursed through him, and his arms tightened around Aiyanna. The strange surge of affection he felt for the woman in his arms sent shivers of fear radiating over him.

By the gods, what the hell had he done?

By sanctifying the union, had he opened the door for her death?

Aiyanna caressed his bare chest; she twirled the curly hair. "You didn't," she whispered.

He covered her hand with his own and gave it a squeeze. "I thought we were going to give each other moments for our private thoughts, eh?"

Her eyes widened in alarm, and she bolted upright. A blush like a shadow ran over her cheeks. "I'm sorry. I didn't mean it. They kind of jumped out at me. I'll try to get control over that, I promise."

He chuckled, pulled her back into his arms, and pressed a kiss to her forehead. "I know ye will." He glanced toward the window. "I suppose we should get up."

"Do we have to? Can't we just stay here?" she murmured, pulling the covers over her head, curling up to him.

Cameron closed his eyes and enjoyed the warmth of her bare breasts against his naked skin.

"A nice notion, but we canna lie abed all day." He chuckled and slid to the edge of the bed where he dropped his feet to the floor.

She moaned and stretched. Her head peeked out from beneath the comforter. "Where are you going?"

"Come on, lass, 'tis time to get up." He brought his hand down on her butt and delivered a stinging slap.

"Ow!" Her eyes widened. She shot him a grave look.

Aye, there was that bitchy side.

He threw back his head and released a great peal of laughter at the expression on her face.

When her frown deepened, he regained control, grinned and winked. "Come on, lazybones. I'll kiss it later."

****

Cameron walked across the room where he bent over to pick up his jeans. Aiyanna's gaze followed his every move, and desire flashed over her.

Oh Lordy! What a taunt, tight—

He stood and turned around. His golden eyes captured hers, and he smiled with beautiful candor.

Sexy, sexy man! He would make a great pole-dancer.

An eyebrow arched, and his eyes twinkled with mischief.

Uh oh!

In the next instant, his arms shot outward at his sides, and he jiggled his hips before he spun in a three hundred sixty degree circle.

Her blood pounded, and her face grew hot with humiliation.

Crap!

At his deep chuckle, she grabbed the comforter and yanked it over her head.

"You promised not to listen?" she muttered, angry at herself for being embarrassed.

She would have to find a way to block the man from reading her intimate thoughts.

"It kind of jumped out at me." He chuckled, uttering the very same words she'd used moments before. "I promise I'll try no' to eavesdrop too often."

A blast of chilly air brushed over her, and she lowered the covers. Cameron waved the comforter in the air. Only the thin sheet covered her.

"Hey!" Aiyanna pouted, grabbing for the fabric.

Featherlike laugh lines crinkled around his eyes. He lifted his hand and the quilt out of her reach.

She shot him a withering glance and was rewarded with a deep chuckle and a raised eyebrow.

"Time to get up, lass," he said, in a velvet

187

murmur.

"All right already," she muttered.

Maintaining her hold on the sheet, she slid off the edge of the bed. When her feet touched the floor, the material caught. She gave the sheet a swift jerk pulling the material free. Standing, she wrapped it around her body.

Something clicked in her mind. Was it possible? Her gaze shot to his face. She was startled by the notion that flashed through her mind.

He must have sensed her hesitation and then read her mind. In the next instant, he stiffened. His shoulders straightened, and he held up a hand as if to stop her next words.

He was too late.

"I love you." The words spilled from her lips without conscious thought.

He stilled, his expression stunned. His eyes turned dark and unfathomable. An inexplicable look of withdrawal settled on his face, and he turned away.

Always one to speak her mind, she wondered if perhaps she'd chosen the wrong moment to free her tongue. His genuine astonishment made her regret her candidness.

She laughed, the sound edged with nervousness.

"It's too bad I don't have a camera. The look on your face is priceless." Aiyanna tried to put a teasing lilt into her tone, yet her voice came out in a hoarse whisper.

"I doona take pictures."

"Oh."

He whirled to face her, his eyes hooded like those of a hawk. "Ye canna be serious, lass."

A hint of a smile curved her mouth, and she shrugged. "I've heard that it's best to be honest with those you love."

"Ye doona know anything about me."

"I know everything I need to."

Cameron waved his hand toward the bed. "This? Is this what ye know?"

Shaken, Aiyanna lowered her head. Her stomach knotted in pain, and bile rose in her throat. She raked her fingers through her hair uncertain what to do next, but then, hostility filled her.

He thought so little of her?

"Is that what you think I'm all about? Sex? Perhaps I should say, wham bam, thank ye, sir for the great night."

"Aiyanna, doona do—"

Aiyanna clutched the sheet between her knuckled fists. Hysteria rose in her voice. "Do what, Cameron? You started this. Let's finish it."

"Let it go, Anya." His jaw clenched, and his eyes flared with anger.

She released a deep breath, and her shoulders dropped. "Yeah, whatever." She set her chin in a stubborn line and, through stiff lips, asked, "You don't know me very well at all, do you?"

"No, I doona."

His words cut deep, and tears filtered from her eyes.

"I guess that's it then. Thanks for the great sex. It was...memorable." And with those words, she spun on her heels and headed for the door.

"Aiyanna—" His words sounded behind her, but the slam of the door cut them off.

****

Damn that man!

She'd worn her heart on her sleeve, had even spoken the words, and, once again, her heart had been ripped out and lay at her feet. She'd retreated before he took the opportunity to stomp on it.

Stupid! Stupid! She admonished herself.

Aiyanna hadn't spoken a word to him all day. Whenever he walked into a room, she walked out, avoiding him like the heart-breaking plague that he was.

She acted the spoiled brat. This she knew, but she considered her reaction appropriate. Besides, self-perseverance raged through her like a wild fire. If he dared to mutter so much as one word to her, she would, most likely, burst into tears.

She wasn't prepared to display that side of her nature. Not to him. Not yet.

Aiyanna stood on the porch and watched the stars twinkle against the dark backdrop of the sky, a mug of hot chocolate clasped between two hands. She gasped as a lone star shot across the sky.

She closed her eyes and made a wish or two; although, she never uttered them aloud. One selfish, the other not. She wouldn't choose between Cameron and Cheyenne. She couldn't.

Even though she cursed Cameron MacLean, she ached for his strong arms around her, his hands on her hips, holding them, preparing her for his hard penetration. Memories of his masterful kisses were crystal-clear. Even now, her body tingled at the reminiscence.

She opened her eyes at the realization she would never experience his wild, fierce class of lovemaking again. Not only had she responded to his touch without shame, but also no other man would ever compare to him or his skilled hands again.

Naïve little Anya. She walked into this with her heart wide open.

She took a sip of hot cocoa and listened to the clatter of the night animals' songs that rang out in the forest, soothing her raw nerves. She imagined the crickets calling to their mates with the simple gesture of rubbing their legs together.

If only it could be that easy for her.

Strong arms wrapped around her from behind. Her eyes widened, and she tensed. So focused on the echoes of nature, she didn't hear the door open behind her, nor had she heard his footsteps cross the deck.

"How can you love me?" His whispered words sent a thrill through her.

The incredulity in his tone pulled at her heartstrings, and she turned to face him. Reaching up, she smoothed a golden strand of hair from his forehead. He grasped her hand, stilled its motions, and then pressed a soft kiss to her palm.

"How can I not? You're thoughtful, kind, smart, and handsome. I could continue on, but it wouldn't make any difference. Starr always told us girls that we'd never see it coming until it was too late."

"See what?"

"True love."

Cameron grew quiet, and Aiyanna squirmed beneath his intense stare. His eyes scrutinized her as if trying to read the truth of her emotions, to glimpse deep into her heart.

Without a hint of warning, he grabbed her by the back of the head. She sucked in a startled breath when his hand fisted in her hair, and he pulled her head toward him. From the intensity on his face and the hungry gleam in his eyes, she swore he would devour her alive. Instead, his mouth swooped down on hers in a kiss meant to claim, to dominate.

When he released her lips, he pulled her into his arms. "Ye make me want to believe in miracles again," he whispered against her hair.

"Believe," she encouraged. When he didn't rely, she pulled from his arms. "I can't make you trust the future, and I can't make you love me. You've told me we're bonded together. Our destinies are intertwined. To believe we can make it work means you have hope." She stepped back and walked around him. Before entering the house, she stopped and glanced over her shoulder. "Without that, life is nothing."

Aiyanna walked in the kitchen, snapping the door shut behind her. Her knees weakened, and she stumbled to the kitchen table where she dropped into the chair. She closed her eyes and willed the tears that clung to her lashes to go away.

After a few moments, she pushed herself upright, turned and peered out the window to where she'd left Cameron.

He was gone.

Had she'd scared him away?

Medieval warrior, the gods' chosen, whoever Cameron MacLean was, it made no difference. To her, he was an incredible man who had survived the worst pain a human could suffer. Instead of buckling beneath its weight, he grew stronger.

He deserved love, and he had hers regardless of the barrier he'd hung up between them.

She had hope, but would it be enough for them both? To believe in a dream and fight for a future required the non-magical belief that anything can happen.

Aspirations for a happy future brought her to this point in life, and she refused to give up on them now.

Maybe, someday, he would come to love her in return.

Chapter Twenty-Five

A loud crash penetrated Aiyanna's sleep-drugged mind. She woke with a start, her heart pounding. Seconds later, heavy footsteps sprinted up the wooden steps. She recognized Cameron's wide stride, followed by a resounding thud that shook the walls when his bedroom door closed.

Damn, the man had no manners.

A quick glance at the clock revealed the hour: twelve fifteen. What brought him home early?

She pushed the comforter aside and scooted from bed. She wedged her feet into the pink, fuzzy slippers on the floor and grabbed her robe from the bedpost.

Tossing the robe over her shoulders, she opened the door a crack and glanced down the hall. Light seeped from beneath his door. Her heart squeezed in anguish when she realized he thought her good enough for sex but not cuddling.

She took a step back into her room, closed the door with a soft click and crawled into bed.

She closed her eyes and hugged the pillow against her chest. Tears clung to her lashes.

After a few moments of self-pity, she regained her composure enough to arrive at a difficult decision. She wouldn't let Cameron nor her feelings for him interfere in the search for her sister. Through all of this, she'd lost sight of what she needed to do.

Her new resolution left her empty. She drew a deep breath and dug deep for determination. The raw sores of an aching heart lingered, but she vowed to survive.

Let him fight his own damn battles. She had her sister to find.

Less than a half hour later, Aiyanna, wide awake now, walked into the kitchen. Perhaps a nice, hot cup of tea would ease the tenseness in her muscles and make her sleepy.

At the sink, she settled the teakettle beneath the spout and flicked on the water. While the liquid filled, she glanced out the window but found the view unsettling. Darkness engulfed the back yard, and a murky gloom consumed the swing.

While the water heated on the stove, she sat in lonely silence attempting to swallow the lump that lingered in her throat. She planted her elbows on the table and ran her hands through her hair.

A loud knock sent a chill up her spine. Her body tensed, and she shot upward. Her gaze jumped to the back door, yet she didn't move from the table. Her hands clenched around her empty teacup, knuckles white.

"Mayhap ye should answer the door, lass?"

Aiyanna turned toward the hallway where Cameron leaned against the doorframe. His tee molded to his muscular chest. Her mouth watered. He looked scrumptious. Her gaze traveled the length of his body before it returned to his face where a cocky smile met her eyes.

She glanced toward the clock on the stove. "It's one o'clock in the morning. Who would possibly be visiting at this time of the morning?"

Cameron shrugged in unconcern. "Mayhap someone's car broke down. They saw yer lights on, and needs to use the phone." He walked over and sat opposite her.

"What if it's—?"

Cameron's hands stretched across the table and

grabbed her hands in his. "It isna. Between the two of us, we would have sensed evil. No' to mention, Starr's senses are razor-sharp. Surely she would have kicked up a stir."

"I suppose, but—"

The knock sounded again.

"Ye're never going to know who's there unless ye answer the door."

She chewed her bottom lip in hesitation, and he gave her hands a supportive squeeze. "'Tis okay. I'm no' going anywhere."

"I suppose."

"Then what are ye waiting for?"

Aiyanna squared her shoulders and rose from the table. She struggled to control the shimmer of terror that streamed over her. Her breath caught in her throat.

Just as she opened the kitchen door and prepared to step onto the porch, fear prickled her flesh. Goosebumps formed and ran the length of her back, and a cold knot formed in her stomach. She paused to catch her breath, glancing over her shoulder at Cameron.

He nodded and winked in reassurance. His lips curved into an encouraging smile.

She turned away and closed her eyes. With a shiver of vivid recollection, the memories of the past slammed into her like a sledgehammer.

A night just like tonight...

Three years ago, she met Harris Wade at a faculty meeting. Newly hired as the Psychology II professor, his charm won her over. With his sandy brown hair and bright blue eyes that twinkled when he smiled, Aiyanna couldn't resist. They hit it off. Despite her tenuous lifestyle, they began dating less than three weeks later.

Six months after their first date, he went to visit his family in Florida for the Christmas holiday.

Gone for a week, Aiyanna missed him terribly and counted down the days until his return.

When he arrived back into town, he called her from the airport. His eagerness to see her echoed through the phone and made her toes tingle.

A half an hour later, his car pulled into the drive. When the car door slammed shut, she rushed to the door and whipped it open. A strange man, donned in black from head to foot, stood at Harris' side. Dark, emotionless eyes dominated the man's face, and he radiated of evil intentions.

"Harris, what's going on?" Her voice broke with unease.

"Anya...Anya..." Even Harris' voice sounded strange, bitter and hostile. "This is Dr. Jakowski. He's here to purge your evil from this world."

"Harris—" Fear and anxiety rose in her throat. She pushed it down. "You want to kill me?" she asked, in a choked whisper.

At his determined stare and cocky grin, she got her answer. She jerked the door and attempted to slam it shut. Harris stuck his hand in the crack and blasted it open. Aiyanna hurtled backward, and the two men stormed into the house.

"Why are you doing this?" she cried.

He laughed. His tone carried a sharp edge that sliced her heart open. He never loved her, setting her up for this witch hunter to kill her.

"Anya, who's at the door?" Cheyenne entered from the hall, her eyes red rimmed from sleep.

The man beside Harris raised a hand.

Aiyanna screamed. "Watch out." Cheyenne ducked a second before a lightning bolt shot past her head and smashed into the cabinets behind her. Wood splintered and splayed across the countertop.

"Anya, quickly." Cheyenne stretched out her hand.

"Do not let them grasp hands," the witch hunter

shouted, in a raspy voice tinged with panic.

His warning came too late. A jolt of power radiated from their clasped hands and soared up Aiyanna's arm empowering her. She closed her eyes and murmured the chant that would place a protective field around them. Cheyenne's voice joined hers until the room shook from the force of their incantation.

When Aiyanna opened her eyes, a bright white light circled Harris and the hunter. It radiated from the inside out. Harris' face twisted and melted like snow on a furnace fire. He screamed in pain, the sound horrifying. The torment didn't last long before both men's bodies split and evaporated into a cloud of gray ash cinders.

Pain ripped through her. Violent sobs tore through her and sent her to her knees. She'd loved him so much, and his betrayal nearly destroyed her. Cheyenne knelt beside her, caressed her hair and drew her into her embrace.

"I'm so sorry, sis," she murmured.

The knock rapped again, louder this time. Aiyanna returned to the present. She reached the outer porch door, stopped and glimpsed through the screen.

A woman, her back to the door, stood on the steps. She stared out across the backyard.

"May I help you?"

At Aiyanna's question, the woman spun around.

A bright smile lit up a perfectly symmetrical face. Rose-pink cheeks accentuated equally proportioned lips. The woman's hair flared like a fiery inferno, and Aiyanna believed her the most gorgeous woman she'd ever seen.

"Hi. Is Cameron around?" The woman's voice held the same musical brogue as Cameron's, the sound as striking as its possessor.

Aiyanna floundered in an agonizing maelstrom

of raw and primitive emotions. Jealousy impaled her and, as each moment passed, the barbs dug in deeper. Aiyanna swallowed past the lump that formed in her throat and managed to stutter, "Is he expecting you?"

"I doona think so. I heard he was in the area and thought I'd stop by to say hello." The woman peered over Aiyanna's shoulder inside. "Is he here? Or did he go out?"

Aiyanna pushed the screen door open in invitation at the same time Cameron poked his head out the main door into the porch.

"Cookie? Is that ye, lass?"

The smile on the woman's face grew brighter at the sight of him. The next thing Aiyanna knew, "Cookie" jumped into Cameron's arms. He caught her and spun her around a few times before he settled her on her feet.

Cameron's exuberant greeting and the sparkle in his eyes when he looked at the other woman sent a sharp knife through Aiyanna's heart. The pain intensified when he pressed his lips to hers in a quick kiss.

He never looked at her like that, and any spark of hope Aiyanna held onto extinguished in a puff of cloud vapors.

"What brings ye to the area?" Cameron asked. He held her hand and led her into the house to a chair at the table.

Aiyanna followed yet remained out of the spotlight.

"We've all been summoned here."

"So they know?"

Rising fine, arched eyebrows, the woman asked, "What?"

"About Deidra's presence here."

An intense but secret expression lit "Cookie's" face. Her gaze shot to Aiyanna who remained motionless in the corner before returning on Cameron, her lips pursed in disquiet.

Cameron nodded. "'Tis okay. Cookie—" He cleared his throat. "Cara, this is Aiyanna. Aiyanna, Cara."

Cara broke into an open, friendly smile and glanced at Aiyanna. "'Tis nice to meet ye. Any friend of Irish here is a friend of mine."

Friend? Aiyanna grimaced inside but pasted a welcoming smile on her face. "It's my pleasure. Welcome to Arlington." Her gaze shot to Cameron. "Irish?"

He chuckled. "Aye, I was born in Scotland but lived most of my life in Ireland."

Cara cleared her throat, drawing Cameron's attention. "Devlin and Fallon are scheduled to arrive before the sun comes up."

"I bet Fallon wasna happy about leaving Lizzie."

"Ye know the deal. When duty calls—"

"We answer," Cameron finished for her.

Cara nodded.

"So how have ye been, Cookie?"

"Fine, and for the record, *Irish*, call me Cookie again, I'll—" She left the sentence dangling, the ominous threat of her tone reinforced by the anger in her eyes.

Cameron appeared unconcerned and chuckled. "Aye, ma'am."

Cookie wrinkled her nose. "Ma'am? Hmmm, that's even worse than Cookie. Cara is my name. It works for me. Always has."

Aiyanna watched the interplay between Cameron and the woman called Cookie/Cara and suddenly felt like an intruder in her own house. She no longer existed in Cameron's eyes.

She swallowed hard and bit back the tears. Without a word, she turned and walked from the room.

Once in the hallway, Aiyanna turned and glanced back into the kitchen. He hadn't even realized she'd left. Cara held his full attention.

Aiyanna turned to the living room where she plopped onto the sofa and listened to the muffled sounds of their cheerful voices.

After a few minutes, she jumped to her feet and walked upstairs to her room where she lay on the bed and yielded to uncontrollable sobs. She grabbed her pillow and covered her head to smother her cries, rocking back and forth. Her body shook.

To hell with the both of them.

Chapter Twenty-Six

The voices downstairs faded until Aiyanna barely heard them. She doubted they were even speaking anymore.

She held no doubts that Cameron loved the red-haired beauty. The look in his eyes...

Stupid! Stupid!

She berated herself, norm to the fashion these days.

The door to her room opened, but she remained motionless.

"Aiyanna," Cameron's voice a soft whisper, as though hesitant to wake her up.

"What?" she asked, her voice muffled against the pillow she hugged close.

"I wondered where ye disappeared to. Why did ye leave?"

That did it.

Aiyanna moved so fast, she figured he never saw her coming.

One instant, she laid across the bed, fatigued from emotional exhaustion, and the next she stood in front of him. She glared at him one full second before she slapped him across the face.

Her open palm connected with his cheek, the sharp crack thunderous in the hushed room. His head turned with the blow. She heard his quick intake of breath. When his gaze met hers, his mouth spread into a thin-lipped smile, his eyes dark and unreadable.

"Do ye mind telling me what that was for?" He

asked, his gaze steady, but his jaw clenched and unclenched with each word he spoke.

She flipped her hair across her shoulders in a gesture of defiance and raised her hand to strike again. This time, he caught it before she connected and held her wrist in a loose grip which none-the-less proved impossible to break.

"Was I just a one night stand, Cameron?"

They stared at each other across the sudden ringing silence, his eyes dark.

She jerked her hand from his grip, swiveled, and turned her back to him. He caught her elbow and yanked her to a stop before she stormed away. She glanced down where he held her and snorted. When she lifted her gaze, she shifted indignantly, debating on whether to kick him or not.

Deciding against kickboxing, she tugged her arm. When he didn't release it, she spat out between clenched teeth, "Let me go!"

He jerked her arm, bringing her hard against his chest. His head lowered, and his lips covered hers in a short, hard kiss before he thrust her away him.

"What the bloody hell is yer problem?" he growled.

"My problem? You're just like every other man. You have no morals." She threw the words, and they dropped like stones.

A warning cloud settled on his features.

"Doona do this, lass," he warned.

"I'm doing nothing." She seethed with anger and shame, unmindful of the words that spilled from her mouth. "Go away, Cameron. Just go away. I can't even stand to be near you." She wanted to hurt him as much as she hurt.

"Aiyanna." Cameron reached out and caught her arm.

Wrenching free, she spun to face him. "What? I

spilled my heart out to you. I loved you. You got what you wanted from me then decided to invite your *friends* over." She spat the words contemptuously. Her shoulders drooped, and her final words came out as a whisper, "You could have told me—"

"Told ye what?" he interrupted. His body stiffened. "Look at me, lass."

She glanced into his eyes, shocked by the tenderness she saw there. "Ye canna possibly think Cara...that Cara and I..."

"Are involved. Aren't you? I saw the way you looked at her, Cameron." She stopped as the truth assailed her and knotted her stomach. He made her no promises. "I'm sorry. I have no right to say anything." She looked into his eyes and held on rigidly to the tears that threatened to fall. "One night. I asked for one night, and you gave me that. I'm sorry. I shouldn't have expected any—"

Cameron reached for her and pulled her into his arms. Her forehead rested against his chest.

The tears fell in earnest then, and she sniffled against his chest.

"Aiyanna, doona." With his left hand, he tilted her chin so she couldn't avoid his eyes. "I doona love Cara. No' in that way."

Aiyanna searched his eyes before asking, "You don't owe me an explanation."

"I do, and I'm telling ye I doona love her."

"But I saw—"

"What ye saw is a friendship as old as time. She's a guardian."

Her eyes widened, and her brows shot up in surprise. "A guardian? Cara is a Síoraí?" she asked warily, watching him.

He smiled at her as if she were a small child. "Aye, if ye had listened to our conversation, ye would have figured that out."

She hadn't listened to their words, only her heart. And now, shame burned through her like active volcano. "But a guardian?"

"There are four guardians in existence. One of which is a woman. Dinna yer research tell ye that?"

She nodded, saying, "Yeah," then shook her head. "No." She hesitated and drew a calming breath. "I mean, yes, I knew there were four, but no, it didn't tell who you are, only that you existed."

He pulled her back into his arms and kissed the top of her head.

She melted.

And then, without warning, another notion struck, and she pulled away. She bit her lip.

Cameron rushed out, "What is it?"

"That makes two guardians here in Arlington. Why?"

He chuckled. "Ye really werena listening. The others are expected to arrive by morning." She opened her mouth to speak but stopped when he shook his head. "Doona concern yerself with the details, lass. Lie down and get some rest. It'll all work out."

"But—"

Cameron stepped forward and pressed a sharp, quick, silencing kiss to her lips.

"Rest," he said, before he spun away and left.

****

Cameron walked into the kitchen and found Cara at the sink looking out the window. She must have sensed his presence because she twirled around to face him.

"Where did ye go?"

"I had to make sure Aiyanna was okay."

Her left eyebrow raised a fraction. "Strange name."

"Aye, I thought so too until she explained 'tis a Cherokee name."

"She's a bird?"

Cameron laughed aloud at the stunned expression on Cara's face. "I wouldna say that too loud. Despite her size, Aiyanna will knock ye on yer arse."

Cara snorted, her hands rested on her hips. "I doona think so."

"Ye'd be surprised."

"For calling her a bird?"

"Aye, I did, and that wee lass took me down. Cherokee is a breed of Native American, Cara. 'Tis her heritage. Parakeet is a species of bird. To be honest, I was a wee disappointed in myself that I dinna remember the teachings of the Druids."

She snapped her fingers. "That's right. Now that you mention it, I do remember reading that somewhere before. I can see why she'd want to thump yer arse. No one bad-mouths the birthright."

Cara tilted her head to one side and stole a slanted look at him. "Something's different about ye, Cameron. What's happened?"

He didn't reply.

"Cameron?" she asked, her voice laced with concern. She ambled toward him, reaching for his T-shirt. He didn't stop her as she lifted it over his head.

A crooked grin split his lips when her eyes widened, and her mouth formed a perfect "O".

When her eyes met his, she murmured, "Oh no—"

****

Aiyanna leaned back against the wall outside the kitchen. She didn't know if she were more angry or hurt. Tears welled in her eyes, and she bit her lip to foil the sobs that threatened to escape.

Heartbreak settled inside her and formed an excruciating knot. Bitterness welled in the pit of her stomach. She'd believed him when he told her he didn't love Cara.

And she wanted to believe him still. She couldn't imagine he was the type of man who would bring another woman to her house, especially after what they'd shared, but...

That woman was undressing him, in her house!

Her pulse quickened. Perhaps he'd been hurt, and she was checking his injuries. Maybe, just maybe...

She shook her head.

In his own twisted way, Harris thought her death would shelter the world from evil, but he didn't understand the true nature of her craft. As a white witch, discipline bound her to be virtuous. His mind-set blindsided him to the good she did.

Cameron understood, even accepted her heritage, but that didn't make her worthy of being a guardian's mate. Take a good look at Cara. Now, that woman exuded strength and power, not to mention beauty. Aiyanna couldn't compete with that.

A flash of wild grief ripped through her, and the harder she tried to ignore the truth, the more it persisted.

She wasn't what Cameron needed.

Drawing a deep, tortured breath, Aiyanna stepped out the front door onto the porch. She needed to get away from Cameron. Maybe with a little time to herself, she would find the courage to put things in perspective.

And then, she did something she rarely did except in her dreams.

She changed into an eagle with a hooked beak and sharp talons. Perched on the wooden rail of the porch, she took a quick look toward the house before ascending into the sky.

It always amazed her, this sensation of sheer freedom she experienced when she spread her wings and soared across the heavens.

As forecasted, the weather conditions provided for heavily overcast skies, and periodic showers fell.

Gloomy!

Aiyanna searched the rest of the night and into the next day, among the trees, creeks and hillsides of all local cemeteries. She spent the better part of the day at Arlington, but with no luck.

By early afternoon, a hard, steady rain pelted her, and the sky misted over until she could hardly see two feet in front of her even with her eagle vision.

She didn't give up.

She couldn't.

When dusk settled, she decided to go home. By this time, the rain dwindled to a faint trickle, and the temperature dropped.

A stab of disappointment raced over her. She'd failed.

As she flew over 32nd Street, a small group of vampires emerged from the murky shadows of the trees. They wore dark clothing, and cloaks to hide their pale, blue-tinted, dying flesh covered their faces. They jumped the six-foot fence that surrounded Arlington Cemetery.

She swooped low and landed on the pavement ten feet in front of them.

She shifted into human form and snickered when their mouths dropped open in surprise. Kneeling, she lifted her chin, and her hair swirled wet and wild around her face. With one hand, she tucked the wayward strands behind her ears. Her gaze flickered over each one of them.

"Where is she?" Aiyanna demanded. "Tell me where the other witch is, and I'll make this quick."

"I think you are a bit overconfident in your abilities. You are one. We are many." The largest of the vampires lowered the hood covering his face and smirked at her. His tongue flicked across his lips. Red bloodshot eyes challenged her.

Bile rose in her throat, but she refused to back down from this monster.

He nodded at the others, and they closed in around her.

Aiyanna forgot all the rules, forgot everything she'd been taught in a split second of white fury. Perhaps it was a combination of Cameron's betrayal and her own inability to find Cheyenne, but she was pissed. Rage coursed through her veins like boiling fire.

She pointed her hand at the leader, and a jagged line of crackling fire exploded from her fingertips like a lightning bolt. It hit him square in the chest. A surprised then shocked look rippled across his face before he burst into flames.

The rest of the group turned and attacked.

Chapter Twenty-Seven

By the time Aiyanna flew into the yard, the rain had cleared, and stars lit up the skies.

She landed on the bench of the swing and changed into human form. Memories of the time she spent time with Cheyenne right here inundated her. She kicked at the ground with one foot rocking the swing back and forth. A sense of inadequacy filled her, and she swiped at the tears that fell down her cheeks.

She was getting closer; she could feel it. The demons she'd fought tonight were a tad bit more defensive for ones who were only out to feed. They hid something and weren't about to spill it regardless of their pending annihilation.

Persistence. She vowed to be more vigilant in her search.

Well, it was time to face the music. She grabbed a hold of the linked chain that supported the swing's bench. Just as she pulled herself up, a sharp, stinging pain speared down her arm and sent her slumping back to the seat with a moan. She glanced down and grimaced at the stream of dried blood that trailed from her shoulder to her hand.

Funny, she hadn't felt anything before. Probably, the adrenalin rush during the fight masked the pain. Now, with the battle over, she was certain to feel every twinge.

"Oh, this is just friggin' ducky! A brand new shirt shot to hell." She lifted up the torn sleeve to discover a deep cut two inches long on the fleshy part of her upper arm. "Damn it!" She poked her finger at the ragged edge of the wound and grimaced. It would need stitches for sure, but she'd see to them after her shower. Right now, she needed to make her way inside.

With one last glance at her injury, she pushed herself to her feet and walked across the drive, her movements stiff and awkward.

She ran a hand through her hair and trudged up the steps that led into the porch. Loud, muffled voices radiated from the kitchen. She paused and pressed her ear to the door, straining to listen to the commotion going on inside.

She bit her lip to stifle the outcry when she bumped into the shelf by the door.

Cameron's deep voice mingled with Cara's in a heated discussion. A warm glow of contentment flowed through her. A lover's spat? And so soon after their reunion?

Ah, nuts! She stifled a grin.

But then another voice joined the dispute. The rich timbre of a man's voice spoke in a low, composed tone that carried through the wall.

Aiyanna snuck a peek through the window and saw Cameron and Cara speaking to two other men. Cameron's hands waved in agitation, and he spoke in a tense, clipped voice that forbade any question.

"Calm down, Cameron. The lass will return in due time."

"Dev, ye doona know that. What if she's hurt and needs my help?"

Oh Crap! Hadn't Cameron said the guardians would be coming to Arlington? So that must be who sat at her kitchen table. Worse yet, they were discussing her.

She inhaled a deep, unsteady breath and squared her shoulders. Turning the knob, she pushed the door open and stepped across the threshold. In an instant, Cameron swung around. She cursed the squeaky spring that gave her away.

Her heart jumped against the wall of her chest at the undisguised concern on his face. In the space of a heartbeat, she watched apprehension change to anger.

Without a word, he stepped around her and strode to the door. He slammed it shut. Her body jerked at the sound. She grimaced, and her nerves twitched.

He was not happy.

His golden eyes returned to her face, and he gave her a black-layered look. "Where the hell have ye been, lass?" he demanded. "We've been waiting up for yer return."

Aiyanna swallowed hard, lifted her chin, and met his eyes. "Out," she responded in a tense, clipped voice, abandoning all pretenses. She turned her back to him and gazed at the other occupants of the room.

It was amazing what three pairs of eyes could do especially when they were staring at a person in stunned disbelief. Her determination faltered, and she struggled to maintain an even, sophisticated tone. Shrugging, she asked, "What?" When no one responded to her question, she said, "So shoot me. He is not my keeper."

To her surprise, the room erupted into laughter, which lessoned some, but not all of the tension in the air.

The largest man stood from the table and strolled in her direction. An air of command exuded him. Aiyanna sensed the power that coiled inside him. Oh Lord, if she thought Cameron tall, this man stood a good six inches taller. Thick black hair hung straight around his face. Striking blue-eyes offset full lips. A light scuffle of whiskers framed distinct cheeks. His handsome face was kindled with a sort of passionate beauty. He extended his hand, and his lips parted in a dazzling display of straight, white teeth.

"Ye must be Aiyanna. I'm Devlin, and the oldest of this bunch. 'Tis a pleasure to meet ye."

Not what she expected, he looked like a biker, dressed in black leather pants and a tight T-shirt. Despite his harsh exterior, she took an instant liking to the eldest guardian.

Aiyanna slipped her hand in his and returned his grin. "Hi, Devlin. The feeling's mutual."

"Over there next to the sink is Fallon."

Aiyanna followed the inclination of his head to the man who lounged against the counter. A few inches taller than Cameron, this man possessed laughing eyes and an easy smile. His hair, darker than Devlin's, hung to his shoulders. Dressed like a cowboy in denim blue jeans and a button-up pocket shirt, the only thing he lacked was a cowboy hat.

"Ye remind me of my Lizzie," he commented. He stepped forward and extended his hand. "Nice to meet ye."

She smiled and placed her hand in his. Aiyanna noticed the golden wedding band on his finger.

"You're married?" she asked, in surprise. Her gaze shot to his eyes.

He nodded, his eyes lit up. "Aye, my Lizzie came along and changed my world."

"Is she here with you?" she asked in curiosity, her gaze shooting around the room.

He chuckled and shook his head. "Nay, Lizzie's a bit indisposed at the moment."

"Indisposed?"

"Aye," he said, before his attention returned to the group behind her, successfully ending their introduction.

"Lizzie is expecting their first child in less than two months. Fallon wouldna risk her or the babe."

Cameron's whisper in her ear sparked goose bumps.

She nodded in understanding. "That's reasonable."

"We need to talk."

She ignored Cameron's remark and turned to Fallon. "Congratulations."

"Thank ye. I'm sure I speak for all of us, but ye have our gratitude for allowing us to invade yer home. For myself, this is a mini vacation for me. The bigger my Lizzie gets, the grumpier she gets. I was due for time away."

Suddenly, he flinched and held his shoulder. His face clouded with uneasiness.

She started forward, concern in her voice. "Are you all right?"

Cameron caught her arm and pulled her to a standstill. "Nay, lass. 'Tis best ye stay out of this."

"Out of what? What's going on?"

A female voice echoed in the room. "You are not so far away, my love that I cannot hear the words you speak."

Confused, Aiyanna glanced first at Cameron then to Devlin and Cara. Each one of the guardians smiled, their lips curved, and their eyes fixed on Fallon, whose face creased with discomfort.

"Ah sh...ugar." Fallon spoke to the air. "Lizzie, I dinna—" He never finished his sentence, gritting his teeth. He faced the group and murmured, "I'll be right back."

And then he was gone. The man simply vanished.

Her mind reeled with bewilderment, and she waved her hand in the air where Fallon had stood moments ago. She turned to the group and asked, "Where did he go?"

Cameron laughed. "To make amends to his pregnant wife."

"Poor Fallon. He knows better. Lizzie's powers

have increased three-fold since she's been with child. She can track him anywhere." Devlin laughed.

Cameron nodded in agreement.

"Poor Fallon? Ye have got to be kidding me. I hope she skins him alive." This comment came from Cara who stood in the corner of the room, her hands propped on her hips. A scowl warped her forehead.

Devlin and Cameron both stopped laughing at her expression.

"I pity the man who bonds to ye, Cara," Devlin commented, shooting her a twisted smile.

"Save yer pity, Dev. I wilna ever be bound to anyone. I'll grant no man that kind of power to control me."

Devlin smiled and shrugged. "If ye say so, lass."

"I do." Cara's gaze lit on Aiyanna. "What do ye think? Do ye think a man has the right to treat a woman who carries his child as if she were no more than a piece of baggage?"

"Come on, Cara," Devlin defended. "Fallon doesna treat Lizzie like baggage."

Cara laughed. "It was just an analogy. But, ye must admit, the way he spoke of her and the need of a vacation, well..." She turned to Aiyanna. "What do ye think?"

Aiyanna's lips parted in surprise. "I don't believe any person has the right to control another, whether they're married or not. Vacation?" She glanced over her shoulder at Cameron and shook her head for emphasis. "There are *no* vacations, especially when a woman carries a child. A man needs to offer his support to his wife, no matter what it costs. And then after the baby's born, I believe midnight feedings and diaper changes are duties that could be equally shared."

Cara broke into an open, friendly smile, as if quite satisfied with her response. She turned to Cameron. "Oh, Irish, ye have chosen quite well indeed. I like her."

Aiyanna gazed at Cameron and noted his set face, his clamped mouth and fixed eyes. A muscle quivered at his jaw, but the beginning of a smile tipped the corners of his mouth. It was difficult to say whether he was pissed or pleased.

Her cheeks burned when he glanced at her. The heat intensified beneath his stare, and she turned her face away.

In the next instant, his loud-mouthed curses filled the air, and her gaze shot back to him. His eyes widened, and with a few swift steps, he closed the distance between them.

Startled, she jumped back in surprise.

"What the hell happened to ye?" he asked, in an anxious tone.

"What are you talking about?"

He grabbed her hand and raised her arm. "Yer shirt's been torn, and the area's coated with blood."

In the excitement, Aiyanna had forgotten all about her wound. She shrugged. "It's nothing."

"Let me take a look."

Aiyanna yanked her hand away. "I said it's nothing, Cameron. Leave it be."

"Ye need to take care of that before it gets infected."

"Och Irish, ye heard her. Leave her be. I'm sure she can take care of it herself. Stop *mothering* her, would ye?" Cara giggled at her pun. She walked to the table and flopped down in a chair.

Aiyanna smiled, beginning to like the other woman. "Thank you."

She walked around Cameron who shot angry dangers at Cara. Cara smiled then winked at the angry man. Wow, the woman was brave.

"I told ye no' to go out alone."

"You've said a lot of things I try not to listen to." Aiyanna walked to the counter. Before she reached her destination, Fallon reappeared in her path. She jumped and took a quick breath of utter shock. "Do you have to do that?"

Fallon rubbed his cheek. "Aye, well, sorry about that. I dinna mean to scare ye."

"Everything square?" Devlin asked, coming to Fallon's side.

"Aye, it took a wee bit of convincing, but I think she forgives me." His gaze shot upward, and he asked, "Right darlin'?"

He grinned. A twinkle radiated in his eyes when he looked at the group and nodded. "All better."

Confused, Aiyanna frowned. Who the hell was the man talking to? Worse yet, was someone actually talking back?

She shook her head, decided it best not to ask, and stepped around him where she reached into a drawer to grab a washcloth. After tossing it into the sink, she flicked the faucet upward and waited for the water to heat up. A moment later, steam rose from the depths of the steel basin. She grabbed the cloth, wrung out the excess liquid and placed it against her shoulder, grimacing at the stinging pain.

"Here, let me help ye, lass," Cameron said, reaching for the washcloth.

Aiyanna held the material tight and pressed it to her shoulder, taking three steps around him. "Thank you, but I'm fine." She turned to the other occupants of the room. "I'm going to shower and sew up my arm. Please help yourselves to the guest rooms upstairs. Cameron can show you. It was a pleasure to meet you."

"'Tis our pleasure as well, lass." Devlin stepped forward. "Thank ye again for having us in yer home. We hope this is only a temporary situation."

"Take as long as you need."

"Anya!" Starr's high-pitched shout radiated from the hall. The cat rushed into the room and pounced onto the table. Her long white fur swished over her face. She came to an abrupt stop. With her paw, she brushed the errant pieces of fur from her eyes. Her gaze shot around the group, and she asked in a timid voice, "What did I miss?"

"Starr—" Aiyanna started forward, but at the same moment, Cara shoved her chair back from the table and jumped to her feet. The action caused the chair to topple over, hitting the floor with a loud *thud*. "By the gods, what the bloody hell is that?"

Startled, Starr rose up on her back feet. She hissed. The fur on the back of her neck rose. Her front paws, claws bared, waved through the air in warning.

A sword suddenly appeared in Cara's hand, and she aimed the point at the center of Starr's chest.

Aiyanna rushed forward, putting herself between the tip of the sword and the cat.

At the same moment, Cameron slapped his hand on the blade and pushed it down. "Cara, no!"

Aiyanna swept the cat up in her arms, cuddling her close. She stared at Cara, her brows drawn in an affronted frown.

Cameron chuckled at Cara's wide eyes and pale face lined with confusion. "Havena ye ever seen a talking cat, Cookie?"

Cara shook her head, speechless, her eyes still transfixed on the cat in Aiyanna's arms.

Devlin laughed, walked over and waved a hand in front of Cara's eyes. "Hello in there."

Anger flashed in her eyes, and she slapped Devlin's hand away. "I was a wee bit surprised." She looked at Aiyanna and Starr, and murmured, "I'm sorry, but—" Her voice cracked, and she shook her head.

Aiyanna smiled in understanding. "It's okay, Cara. Starr has that effect on people. I'm going to go get cleaned up now."

Aiyanna spun around, taking the cat with her. At the doorway, she glanced back over her shoulder. Her breath caught at the sight of the guardians standing in her kitchen.

The three men looked absolutely gorgeous. Cara, a pink shade coloring her cheeks, still represented a goddess. Amazing! Every one of them, and they were here in her house.

And then reality hit like a brick wall.

Four guardians, one evil Vampryss, a lost sister, a talking cat and little old her...

Chapter Twenty-Eight

Fallon clasped Cameron's shoulder. "Ye've done well for yerself, Irishman."

Cameron stiffened, jerked away from the hand, and shot the other man a narrowed look. "Shut up, Fallon!"

Fallon threw back his head and released a peal of laughter that grated on Cameron's nerves.

After a moment, the irritating sound faded to a hearty chuckle when the man asked, "What's the matter, Cam? Surely ye can see what I'm talking about? She's feisty, determined, and doesna know how to listen, eh?"

Astounded by Fallon's description, Cameron quirked an eyebrow and asked, "And how would ye know that about her?"

Fallon smiled and shrugged. "I live with a woman just like her. Ye doona need to worry about her. She has all the good traits to be a guardian's mate."

Devlin stepped forward and held up a hand. His gaze shot between the two men. "Did ye say mate?"

Cara stepped forward. "That he did. It would seem our Irish has chosen."

Devlin turned to Cameron. "Is that true?"

Cara piped up, her tone chipper. "I saw his mark myself. He's bonded."

Annoyance creased the look Devlin shot Cara. "Can I talk to Cameron, please?"

She gave the elder a disgruntled look and flipped him off. "Sure, boss man, go ahead, but I'm telling ye they're bonded, and they've even consummated the deal."

"Cameron, is what Cara says correct?"

"Aye," he replied, with heavy irony.

Devlin's tight expression relaxed into a smile. "Well then, I suppose congratulations are in order."

"Sympathies might be the operative word," Cameron muttered.

Fallon nodded smugly. "All right then, ye have my condolences, Irish." He grinned. "On the other hand, ye have my best wishes. To be mated with a white witch—"

A probing query entered Devlin's eyes, and he asked, "Aiyanna's a white witch?" At Cameron's nod, the elder released a resigned sigh. "It is no wonder Deidra Sidhe has been drawn to this part of the country."

"Deidra holds Aiyanna's sister captive. She tries to draw Aiyanna from the safety of the house with promises that she'll release her."

"Aiyanna canna go after her sister. If Deidra taps into her powers—" Devlin broke off.

An ominous warning lay heavily in the air, the threat unnecessary, for they all knew the consequences if Aiyanna were captured.

"Do ye think we can release her sister?" Cameron asked. His voice remained calm while his gaze roamed over the group.

"Where is she being detained?"

"In a cemetery, but we doona know which one." Cameron's eyes turned toward the ceiling. "I wonder if Aiyanna discovered anything new tonight."

"Do ye think that's where she went?"

"The one thing I've learned about the lass, she isna afraid to take on a whole lot of vampires alone if she thought they could give her the answers she seeks."

Devlin studied his face with an enigmatic gaze

before he inclined his head. "Go see to yer woman, Cameron. 'Tis been a long day, and we need to rest. Tomorrow, we'll search the city after the sun sets."

"I can see what I can find out," Fallon volunteered.

All eyes in the room shot to him, and he laughed. "What? I would say I'm sorry I fell in love, and my bond with Lizzie gave me back the ability to walk in daylight, but I'd be telling a fib."

"Zip it, Fallon. We have plans to make, and we canna do that if ye're exhausted from traipsing the countryside during the daylight hours. Get some sleep."

"Party pooper," Fallon grumbled, rolling his eyes.

Cameron strolled to the door, anxious to check on Aiyanna. Before he left the room, he hesitated and turned to face the group. "One thing I should mention. Aiyanna's sister is a white witch as well."

Devlin blew out a deep breath and said, "Oh shit!"

"Damn! Damn! Double Damn!" Fallon burst out.

****

Out of sight, out of mind hadn't worked so well.

"Where did you go tonight, Anya? Did you find Shy?" Starr sat in the center of the bed. The cat's green eyes followed her movements.

"I didn't find her, Starr, but I'm not going to give up," she said, with a grimace.

"Are you all right?" Concern laced Starr's words.

"I'll be fine." She covered the wound with a wet cloth and released a deep sigh at the cooling sensation that eased the throbbing pain.

Starr jumped to the floor and padded to the doorway. Over her shoulder, she said, "Next time, you should take *him* along." Then she was gone.

Aiyanna giggled at Starr's reference to Cameron as "*him*", but "*he*" couldn't fly, and she couldn't carry him.

She walked to the armoire, pulled the doors open and searched for her healing potions.

Images of Cameron's face popped into her mind. His display of emotions was a rollercoaster ride: concern over her injury, anger at her disobedience, then the overwhelming fear on his face when he thought Cara might stab her, but those pictures were overshadowed by his amazing body...all brawn. Absolutely no fat blemished his god-like body. His thighs and buttocks were pure masculine muscle. She could attest to that.

Stop thinking about him. Stop thinking about him. The words chanted in her head.

The door opened. She tensed and twirled around. Cameron stood in the doorway, his arms folded across his chest. The thunderous expression on his face drew her attention.

His eyes blazed amber fire. "Well, lass? What have ye to say for yerself and yer fiasco?" he asked, gritting his teeth in anger.

"Cameron, please. I don't want to argue with you. Not tonight." Her eyes locked with his. "Don't you have some place you'd rather be than here, with me?"

"What's that supposed to mean?"

"Well, I thought you and Cara—" She left the sentence hanging.

He gazed at her with a bland half smile and shook his head. "And I told ye there is nothing between Cara and me. We're just friends."

"But I saw you and her—" His dark, angry expression silenced her words.

"Look, lass," he sighed deeply, and lowered his hands to his sides. "I doona care what ye saw, or what ye think ye saw, but there is nothing between us."

"But—" Her words were cut off as he crushed

222

her to him and pressed his mouth to hers. The kiss dominated her senses and sent the pit of her stomach into a wild swirl.

He stepped away. She blinked. Lightheaded, she stumbled on weak knees.

He studied her face with his enigmatic gaze for an extra beat. "I realize that ye doona have much faith in others, but please trust in me. I wouldna hurt ye, no' in that way," he whispered.

Tears welled within her eyes at the tenderness of his expression and the earnestness in his expression.

God help her! She believed him and gave a quick nod. Her voice choked when she replied, "I'll try."

He smiled and pressed a quick kiss to her forehead. "Good. Now, I'll have yer promise that ye wilna go out at night again."

"No." The denial flew from her lips.

He sighed with exasperation. "Aiyanna, I'll have yer promise. This time, I'll expect ye to stick to it."

"No," she repeated.

"Anya, this isna about ye or yer sister. If Deidra were to find ye—"

"Do you think I don't understand the gravity of the situation? Believe me I do, and I was careful."

He passed a glance at her shoulders. His eyebrows rose in inquiry. He released a long, audible breath when his eyes connected with hers. "Why do ye have to be so stubborn?" With a nod toward her injury, he asked, "How bad it is?"

"I'll live."

"Aiyanna!" he ground her name out between his teeth. "Canna ye just answer the question?"

"A semi-minor cut. It'll need a few stitches and be sore for a few days, but it will heal."

He nodded, as if satisfied. "And how did ye receive such an injury?"

Aiyanna dropped her chin, refusing to look in

his eyes. He slipped his fingertip beneath her chin and forced her meet his gaze. His eyebrows rose in question.

Heat rose up her neck into her cheeks. "I met up with a group of vamps. Let's just say, they weren't very cooperative."

A wry but indulgent glint appeared in his eyes. "And what did ye discover in yer travels?"

"What is this? Fifty questions?" she chirped. Her mouth quirked with humor.

"Are ye being a smart-ass?"

"Fifty-One."

"Would ye just answer the question?"

"Fifty-Two." Aiyanna giggled at his scowl. "Okay, Cheyenne is somewhere in Arlington Cemetery."

"Whew! Big place. Are ye sure?"

"Fifty-Thr—" His glower deepened. He didn't want to play anymore, so, instead, she nodded and replied, "I searched half the park. Tomorrow, I'll—"

"Like hell ye will. Ye're no' to go anywhere near that place," he demanded, his tone velvet, yet edged with steel. As if suddenly struck by another thought, he came to a standstill. His eyes were full of questions when he glanced at her. "Half the park? How the hell did ye manage that?"

She brought her hand up to stifle her giggles. "I soared."

His lips twitched, and a slight hesitation filled his hawk-like eyes before he waved a hand. "Never mind, I doona want to know."

Pain shot up her shoulder, and she grimaced. As if sensing her agony, he stepped toward her and settled shaky hands on her shoulders. A vein pulsed at the nape of his neck, and he swallowed hard.

"A little to the left, and ye could have been killed." He remarked, his voice a tortured whisper.

She stroked his cheek and encouraged his eyes

to meet hers. "I'm fine. Really I am."

He gave her a crooked smiled. "I know, but the thought of anyone hurting ye—" His voice trembled.

She covered his lips with her index finger. "Let it go, Cameron."

His brows drew together in an agonized expression. "I wilna let anyone harm ye."

Cameron's voice shook with the intensity of his promise, and a shiver of apprehension coursed through her.

****

Aiyanna pushed herself away from the kitchen table, achy and stiff. Her temples pounded. Every bone and muscle in her body throbbed, as if someone had stomped all over her.

Oh yeah, right, someone had—a whole bunch of vampires.

The other guardians had bedded down for the day. If they followed Cameron's normal routine, Aiyanna knew she wouldn't see them until after dark tonight.

"Where are ye going?"

"I'm going to lie down for a bit," she replied, raising tired eyes to Cameron who walked into the room. She read concern in his expression. Did she dare hope the scene she witnessed between Cara and Cameron nothing more than...? What? Aiyanna couldn't presume to understand their relationship, but she did arrive at one conclusion. Here with her now, she'd hold onto him for as long as it lasted.

"Tired?"

"Yeah, yesterday was rough."

"Well, if ye dinna try to take on a whole army of—" Cameron stopped when Aiyanna shook her head. He frowned. "What?"

"Let it go, Cameron."

"Let go of what, Aiyanna?" he asked in a neutral tone, but she recognized the teasing sparkle in his eyes.

She stared at him and shook her head again.

"What?"

"We'll talk later," she managed to say, before she turned to leave the room. She hadn't hobbled more than a foot before she was lifted and settled against his strong chest.

She squealed. "What are you doing?"

"Taking ye to bed, lass. I thought that would be obvious."

"I'm capable of walking," she declared. She wiggled in an attempt to squirm out of his arms.

His hold tightened. "I know ye are. Settle down, will ye?"

"Cameron?"

"Anya, ye're exhausted. Let me help."

Her head pounded, and she calmed at his soft-spoken plea. His words made sense and she nodded, resting her head against the crook of his shoulder.

He pressed a kiss to her forehead. "Good girl."

Within moments, he settled her on the bed, the comforter tucked in around her.

"Rest well, love," he whispered.

Chapter Twenty-Nine

Lightning exploded across the darkening sky followed by a rumbling roll of thunder. A storm brewed. It wouldn't be long before the clouds burst, sending a downpour of rain over her.

Her arms weighed down by grocery bags, Aiyanna stood in the middle of the grocery mart's parking lot, struggling to remember where she parked her car. The answer came in a flash. Aisle C.

She dashed across the lot. Head lowered, her chin pressed to her chest. She pushed against the wind, stumbling as it shoved her backward.

Crap! She'd hoped to be home before Cameron woke. He'd be pissed she left without telling him, and now with the weather, double crap!

Since the guardians' arrival two days ago, things have definitely changed at her place.

For the most part, the warriors disappeared at night and slept during the day. Except Fallon who set his own schedule. He was distinctly different than the others. Aiyanna came to the conclusion that it had something to do with his wife and his marriage, but what? She had yet to figure that out. While Cameron, Devlin and Cara didn't eat regular food, Fallon cleaned out her cupboards, fridge, and pantry on a daily basis. The man had an insatiable appetite. Hence, the impromptu shopping trip.

The purr of an engine sounded above the splattering rain on the pavement. It grew steadily closer bearing down on her position.

She seethed with anger.

Damn people! Didn't they know there was a five mph speed limit in this parking lot? And especially in this rain, visibility was near to nothing.

Aiyanna twisted around, prepared to give the driver one her "shame on you" looks.

At first glance, she assumed the SUV would steer around her, but it actually picked up speed and headed directly toward her. Her eyes widened, and panic seared through her. He wasn't going to stop!

She dropped the groceries and waved her hands in the air to warn him. Whether he didn't see her or chose to ignore her, he continued his path.

At the last second, she threw herself to the ground between two parked cars. She landed on the blacktop, flinching at the stinging pain in her knees and palms.

The car sped by. A gust of wind brushed over her. She groaned and pushed herself upright where she landed on her butt, her back pressed against the car behind her. She took a moment to access the damage. Small pebbles stuck to her palms, and she brushed them away. The fabric of her jeans was torn. Long, striped scratches marred the fleshy area below her kneecaps.

The distinct hum of the automobile's engine continued down the lot. He hadn't even bothered to stop and see if she were all right.

Idiot!

She drew a deep breath, leaned around the front fender of her barricade and squinted into the back window of the SUV but couldn't see past the black-tinted windows. She shook her head when the vehicle turned the corner on two wheels. Too damn bad he didn't flip it. That would teach him a lesson. As long as he remained unhurt, Aiyanna quickly corrected. Teenagers and their joy rides...they were going to kill someone one of these days.

"What a jerk," she muttered.

Jumping to her feet, she quickly assembled her groceries and tossed them back into the soaked plastic bags. She couldn't care less if the eggs got broken or the bread squashed. She sure as hell wasn't sticking around here.

She scrambled through the parking lot, her gaze searching the area. Relief rushed over her when she spotted her car two aisles over.

She sprinted the rest of the way over the parking lot. Before she reached her car, she pulled the keys from her jacket pocket. Using the remote on the key chain, she popped the trunk.

She set her groceries in the trunk and had just slammed the hood when she heard the familiar squeal of tires again. Spinning around, she spotted the same SUV barreling through the lot four rows over. He slowed down a couple of times then increased his speed again. It appeared as if he were looking for someone.

She bit her bottom lip, overcome with an uneasiness that made her breath catch. Was he looking for her?

The SUV headed down her aisle again. She lunged to the payment just as the vehicle sped by. Grimacing against the second sting of pain to her kneecaps, she gasped for breath, flinching at her bruised and bloodied knees.

Nervously, she ran her hands through her hair and crawled to the front of her car to peer down the aisle.

Empty. The SUV was gone.

Regardless of the pain, she crawled on hands and knees to the driver's side door of her car. Without getting to her feet, she unlocked the car, opened the door, and scooted inside.

Her hands shook so hard she could barely put the key in the ignition. Once the key slid in, she turned, and the car purred to life. Aiyanna gripped the steering wheel in both hands and dropped her forehead against the leather steering wheel cover. The tears she'd been holding slipped down her cheeks.

****

With groceries filling her arms, Aiyanna leaned against the kitchen door. She struggled to reach the doorknob. Her hand touched the cold brass handle, and she was about to give it a twist when the door swung open.

Caught off guard, the door no longer supported her weight, and she lost her balance. She gasped and would have landed on the floor if not for the hand that reached out to steady her.

Aiyanna glanced from the hand to its owner. Cara bit her bottom lip, her expression contrite.

"Sorry," Cara murmured, then shrugged. "I thought you could use some help."

Cara's eyes suddenly widened and swept over her, taking in her tattered clothing and wet look. She gazed at Aiyanna speculatively before she asked, "What the hell happened to ye? Ye're a mess. Did ye crash yer car or something?"

Aiyanna laughed. "Thank you, and no, I didn't get into an accident. It was more like the accident almost found me."

Cara stared at her with rounded eyes. Aiyanna grimaced at the confusion on the other woman's face. She walked around Cara and set the groceries on the table.

As much as she wanted to dislike the woman, she couldn't bring herself to do it. She liked the rough and tough Amazon woman.

Cara represented beauty and power. Although he denied it, how could Cameron not love Cara?

"He doesna, ye know?"

Aiyanna jumped, startled and spun around. "What?"

"Cameron doesna love me."

"How did you know what I was thinking? I thought that was only when two people were mated."

"'Tis the strongest when ye're mated. All of us have the power to read other people's thoughts if we want to." Her lips curved into a lop-sided grin, and she said, "Most of the time, we choose no' to."

Aiyanna put the milk in the fridge. She turned back around, nodded then laughed. "I guess I wouldn't blame you for that, but why would you want to read mine?"

"Truthfully, I didn't. Strong thoughts jump out, and naturally, I latched onto them." Cara's lips twisted into a crooked smile. "And I like ye, too."

Aiyanna reached into the bag for the eggs, but at Cara's comment, her head jerked up in surprise. Cara portrayed a woman colder than ice, but, in this moment, she displayed her real side. Cara was a common person, and Aiyanna developed a sudden respect for her. After all, she might be a half god, but she was still human.

"If ye tell anyone, I will kill ye."

Aiyanna laughed. "Your secret is safe with me."

"I know," Cara said with quiet confidence.

Both women grew silent. Cara sat at the table while Aiyanna rushed around the kitchen and put the rest of the groceries away. Once done, she sat at the table across from the female guardian.

After a few moments, Cara cleared her throat. "Seriously, Cameron and I, we're friends." She crossed her arms over her breast, and her shoulders bobbed up and down. "I love him. I do, but no' in the romantic sense of the word."

"You seem so close."

"In our line of work, we doona make friends easily. If we make a friend or two, they age. After they've lived their life, their bodies give out, and they die." At Aiyanna's soft gasp, Cara laughed. "I know it sounds harsh, but we've seen it so many times. That's why we doona form attachments. It hurts too much to say goodbye. So, we hold on to the friendships we found in being a guardian. Our responsibilities as the Síoraí are the only things we have in common." She wrinkled her nose. "And to be honest, Cameron isna my type. I prefer the strong, silent type, and I wouldna use silent to describe that man."

Aiyanna laughed. "You've got a point there." And then, she thought about what Cara told her. Confusion filled her. "But why would a guardian mate with a human? I'm going to die. Why did he choose me?"

Cara shook her head. "I doona have the answers ye seek. I'm sorry."

Aiyanna shrugged. "It's okay." She placed her elbows on the table. "So, tell me, how long have you known him?"

Cara smiled and shook her head. "Cameron and I have known each other a verra long time. In fact, you might be surprised to know that he's the baby of us all."

"Baby? Really? You're kidding, right?"

Even as Aiyanna spouted the questions, Cara nodded. "He is."

"I have a hard time believing that."

Cara giggled. "So does he."

"There are times when I can't grasp how to take him. Do you think you can help me to understand him better?"

Cara's face turned thoughtful. "I doona know that I can help ye with that. Cameron, Devlin, Fallon, we have chosen different paths. As much as allowed, we keep parts of ourselves isolated from each other."

"What happened to Fallon? He's different than the rest of you. Good Lord, look at the food he eats," she said, barely able to keep the laughter from her voice.

Cara smiled. "Yeah, well, he fell in love."

"Falling in love changes you?"

"I doona know if it works the same for all of us." Cara leaned back in the chair, folding her hands together on the table. "'Tis what happened to him. And believe me, he's a pain in the ass about it. He likes to remind us," Cara leaned closer as if telling a deep secret and said, "ye know, rub our noses in the fact he isna a vampire look-a-like, act-a-like anymore. He can eat real food and walk in the sun, but we have Liz on our side, though, and she keeps him in line."

"What's his wife like?"

"Smart, powerful."

"Powerful?"

"Aye, she's a lot like ye. She's human, but her psychic powers make her more than what she portrays. Deidra tried to kill her too."

"That woman gets around, doesn't she?"

Cara's eyes narrowed and darkened. "Deidra isna a woman, Aiyanna. Doona ever forget what's she capable of doing. She can manipulate humans where they have no choice but to do what she demands."

Aiyanna grew silent. She bit the corner of her lip, her focus returning to the events in the parking lot.

Cara must have caught the slight movement, for she reached across and tapped her finger on the table in front of Aiyanna to draw her attention. "What are ye hiding?"

Aiyanna's gaze flashed to Cara. "What do you mean?"

"Something's bothering ye. What happened when ye went out today?"

Shaking her head, she stuttered, "I'm not sure."

Even as she uttered her words, the nagging in the back of her mind refused to be stilled.

"Tell me," Cara demanded.

"I thought they were teenagers joyriding around the parking lot."

"Who?"

"After I finished shopping, I walked across the parking lot to my car. I heard a loud engine and turned. An SUV came barreling down the aisle. They saw me, they had to, but they didn't stop. If anything, the driver seemed to punch on the gas."

"Is that why ye're all skinned up?"

"Yeah." Aiyanna grimaced. "I hate to admit it, but I flung myself to the parking lot in a fit of panic. Between you and me, I'm a chicken shit at heart."

"Aiyanna, this is serious. Ye need to tell Cameron what happened today."

"No!" The word came out a little more forceful than Aiyanna intended, and she quickly apologized. "I'm sorry. No, I don't want him to know. Please don't tell him."

"Why? That man will do anything to keep ye safe."

"Except forget the past." Aiyanna pushed herself away from the table and stood. She glanced at Cara and said, "Thank you."

"For what? I havena done anything."

"You listened. Promise me you won't tell anyone about my accident."

"Do ye realizing what ye're asking?"

"I do, and I'm sorry to put you in this position, but I need time."

"Ye love him, doona ye?"

Tears filled Aiyanna's eyes. "Yes, no, I don't know. I think I do, and even went so far as to tell him I did. You should have seen the expression on his face. He looked at me as if I'd suddenly grown three heads."

"Three heads?"

"Oh yeah. He didn't believe me and even had the nerve to tell me—" Realizing where this headed, Aiyanna stopped, her hands clenched in front of her. She shook her head. "Never mind. Whenever he's nearby, I feel like a lovesick teenager. All he'd have to do is ask, and I'd willingly jump into the backseat of a car. Is that love or lust?"

Cara's lips curved in understanding. "I think ye know the answer to that, Aiyanna. But I imagine ye both have the same problem."

"And what's that?"

"Ye refuse to let yerself believe."

"In what?"

"That love truly exists."

"Do you believe in love?"

A momentary look of discomfort and sadness crossed Cara's face. "I did once."

Chapter Thirty

That evening, Aiyanna trudged up the stairs with Cara's words ringing in her head. The weight of doubt pressed heavy on her shoulders. Did she believe in love? Did she truly love Cameron? Or had it been the heat of the moment that spurred the words?

Mentally, she shook her head. Only superficial people spoke words without meaning. She wasn't shallow, was she?

Preoccupied with her thoughts, she ambled down the hallway toward her room.

A brief shadow caught her eye a split second before strong hands caught her shoulders. Her head jerked up to discover a quirky smirk on Devlin's handsome face. Startled, she sprang back a couple of steps. She hadn't heard the guest door open. Thank God he'd stopped her before she ran headlong into his broad chest. She could have broken her nose.

"Whoa there, lass," Devlin said, his voice laced with laughter.

"Oops, sorry, I didn't see you there," she blurted, over her pounding heart. The heat of embarrassment flared into her cheeks, and she lowered her eyes, prepared to step around the man and continue on her way.

"Aiyanna."

She glanced up. Unease lurked in his bright blue eyes, and she asked, "Did you need something?"

"Nay, I'm good, although, I'm a bit concerned about ye. Are ye all right?"

"Why do ye ask?"

"Ye seem a wee inattentive to yer surroundings."

Her lips curved up into a slim smile, and she conceded, "A little distracted perhaps, but I'll be fine. I was headed for bed."

He nodded as if in understanding, yet his expression remained one of disbelief.

"I'm fine." He still appeared unconvinced, and she reassured, "Really I am." She turned from his irritating stare and added under her breath. "I'm tired. Unlike you, I need to sleep."

He chuckled. "Ooh, an attitude to match yer fiery temper. No' bad characteristics for a guardian's mate."

She stopped and pivoted on her heels to face him, suppressing a sigh, tired of hearing about her great qualities. "Cameron and I are not truly mated. Not yet anyways."

His eyebrows rose in question, and the beginning of a smile tipped the corners of his mouth. A smile without malice, almost apologetic. He released a long, audible breath. "So, ye know about that, eh?"

"I do, but what I don't understand is why such an important detail is left out. Shouldn't I have been told that to fortify this union and become a Síoraí mate, I have to die? The bite and the sex are just preludes to the final culmination...death."

"That is a well-kept secret. No one is supposed to know until it happens."

"What? You mean Cameron doesn't know?"

Devlin shook his head. "Nay, he doesna, and he canna find out, lass. It is part of the process for him as well as for ye."

"Did Fallon travel this same course?"

"Aye, and it nearly ripped him to pieces. If ye're worried about it, there's no need to be. Ye will be in good hands."

"I'm not afraid."

Devlin smiled. "Aye, I can see that, and I'm impressed."

"Don't be. I didn't say I was ready to jump off the bridge."

"Ye canna prepare for such a thing. The timing canna be predicted. No one knows when it will happen."

"But it will."

The warmth of his smile echoed in his voice. "Aye, lass, it will."

"Will it happen to Cara?"

He nodded. "When the time comes, aye."

"And you? But you know."

This time, he inclined his head. "That I canna answer, lass. My past and my future are a little different than the others."

"But my path is set?"

Once again, he nodded.

Raising her chin, she assumed all the courage she could muster and strolled down the hall. At her bedroom door, she hesitated and called over her shoulder, "Good night."

"Good night, lass."

Devlin's footsteps thundered on the steps as he went downstairs.

****

An hour later, she stared at the ceiling, struggling to find answers to her questions. She rolled onto her side and tucked her hand beneath her cheek. Tears lingered on her lashes, and she tried to swallow the lump that lingered in her throat.

The door opened.

She tensed when footsteps crossed the room, until the heady, rich scent of Cameron infiltrated her sense of smell.

Since the other guardians' arrival, the upstairs

rooms had filled up quickly. Cameron moved from the other bedroom into her room and into her bed.

She hadn't been disappointed with his choice.

The bed dipped, and the breadth of his weight settled beside her. His arms surrounded her, and he tugged her against his chest. She let him. Every fiber in her body tingled at his nearness.

His breath touched her ear. She rolled over, glancing up at him. A shadow above her, his eyes glowed in the darkness. Her mouth parted on a sigh, and she rose up to meet his kiss.

His hands roamed over her with tantalizing persuasion. They caressed, massaged her, filling her with a burning desire, an aching need.

With a low growl, his mouth plunged downward to capture and devour her lips. He drugged her senses with his gentle massage. Currents of desire raged through her. The touch of his hand on her ribs stoked the already growing fire. Her insides melted.

And then the kiss changed. He nudged her lips open with his thrusting tongue and launched a sweet exploration of her mouth. The pit of her stomach lurched into a wild swirl.

When he moved away, she burned in the aftermath of his fiery possession. His hand slid the strap of her gown off her left shoulder, baring her breast.

He dipped his head and took her nipple in a gentle suckle. She moaned, her body arching to meet his mouth. He drew away long enough to rid her of the short gown, completely exposing her body.

His gaze roamed over her. He brushed a hand along the curve of her hip, over her soft thigh, and through the moist tangle of curls nestled at the apex of her thighs. She whimpered in delight when he separated the tender folds to expose the swollen bud where he rubbed the pad of his thumb across her core. Her breath came in long, surrendering moans

Victoria Noxon

at the spasms that rocked her.

Aiyanna pulled his head to her breast and opened her legs wider, surrendering to his masterful seduction. She ached and throbbed where his hands stroked her. When he plunged his fingers inside, her body instinctively vaulted toward his hand, and she cried out in erotic pleasure. Her body vibrated with liquid fire. The tender strokes of his fingers sent erotic jolts through her veins.

She trembled with need.

Unable to wait for him any longer, she grasped his hair and pulled his lips to hers. She gave him a "let me show you how to do this right" kiss before she gave his shoulders a rough shove and pushed him onto his back.

She climbed on top and rubbed her warmth across his stomach. In control, Aiyanna reached between their bodies and guided him inside her.

Aiyanna arched her back to draw him deeper. So hard and hot, he filled her. His hardness electrified her.

He gripped her hips and guided her over him, slowly, deeply in an undulating rhythm that made her writhe from the intense pleasure of his intimate strokes.

"Ye're beautiful," he breathed. He rolled his hips, thrusting harder and deeper within her.

His eyes darkened. He reached a hand between them to tease her. His fingers stroked her swollen bud in unison with his thrusts. His hips moved, and he slid in and out.

Waves of ecstasy throbbed through her. The world spun and careened on it axis. The pleasure pure and explosive, her orgasm so intense she screamed, her body vibrated with liquid fire.

****

With a deep growl, Cameron rolled her onto her back, maintaining the connection of their bodies. He slowed his movements, enjoying her tightness. When her nails dug into his back, his own release escalated to its crescendo. He gripped her hips and held her still while he pounded into her again and again until he slid over the abyss where pleasure claimed him. He groaned against her neck.

With his body numb with release, he collapsed. He lay still, attempting to regain control of his breathing.

After a moment, he moved off her, drawing her head into the crook of his shoulder. His heart beat a brisk pace in his chest. Never before had he experienced such elation.

Her fingers traced the lines of his upper body, twirling his chest hairs in her fingertips. The tenderness of her touch surprised him. He caught her hand in his and brought it to his lips where he kissed her fingers one by one.

And in the next moment, the dam he'd constructed around his heart broke, and all his pent-up emotions spilled free.

He could scarcely breathe with the realization. For the first time in two hundred and fifty years, he made love to a woman, and it was a purely sensual experience. He wasn't satisfying a primitive urge with meaningless sex.

By the gods! Nothing this connected, this poignant could ever be considered meaningless.

Until he met Aiyanna, he merely existed, never truly lived. Even with Sarah, they shared love, a life, and children but not this soul-binding connection.

He never wanted to let Anya leave his arms.

What was the matter with him?

Did he love her?

No, it couldn't be.

He had to be wrong. He had to be.

What they'd experienced was the progeny of a hundred-year abstinence. Lust brought them to this point.

Sheer, unadulterated lust.

Wasn't it?

Even as the voice whispered in his head, his heart told him something entirely different. He had finally irreversibly reached the point of no return, and he could no longer deny the obvious.

He was in love with Aiyanna Grey.

Her lips seared a path across his chest. Butterfly kisses heated his flesh. Her palms traced his nipples. He closed his eyes and held her tight, enjoying the pleasures she evoked.

He pressed a kiss to the top of her forehead and placed his hand over hers to still her hand's travels. "If ye keep on with that, lass, there wilna be any sleep for either of us tonight."

She lifted her face, resting her chin on his chest. A saucy glint lit up her eyes. "Your point being?"

"Och, love, do ye know what ye're saying?"

In response, her tongue slipped from between full lips, and she licked her lips, her eyes teasing, tempting until he felt obligated to react.

In the next instant, she lay on her back, and he rose above her.

"In that case—"

His words were hindered as her hands laced through his hair, and she pulled his lips to hers.

Chapter Thirty-One

A haze marred her vision, blurring the images around her. Aiyanna rubbed her hand across her eyes and swiped away the fog. When her vision cleared, a granny knot settled in the pit of her stomach at the sight that met her eyes. She gasped aloud and immediately clapped one hand across her lips to prevent another unconscious outburst.

Beside an aged burial chamber, her sister hung between two wooden posts. She struggled against straps that tied her hands to the poles. Vampires surrounded her. A gurgled chant echoed through the trees. They twirled around their prisoner, dancing a bizarre waltz.

Leather whips whizzed through the air and landed with earsplitting slaps against Cheyenne's skin. Cheyenne moaned when each blow struck. Aiyanna flinched at the sound. The sight of blood oozing across her sister's skin brought the bile into her throat. The blue-skinned vampires stuck out their tongues catching the dribbles of blood that trickled toward them.

Aiyanna stretched out a hand but couldn't reach her.

Stop it! Aiyanna screamed, but the words that passed her lips were silent. Anger, fear and helplessness raged through her.

Paralyzed, she couldn't interfere, simply a spectator to the brutality.

From the corner of her eye, movement drew her attention to the east. Through the trees, a misty bluish miasma rolled across the ground headed in the direction of Cheyenne and her tormentors. As it drew closer, it thickened and swelled, writhing like fog around the circle, as if protecting the bloodsuckers from invaders of the outside world.

From within the mist, two reddish glows beamed like stabbing pits of swirling red flames.

Deidra! And the bitch taunted her.

Aiyanna ignored her and focused her attention on Cheyenne. A tiny light, the size of a firefly, fluttered in front of her face. Cheyenne grimaced, yet her lips curved briefly before she nodded. The glow shot into the sky and soared toward Aiyanna who quickly recognized the radiance of a Wood Fairy.

The Fairy fluttered toward Aiyanna and waved her hand, an indication she should follow. With one last look at Cheyenne, Aiyanna turned and followed the pixie to a cement building hidden behind a barricade of creeping plants. She brushed the vines aside to discover an open doorway. Once inside, the Fairy's glow illuminated the darkened area. They passed through each room with ease until they reached a long hallway.

Never one to suffer claustrophobia, the walls closed in around her. Nausea swirled in her stomach. Molten lava raced through her veins, and sweat poured down her face. Her breath burned in her lungs, and she wheezed at the stagnant, musty air.

With one hand flattened against the stone wall, she scaled her way through the passageway. Her gaze continued to follow the light that radiated from the sprite.

She didn't even know her name.

Marissa.

Aiyanna started at the Fairy's soft voice entering her thoughts.

It's nice to meet you, Marissa, she returned mentally, maintaining the audible silence.

Ahead, a light shimmered from an open doorway. She hurried through the corridor, anxious to escape the eerie place. As she stepped forward, her foot caught on the threshold, and she fell forward, landing on her knees in the soft grass.

Head down, she gulped in the fresh, clean air. Marissa's soft twittering whispered in her ear, and the light fluttering of her wings brushed against her hair.

Aiyanna drew another deep breath and turned her head.

Instead of Marissa, her gaze landed on a two-foot white concrete marker that rose three feet above her.

She pushed herself to her feet, brushed her hands on her jeans and walked over to the sign.

"Thank you, Marissa," she whispered. She turned to where Marissa hovered, only to discover the sweet Fairy gone.

Aiyanna turned back to the marker that held the clue she'd been waiting for.

Plot 794.

****

Aiyanna woke with a violent start and shot straight up in bed, instantly wide awake.

"Plot seven ninety-four," she whispered.

She rolled over eager to share her news with Cameron, but his side of the bed lay empty. Running her hand across the sheets, the cold of his absence filtered into her palm. She bit her bottom lip at the realization he must have left shortly after they made love.

She no longer feared a romantic relationship existed between Cara and Cameron. In fact, she trusted the female guardian. Aiyanna didn't know Cara's story but sensed her past mirrored Cameron's, having recognized the sadness in Cara's eyes when she spoke of love.

She whipped the blankets aside and jumped

from bed. Dressed in seconds, she rushed down the steps in search of Cameron and the other guardians.

It was time to free her sister.

****

"Are ye certain it wasna a dream, lass? Ye've been under a great deal of stress lately," Devlin remarked, dropping into a chair at the kitchen table. His tone was laced with skepticism.

"I'm positive. Cheyenne is in Arlington Cemetery, Plot number seven ninety-four. I saw her. I swear I did," Aiyanna cried, rushing to the door. "Come on, we have to leave now."

"Whoa, lass," Cameron called. He took a step forward, blocking her escape.

"What?"

"We canna go out until tonight. The sun will be up in a little less than an hour," Devlin reminded her, gently.

"But...but, we can't wait. The longer we hang around here—"

"Aiyanna, if what ye saw is true then we know where to find yer sister. That's a start, but we canna go barreling in there like a bunch of fools without knowing where Deidra's hiding. That would be suicidal. Chances are she's close by." Devlin released a deep breath at Aiyanna's agonized expression. "Look, Deidra isna going to harm her. Remember, she's her ace in the hole."

"I'll go check it out," Fallon volunteered. He turned his back to the others, sending Aiyanna a sly wink.

"Fallon—" Devlin started, but Fallon held up a hand to silence him.

"I'm only going to scope the place out. Ye're right. That bitch wilna go far from her prize. At least, no' during the day. She'll be resting like the rest of ye. She doesna know about me or that I'm a day walker."

Devlin hesitated. "I'm no' so sure that's a good plan."

"Oh, come on, man."

Cara stepped forward. "Dev, he's got a good point. He can slip in and out without them ever knowing he was there."

After a moment, Devlin frowned but nodded. "Okay, but if ye run across her, keep yer distance. Doona try to be a hero, and, by the gods, doona get caught. I'm sure she'll have humans guarding Cheyenne."

Fallon's eyes twinkled, and he grinned. "That wilna happen. I have too much of the good life."

Cara laughed and slapped Fallon on the back. "He doesna need to worry. Lizzie will send Auntie after him to bring him back."

Fallon grimaced.

"Ah, afraid of the goddess, are ye, Rebel Man?" Cara goaded with dazzling determination.

"No' of the goddess." He cleared his throat. "I mean Aunt Rea. Actually, she's a wonderful ole lass, and I know she would be more than happy to save me from those parasites, but—"

"Who would save ye from yer wife, eh?" Devlin laughed.

A grin overtook Fallon's expression, and he shrugged. "She does hold all the cards."

"And the keys to the bedroom, I'll wager," Cameron chimed in.

With an irresistibly devastating grin, Fallon nodded. "And that, my friend, would be a wager you'd win."

Aiyanna heard enough. Exasperated, she rolled her eyes and said, "Would you guys stop? This isn't helping my sister."

Fallon glanced at Aiyanna, chuckled and nodded. "I'll gather a few things from my room and be off. If I'm no' back by sundown, come looking."

With that, he sauntered from the room.

****

The sun cast golden rays over the treetops that lined Aiyanna's property. Cameron lurked in the shadows on the back porch, careful to avoid the precarious beams.

He thought of Fallon and of the life he shared with his wife.

And suddenly, all his loneliness and confusion of the past centuries welded together in one upsurge of devouring yearning. He wanted what Fallon had, the good life, complete with Aiyanna's love and children if the gods willed it.

He ran a ragged hand through his hair; her name lingered in his thoughts.

He'd been forced to admit to himself a while ago that his relationship with Anya was no longer fused by sex. He recalled the ecstasy of being held in her gentle arms. Making love to her was amazing, yet that was not the adhesive that bound them together.

He didn't want to live without her whatever the future brought.

He impatiently pulled his drifting thoughts together.

Hadn't Fallon's life changed when he bonded with Lizzie?

Could it be?

His eyes widened.

He raised his left hand. His fingers trembled. Determined, he inched his arm up, stretching his hand into the sunlight.

It stung like the fires of hell. He pulled back and waved his hand wildly through the air putting out the flames that shot from his fingertips.

"Mother fucker," he muttered, at his smoking hand.

"Wow, ye've learned the language of the times very well indeed."

Cameron jumped at Fallon's laughing voice behind him. He turned and scowled at the other man who stood in the doorway leading into the kitchen. "I thought ye'd already left?"

Fallon opened the front of his leather jacket. Inside, his pocket held a slew of wooden sticks. "I forgot my stakes. I may not need them, but best to have them just in case."

Cameron smiled and inclined his head. "How long have ye been standing there?"

"Long enough." Fallon chuckled. He drew away from the doorframe, standing up straight. His expression turned serious when he observed Cameron's still smoldering hand. "It doesna work that way."

"What?"

"Just because ye've united with the lass doesna mean ye've regained all the qualities ye lost when ye became a guardian."

"I doona understand. Wasna that the way it worked for ye?"

Fallon smiled and shook his head. "Nay, I had to find peace with my past in the face of the greatest adversity I've ever seen. I finally had to admit to love."

"Admit to love?"

"Ye'll know when the time arrives." Fallon slapped Cameron on the shoulder. "I'm off. I'll see ye in a bit."

"Hey, Fallon—"

Fallon glanced over his shoulder, "Aye?"

"What happens next?"

His expression stilled. "I doona know what's next for ye, lad. I'm sorry."

And then he stepped off the porch and disappeared into the woods.

Chapter Thirty-Two

Fallon returned from his excursion in the cemetery after only an hour. He stomped into the kitchen, dropped in a chair, and ran his hand through his hair.

Aiyanna rushed into the room, followed by Cameron and Cara.

"What did ye find out?" Devlin asked, stepping into the kitchen from the hall.

Fallon's gaze searched the circle of faces around him and grinned. "Wow, I must be an important man to have drawn such a crowd."

"Did you find her?" Aiyanna asked in an anxious tone. Her fists bunched at her sides while she waited his answer.

Fallon nodded. "Well, she is definitely there. Deidra is using humans to guard her."

Cara laughed with no humor. "O' course she is. They're no' affected by the sun like vampires. If she dinna, she'd be unprotected during the daytime hours."

"What about the bitch?" Cameron walked across the room and leaned against the counter.

Fallon grunted. "Aye, she's there too. Plot Number seven ninety-two, two away from where Aiyanna's dream told her they housed Cheyenne."

Cara dropped into the chair opposite Fallon. "So, what's the plan, guys?"

"The sun will set in about three hours' time." Devlin stepped forward. "Whatever we decide, it needs to happen before Deidra wakens for the night.

For the next two hours they planned their strategy. There was no margin for error. If they didn't get Cheyenne out within those first few minutes, then, chances were, all would be lost.

While Cameron and Devlin set up surveillance on Deidra, Fallon and Cara would split from the group and make their way to Cheyenne. Once they delivered Aiyanna's sister safe at home, the guardians would return to Deidra's hideout and take the Vampryss down.

Fallon rested his hands, palms down, on the table. His gaze scanned the others in the room. "Well, that's it, then. Let's gather our crap and hit the road."

Aiyanna headed for the door. "I'll be right back. Don't leave without me."

As she stepped into the hall, a hand gripped her forearm, preventing her from going upstairs. She glanced up into Cameron's determined face. With a soft tug, he pulled her into the living room where he released her, spinning her around to face him.

For a moment, he studied her with a curious intensity.

Unnerved, her hands settled on her hips, and she glared at him. "Listen, there's no time for this. If we're going to free Cheyenne, we've got to leave now."

"Ye're no' going anywhere," he barked, with a significant lifting of his brows as if challenging her.

Aiyanna refused to cower beneath Cameron's bellow. His forehead creased into an insolent scowl, and he glowered down at her, his eyes blazing yellow lightning.

She ignored the warning cloud on his face. With her arms folded across her chest, she stomped her foot and declared, "I'm going, and I don't care what you say, Cameron MacLean."

Cameron's gaze flickered at something over her

shoulder. His lips twisted into a cynical smile, and he glanced at her, eyebrows raised as if to say "Ye're in trouble now." She spun around just as Devlin entered the room.

"Dev, tell her she isna going?"

Aiyanna crossed her arms over her chest, tapped her foot and sent the eldest guardian a defiant stare, daring him to agree with Cameron.

Devlin's mouth twisted at the corners. His eyes moved over her and then traveled to Cameron and back again. This eye contact continued for a few seconds before he took a step back, chuckled and threw his hands in the air. "She's yer mate. Ye deal with it," he commented, then spun on his heels and left the room.

Aiyanna turned back to Cameron and smiled in satisfaction.

His eyebrows rose in question. "Doona look so damn smug. He dinna say aye."

"And he didn't say no. Look, Cameron, I'm not going to argue with you. Either you let me tag along, or I'll wait for you to leave and go by myself. It's that simple."

"Damn it! It isna that simple. Why doona ye realize that?" He spun around and sent his fist blasting into the wall. The plaster cracked, spraying a thin coat of dust into the room.

Aiyanna's nerves twitched at his temper, but she refused to allow him to see her rising panic. If she did, and gave into him, she conceded defeat.

"And why do you refuse to see me as an adult? Despite the way you treat me, I am not a child."

He drew a deep breath and released it by slow degrees. When he spoke, his tone was choked yet gentle. "Aiyanna, please think about this. Ye understand the repercussions if Deidra—"

"I know what could happen, but it won't. What is this all about? Do you have so little faith in me?"

"No' in ye...in me."

"You're not my protector, Cameron. As much as you'd like to believe you are, you're not. I can take care of myself."

He lifted his chin. With his eyes on the ceiling, he swallowed hard, as if trying to gain control. After a moment, he looked at her. "Canna ye see how hard this is for me?"

Her determination was like a rock inside her, and she refused to budge. "You make it difficult on yourself by letting the past affect your present. When are you going to realize that was a different time and you're not the same man?"

"Doona ye think I've tried? But it still changes nothing."

Aiyanna wanted to slap him into recognizing the truth.

Instead, she bit down hard on her lower lip, but even that wasn't enough to stop her next bitter words. "I never believed you were a man who clung to self-pity."

"Aiyanna..."

"I'm going, Cameron. Like Devlin said, deal with it," she stated, with quiet emphasis. On the outside, she kept her features deceptively composed. Inside, she trembled.

Fighting to control her rattled nerves, she turned and walked toward the doorway, holding her head high. At the threshold, she stopped. Without turning, she said, "Oh, and by the way, you *will* be fixing that hole in the plaster."

Outside in the hallway, she collapsed against the wall. She wrapped her arms around her body, closed her eyes, and leaned her head back against the wall. Why did she have to love such an idiot?

Footsteps echoed on the staircase, and she opened her eyes. Cara spied her and rushed to her side.

"Are ye all right?" she asked.

Barely able to speak, Aiyanna nodded. "I'm fine," she whispered.

"Ah, the bloody idiot, eh?"

Again, Aiyanna nodded.

"Forget him. Go freshen up. Let's get a move on."

"Why doesn't he trust me to know what's right?"

Cara wrapped her arms across Aiyanna's shoulders and led her toward the bottom of the stairs.

"Because he's a man, and as such, they believe they have all the answers, but as women, 'tis our deplorable duty to show them otherwise."

Aiyanna giggled then hiccupped. "I'm going to show him a thing or two, and I'm not sure he's going to like what he sees."

Chapter Thirty-Three

Moments after they appeared in the cemetery, the winds picked up in intensity, creating an eerie wail that echoed through the trees and across the cemetery. The ghostly sounds sent chills crawling up Aiyanna's spine. She swallowed hard and breathed in shallow, quick gasps.

The howls rose and fell in a steady rhythm then disappeared entirely only to return a minute later.

As hard as she tried to ignore it, the noise crawled beneath her skin and struck the cord of every nerve in her body. She pushed against Cameron's back. When he glanced at her over his shoulder, she urged her lips to curve into a blithe smile, even though she wasn't feeling particularly blasé at the moment.

"Are ye okay, lass?" he whispered. His brows furrowed in concern.

She wanted to tell him no but instead nodded and murmured back, "Fine."

She gritted her teeth at the odd changes in pitches and tones that bounced off headstones and tunneled through open crevices.

The guardians' strategy placed Aiyanna with Cameron and Devlin outside the building Deidra hid watching for movement. The three would lie in the shadows and wait for the signal indicating that Cheyenne had been released. After that, they would return to the house for the happy reunion.

Of course, Cameron's irritation soared higher at the plan, and he argued, "It isna safe. Aiyanna shouldna be allowed within two feet of that bitch."

Devlin listened to Cameron's ranting for more than ten minutes before he explained in a calm, yet matter-of-fact manner, "Cameron, if ye shut up and think about it, ye'll see the sense of this. Putting Aiyanna in close proximity of her sister isna an option. Their combined powers would create a beacon, most certain a draw to Deidra. With Aiyanna at yer side, ye have the ability to use yer powers to shield her. Combine that with the bond ye share with the lass. She couldna be in safer hands."

"Make her stay here."

Devlin smiled and shook his head. "No' an alternative. As soon as Cheyenne is released, where do ye think the first place Deidra will go?"

"There is a protection spell around the house. She wilna be able to get inside."

"Vampires canna, but that wilna stop a human follower. And with all of us gone, there is no one here to protect her from them."

It had taken some convincing before Cameron finally saw the logic to Devlin's plan. He hadn't necessarily approved, but he agreed to go along with the plan.

Aiyanna hissed in dismay and frustration as the clatter continued. She covered her ears with her hands to block out the noises before they drove her crazy.

She felt a light touch to her cheek and opened her eyes to Cameron's face. He nodded, as if understanding her emotions. His lips split into a smile of reassurance.

She drew a deep breath and bobbed her head.

"Come on," he mouthed.

Tucked close to Cameron's back, she put one foot in front of the other. Suddenly, she smashed into a hard, immovable object. A bruising pain ran through her hip. The collision upset her balance, and her knees buckled beneath her. She grabbed a hold of a nearby headstone to steady her legs. When she looked up, her eyes met Cameron's. His expression was tight with strain, his jaw clenched.

Ooops! She'd run into him.

She smiled and mouthed, "Sorry."

With a curt nod his attention diverted elsewhere.

"Let's go," Devlin whispered.

****

"Creepy crap out here tonight, eh Cara?" Fallon asked with a trace of barely contained laughter in his voice.

Cara snorted. "'Tis just the wind, but nice analogy. I dinna know ye had it in ye."

"Ye'd be surprised what's in me."

"Aye, bunches of BS," she replied through stiff lips. She shifted and took a step forward but stopped when Fallon's hand squeezed her arm.

She looked at him in question.

"Over there," he whispered, inclining his head in the direction of the mausoleum.

From the obscurity of the trees, Cara focused into the darkness. In front of the concrete memorial, a door stood wide open, a silent, erect figure in the threshold. Two more stood guard on each side of the doorway.

She turned to Fallon and mouthed, "Human."

Fallon nodded. "Yeah. They haven't changed shifts yet. I know the one in the doorway from somewhere, but I canna—" His eyes widened, and he jerked upright. "Son-of-a-bitch."

"What?"

"That's the bastard that tried to kill Lizzie."

"Are ye sure?"

"Positive. I'd recognize him anywhere. What was his name? Jim, Jeff, no, Jack. That's it. Jack Stannard, a coroner for the Rapid Rivers Police

Department."

"What the hell is he doing here?"

Fallon's hand moved to his waist where he pulled out a long-bladed knife from the sheath tied to his belt. The sharp edge shimmered in the moonlight. "He isna under Deidra's control. He's out for his own glory."

"Ye canna kill him," Cara rushed out.

"Watch me," he replied, before he disappeared.

Cara swung around in time to see him reappear behind the figure where he dragged him back into the shadows. The other men seemed oblivious to Fallon's appearance. They stood at attention, their eyes faced forward.

A second later, Fallon stepped into the building's doorway, swinging his arms wide. His knuckles connected with the chins of each of the two men. They dropped like stones, unmoving.

He looked in her direction and waved her in. She scanned the area and scooted out from behind the trees. Treading lightly on dried grass and broken limbs, she reached his side. Fallon moved aside, motioning her inside with a sweep of his arm. Without hesitation, Cara took the three concrete steps that led down into the crypt.

"Ye dinna kill him, did ye?" Cara asked, spying the motionless body of the coroner in the dusty corner.

"Nay, but I damn well should have. He'll be out for a couple of hours. When we get back to Aiyanna's house, I'm going to send the cops out for that bastard. If I recall, he's wanted in Rapid Rivers on some embezzling charges."

Cara laughed. "Ye're a bastard, do ye know that?"

Fallon's face split into a wide grin. "Aye, so I've been told."

She smiled, shaking her head. "Come on."

The halls of the mausoleum were sunken pits of gloom and silence, deep beneath rotted timbers. They moved through tunnels of darkness. Cobwebs swept across her face. She shivered and swiped the offending netting away with a brush of her hand.

A loud hiss echoed in the darkness. She came to a standstill tapping Fallon on the arm. Out of the corner of her eyes, she saw him nod. They turned. Her eyes searched the darkness looking for the source of the eerie sound.

Suddenly, two blue-skinned, veiny vampires rushed from the murky corners. She raised her sword and rushed forward, meeting one the vampire head on. Her blade entered the chest of her target. A gray cloud of ash filtered in the air.

She spun around to glance at Fallon. His prey gone, his eyes continued to search the area.

A snap sounded behind them, and they spun around. Two more vampires appeared. Their long skeleton hands reached for them. They hissed. Their fangs dripped blood.

"Change of guard," Fallon shouted. Swiping his blade in a figure eight, he dashed toward them, swiping at their heads. One connected, decapitating a vampire, which evaporated in a burst of flames. He spun around, catching the last one across the mid-section, slicing the bloodsucker in two.

He glanced toward Cara. Breathless, he said, "Come on. Grab the girl, and let's get the hell out of here before company arrives."

Cara nodded, and they headed around the corner. A light appeared toward the end of the passageway, illuminating the dark.

"This must be it," Cara said, in a low tone.

They inched into a large parlor-type area. A candle sat on a busted up wooden table beside a locked door. The bolt barring the door looked new and sparkled silver in the candlelight.

A light wind rushed into the room. The flame flickered. A figure materialized from the bricks and mortar of the concrete hallway. At first, a silhouette of a man appeared, but as he emerged into the room, he turned into a vampire, an ancient bloodsucker dressed in an off-white shirt, black slacks, and dark overcoat. Navy blue tinged veins lined his forehead and ran along his cheeks.

His chalk-colored face was a mask, fixed and vacant, with a dripping, salivating grin curving his lips. Cara cringed at the vampire's rotten black teeth and fetid breath.

He walked with the exaggerated stride of a man who had too much to drink. Eyes wide, they gleamed with an internal fire, his lips wet and red.

The vampire entered the light of the candle, and Cara scowled at the stain that blemished the crumpled whiteness of his shirt—a fresh glistening stain of bright scarlet blood.

The bloodsucker opened his arms and said, "Welcome to my humble adobe." His fanged smile disappeared. His mouth twisted in anger. "It is a shame you will not be staying long."

"No' much for hospitality, are ye?" Fallon asked, chuckling.

"My sanctuary is my home. I did not invite you, and I ask you to leave."

"We will as soon as we retrieve what we came for."

The vampire laughed. His eyes, fixed on Fallon's face, deepened in color, incandescent and dangerous.

Fallon's face spread into a smile. "And I thought this was going to be boring."

Cara leaned back against the wall, maintaining a bored expression. She covered her mouth with her hand and exaggerated a loud yawn. "Wake me up when you're done."

She crossed her arms over her chest.

Quick as lightning, Fallon pulled two sharp knives from his side and flung them at the ancient.

Before they connected to the creature's chest, he vanished. The blades struck the wall behind where he stood, showering the table with a fine sheen of concrete dust, before landing on the ground with a dull *clunk*. The candle flickered but didn't go out.

Alert now, Cara jerked forward. Her gaze scanned the room. "Where the hell did he go?" she shouted. She reached for her sword.

As the weapon slid from its sheath, the air shimmered behind Fallon. The vampire reappeared only to disintegrate less than a second later. Ash and soot filled the room.

Cara stared at Fallon in disbelief. He chuckled and brought two more blades into view. He twirled them with exaggerated arrogance before he slid them into the waistband of his jeans.

He glanced at Cara and raised an eyebrow. "What? I told ye it wouldna be long."

Cara laughed and shook her head. "Sometimes ye amaze me. Let's go." She walked around him to the locked door. "My turn." She removed a small blade from her side pocket, flipped the blade around and brought the butt of the knife down on the padlock.

With a snap, the lock broke and fell to the ground.

"Och, Cara, sometimes ye surprise me," he teased.

"Ye're an ass." She sighed with exasperation.

Fallon pushed the door open and held out his arm. "After ye, milady."

Cara replaced the blade and pulled her sword out. She held it out before her and entered the room, swinging the long blade back and forth, her eyes searching.

At first glance, the room appeared empty until

Cara's gaze landed on a cot on the opposite side where a shape huddled beneath a thin blanket, lay still and motionless. She rushed across the six-foot area and knelt beside the bed. After setting her sword on the floor, she reached out and gently touched the woman's shoulder.

Cara flinched when the woman sat up and covered her face with both hands as if to protect herself from them.

"No!" Her scream escaped as a hoarse cry before she collapsed and rolled away.

"'Tis okay. We're friends," Cara reassured. "We're going to take ye out of here."

"What?" Cheyenne's weak voice pulled at Cara's heart.

Sympathy flooded over her. The vampires had beaten Cheyenne repeatedly, leaving her bloodied and alone in this cramped room.

She turned over, groaning in pain.

"By the gods!" Cara exclaimed. "Fallon!"

Her face was identical to Aiyanna's. A perfect match.

"Twins! They're fucking twins!" he said in a raw, harsh voice.

Certain that Fallon's expression mirrored her own stunned surprise, Cara nodded.

Their mission turned critical. If Deidra tapped into the powers of two white witches so powerfully connected, her control would increase ten-fold.

"You know Anya?"

"Anya?" Cara asked in confusion before she realized she asked about Aiyanna. "We do. She's the one who sent us to get ye out of here."

"She's not here, is she?" Cheyenne asked, struggling to sit up.

This time Cara supported her shoulders and helped her up but kept an arm around her to keep her steady.

Cara's stomach twisted when Cheyenne moaned and grabbed her head. She peered up at Fallon. The blood drained from his face. Ashen, he stared transfixed at Cheyenne.

She followed his gaze and mumbled under her breath, "Shit!"

A multitude of bruises, cuts, and scrapes coated the inside of Cheyenne's arm from her wrist up to her shoulder. She must have realized what they looked at, for Cheyenne whipped her arm against her, hiding her injuries against her stomach.

"Did she do that to ye?" Cara asked, in concern.

"Yeah, well, she wanted to keep me weak, so she set her guards upon me now and again." Cheyenne pushed herself to the edge of the cot and attempted to stand. Unsteady, she fell sideways. Cara caught her before she landed on the floor.

"It would appear her plan was successful," Cara said and turned to Fallon. "Do ye think ye can help here?"

Fallon stepped forward and, with little effort, hoisted Cheyenne into his arms.

"I can walk," Cheyenne protested, her voice mumbled against Fallon's shirt.

"No need when we have a strong man like Fallon here to carry ye," Cara chided. She reached out a hand and covered Fallon's hand with her own. "Get us the hell out of here."

He nodded and closed his eyes.

The three faded into the darkness, leaving the mausoleum empty.

****

Deidra's eyes opened. She shot upward from her prone position at the intense sensation of loss that raced through her.

"No!" she shrieked.

The sound reverberated against the walls, down the halls, and outside across the grounds.

Chapter Thirty-Four

"That's our cue." Devlin glanced over his shoulder at Aiyanna and passed her an encouraging smile. "I'm assuming that means yer sister has been released. And by the sounds of that bellow, Deidra is pissed."

"Thank God," Aiyanna replied, in a suffocated whisper.

"Time to go," Devlin murmured. He crouched near to the ground and crept from the area.

Cameron pressed a soft kiss to Aiyanna's cheek and murmured into her ear, "Come on. Let's get the bloody hell out of here."

Her lips curved, and she nodded.

With his head ducked low, Cameron turned to follow Devlin. He'd traveled less than six feet when the back of his neck tingled, and a chill etched a path down his spine.

He froze then spun around. His gut clenched and knotted. Aiyanna stood in the exact spot he'd left her, her face turned toward Deidra's crypt. A soft breeze whipped her hair across her cheeks.

He rushed back to her side and wrapped an arm across her shoulders, drawing her beside him. In a low voice, he said, "Come on."

She didn't budge, not an inch, her body rigid and inflexible as if she'd been molded in concrete.

"Aiyanna!"

No response.

"Aiyanna!" he whispered, his tone urgent. This time, he grabbed her by the shoulders and shook.

The fringe of her lashes cast shadows on her cheeks. At his shake, her gaze shot to his face. He took a step back. Shock raged through him at the expression on her face. She regarded him with impassive coldness, the color of her eyes no longer the lovely chocolate brown he'd always admired. Now, they sparkled of yellow umber, streaked with white bolts, reminding him of a furious summer lightning storm.

He tried to reach inside her mind, but her thoughts lay hidden behind a black slab, unfathomable.

"Aiyanna, come back to me, love."

For the briefest moment, her eyes cleared. A raw panic glittered in their depths before her body faded away. One minute she stood before him, and the next he stared at empty space.

He spun around at the rustle of leaves behind him only to discover that Devlin had returned. "Where the hell is Aiyanna?" the elder asked, in an anxious voice.

"Gone," he replied. A faint tremor rocked his voice. Grimly, he looked into Devlin's face and swallowed hard before repeating again, "She's gone."

****

Aiyanna stirred and opened her eyes a crack. She lay on a concrete floor. Her hand twitched, displacing an inch of dirt on the floor that sent a spray of dust into her face. She sniffled and pinched her nose, squeezing off the sneeze that threatened to erupt.

Through squinted eyes, she browsed around the area seeing the concrete floors and walls, bare except for a coffin that rested near the wall on the opposite side of the twelve-by-twelve room. The gold-plated casket indicated this to be the final resting place of a much loved, very rich man. A large, hand-painted picture hung on the wall above the coffin and portrayed a smiling elderly gentleman surrounded by, she assumed, his family.

Her perusal of the room continued.

She was alone.

She sat up and groaned at the throbbing pressure in her head, massaging her temples.

A hot brush of foul air swept against her cheeks. She jerked her head upward with a whimper. Beside her stood a creature covered in thick, rank fur. Its foul, putrid stench burned her nose. She gagged, jerked back, and forced her stomach to relax.

The dog creature pursued. It leaned closer as if to sniff. Instead it sneezed, blowing a rancid mist into her face. Disgust swept over her, and despite her weakened limbs, she jumped to her feet and shouted, "Get the hell away from me!"

The creature's yellow eyes bulged, and it emitted a startled gulp followed by a sharp hiss. She cringed when it stood on its back legs, thrashing its fur-covered arms above its head like an orangutan on a rampage. It swung around and peered over its shoulder before turning back to face her. Baring its teeth, heavy black lips drew back in a buoyant smirk.

"Come here, Samuel."

The thing scurried off. Aiyanna's eyes followed its movements where it stopped beside Deidra. Her ruby red lips curved into a self-satisfied grin.

Now, where had she come from?

Deidra's hand settled on top of the animal's head, and she patted its head. A soft growl of pleasure cooed from the beast's throat.

"You humans are so cruel. Samuel was trying to be friendly, and because of his looks, he is scorned and pushed away." Deidra continued to stroke the monster dog even when she turned eyes filled with scorn on her. Long black hair hung to the Vampryss' waist and blended with a deep onyx black gown that trailed across the crude floor when she moved.

"Well, he can be friendly from over there," Aiyanna mumbled. In an attempt to buy some time, she took a moment to brush the dirt from her pants before she looked at the woman again. "Deidra."

"It's a pleasure to finally meet you in the flesh, too."

"Did I say pleasure? How did you get me here?"

"You are not the only one who knows how to chant a spell, witch. I'm familiar with one or two myself, especially the one to tap into a person's psyche and get them to do whatever I want. It was so easy to freeze your thoughts and prevent you from moving. Then I only had to call to you. Once I started chanting the 'call and deliver' incantation," she hesitated, and snapped her finger. "Wa lah, here you are."

"Now that you've got me, I'm no longer any use to you."

Deidra shrugged and strolled across the room to stand before Aiyanna. "I know the gods' precious guardians have released your sister. It no longer matters," Deidra spoke, her voice triumphant. "She was too weak, but you, my dear..." Fingers caressed Aiyanna's hair, her cheek, and Deidra ran one long pointed fingernail across her lips. "...are perfect."

Aiyanna jerked her head away and muttered, "Go to hell."

Deidra yanked Aiyanna's head back to expose her throat. "I've been there and survived. I won't go back."

"I wouldn't sound so sure if I were you."

Aiyanna held her breath when Deidra's mouth parted. Her tongue curled over a protruding lower lip. Sharp, pointed teeth gleamed in the lantern's light.

Deidra stared into Aiyanna's face, her eyes points of vivid fire. With a flick of her wrist,

Aiyanna's feet left the floor, and she flew across the room. Her stomach churned. She struck the concrete wall and groaned at the stab of pain that sliced through her shoulder.

"*I am sure*, and the reason I'm so sure is you're going to help me regain my mortality in this world."

"Like hell I will." Aiyanna smiled smoothly, betraying nothing of her inner turmoil.

Deidra's eyes flashed a crimson color, her face a glowering mask of rage. Her nostrils flared.

Aiyanna's resolve not to give into the fear faltered when the room shook. With a startled squeal, she stumbled and fell to the ground, sprawling face first on the dusty concrete floor.

Suddenly, the grounds erupted into a hollow rumble, followed by the alarmed cries of Deidra's minions. Outside, the rustle and cracks of branches pounded the outer walls of the crypt. After a few moments of shaking, Aiyanna heard trees splinter and snap and then a powerful crash as they dropped against the building.

The ground trembled for several minutes when, all of a sudden, it stopped. Aiyanna rose unsteadily to her feet and leaned, swaying a little, against the wall. She coughed at the dust flying around her face and waved her hand in the air as if to brush the powder away from her face.

Her eyes watered, and she cleared her throat. "Impressive, but the answer remains the same," she choked. "There is no way in hell I'll ever help you."

Deidra moved so fast Aiyanna didn't see her until she stood directly in front of her. The Vampryss wrapped her hand around her throat. Aiyanna struggled to draw a breath, but even that brief act turned into a strangled gasp.

"Get yer filthy hands off of her." Cameron's voice pierced the room with a roar of animal fury.

Chapter Thirty-Five

Deidra whipped around at Cameron's shout. With a flick of her wrist, she released Aiyanna and flung her aside. Once again, she was thrown to the floor where she landed with a burgeoning burst of dirt.

"It's about time you showed up," Aiyanna muttered, and spit out the dust that filtered past her lips into her mouth. She stood and swiped the dirt off her pants *again* before meeting Cameron's gaze.

"Are ye okay?"

She nodded. "I'm fine, but she sure lacks manners. Not the way I would treat a guest."

Devlin stood behind Cameron in the door. At Aiyanna's scathing report, he stepped around Cameron, his eyes fixed on Deidra. "Dee, when are ye going to learn?"

Cameron's eyes widened at Devlin's frank familiarity with the Vampryss. "Dee? Ye have pet names for demons, Dev?"

"We've known each other for quite some time," Devlin answered, with quiet emphasis.

"Still keeping secrets from your friends? I'm deeply hurt you haven't told them about us." Deidra's brows dripped into a frown, and her bottom lip puffed out in a pout.

Devlin threw back his head and released a loud bellow of harsh laughter. His eyes were edged with anger when his gaze turned back to her. "Still as delusional as ever, I see. There never was any *us*, Dee."

269

"And I see you are still in denial, eh?" Deidra's gaze landed on Cameron. She smiled and leaned in Cameron's direction as though she would tell him some deep dark secret. "He doesn't want anyone to know that I threw him over for Ághmach. Ághmach was a much better catch, mind you." Her voice dropped a note lower. "Devlin had a hard time accepting my choice."

Devlin snorted at her pronouncement. "I suppose he would be considered a better catch for someone like ye, Dee. Lunatic, homicidal, bloodthirsty...aye, a match made in Hades."

Devlin's speech proved to be the final barb needed to spur Deidra's anger.

With a piercing shriek, she shouted, "Kill them."

Vampires, their pasty white flesh marred by bluish tinted veins, oozed through the door into the room, their fangs bared in feral growls.

Cameron inclined his head toward Aiyanna. His expression was stern when he mouthed, "Stay out of this."

Aiyanna took a couple of steps backward until her back pressed against the wall. Instead of standing idly by, she called upon the ancient powers of her coven. When the fire surged into her fingertips, she raised her hands and took aim at the open doorway. As the vampires crossed the threshold, they were met with blazing blue lightning bolts that vanquished them to measly puffs of dark ash.

Out of the corner of her eye, she saw three bloodsuckers closing in on the two guardians. She bit down hard on her lip to keep the warning from escaping. They certainly didn't need her shout distracting them.

She shouldn't have worried, for Cameron stooped over, sending the first one flipping over his back. He whipped around, pulled a stake from his jacket pocket and struck the man in the chest before he regained his feet. The vamp burst apart in a cloud of ash and dust. Cameron pulled a dagger from his boot. In one smooth, fluid motion, he swung around and sliced at the second one, catching him across the throat.

****

Not waiting for the vampire's explosion, Cameron spun around, ready to face the third one.

He was gone.

Cameron's body jerked as something landed on his back and latched on. He cursed and bent over so fast that the vampire lost his momentum and went flying through the air. While mid-air, Cameron whipped the knife from his jacket and flung it at him. It struck him in the heart, shattering him in a trillion pieces of gray powder.

Cameron glanced at Devlin. The elder battled each vampire that crossed his path. Satisfied he held his own, his attention focused on Aiyanna against the wall.

Fierce concentration lined her face. Flames shot from her fingertips, and his gaze followed its path.

He grinned.

"Aiyanna!" Mentally, he called her name.

Her eyes met his through the vampire-ashen room.

"Doona ye ever listen?" he asked, in a tone full of frustration.

She shook her head, her lips arched into a slight smile. Without using her voice, she said, *"Nope. Besides I wanted to help."*

In the next instant, her hands dropped, and she sagged against the wall.

Concern rioted through him. *"Are ye okay, lass?"*

Aiyanna nodded. *"I'm fine, but my powers are used up."*

"Where's Deidra?"

271

"I don't know." Her gaze scanned the room. *"Over there."*

He followed the incline of her head. The Vampryss stood behind the casket. A pair of mangy, flea-ridden black and silver werewolves stood in front of her, protecting her.

His neck tingled. He turned sharply, slicing a blue-skinned bastard across the neck. *Damn it!*

A sudden, icy contempt flared inside him, and his powers strengthened. He circled around and raised his hands, releasing all of his fury through his fingertips. If he didn't, it would build to an uncontrollable pinnacle and destroy him. Jagged lightning bolts of fire flew from his hands toward Deidra and her protectors. The werewolves exploded.

Behind him, Devlin fought the vampires that entered the room. Instinct told him they met Devlin's blade before they crossed the threshold. Assured his back remained protected, Cameron turned and focused all of his concentration into fighting the bitch Vampryss.

Deidra faced him. Black anger lit up her eyes. This bitch didn't frighten him. In fact, he sent her a cocky smile that only succeeded in enraging her even more. Her eyes sparkled of vibrant crimson, and her nostrils flared.

Cameron's fingertips continued to flame. Bright white electrical currents shot from his hands aimed toward Deidra.

Before the force of his anger reached her, Deidra's hands rose emitting their own lightning bolt of dark, pulsating red.

The glowing lightning embers merged in the center of the room to form a jagged edged globe. The sphere grew, and the room flushed with a pinkish rose tint.

Aiyanna's apple blossom fragrance rose in his nostrils, an indication she had recovered and stood

272

at his side.

"Aiyanna, get back," he rushed out, his voice strained.

"No. I want to help," she insisted, lifting her hands.

Cobalt blue flames shot from her fingertips, merging with his. The sphere altered to a vibrant violet.

Combined, they were no match.

Deidra's flame brightened to a deep dark red before it faded and transformed from streaks of powerful energy to black feeble smudges that spit useless sparks.

"No!" Deidra screamed when her power fizzled. Defeat in her future, she sent one final blast into the orb.

The sphere exploded.

The bright light shocked both Cameron and Aiyanna, and they jerked back a step.

Using their surprise, Deidra evaporated into a mist of red vapors that floated out the door. Shattered fragments of mortar splattered the room when Cameron and Aiyanna's bolts shot into the concrete wall. At the same time, they lowered their hands and turned to each other.

"Are ye ok?" Cameron asked, his eyes searching her face. Her toes tingled at the concern in his voice and the love in his eyes.

Aiyanna caressed his cheek then traced the line of his jaw. She nodded. "I'm fine, and you?"

"Glad to hear the two of ye are doing ok, but I, myself, could use a little help here." Devlin's strained voice echoed between them.

Cameron laughed and pressed a kiss to Aiyanna's forehead. "Stay here." He leaned back and looked into her face. "And this time, I mean it."

****

Aiyanna smiled. Cameron scooped up his sword

from the floor and ambled over to assist Devlin. For the next few moments, the only sounds in the room were the *"swoosh"* sounds of vampires exploding and evaporating, sliced in two by the guardian swords.

"This isn't over yet. The gods have taken too much from me. I will not let them win." The voice echoed in her mind, and Aiyanna swirled around.

Deidra had reappeared. Her lips twisted into a snarl, and her fangs protruded past her bottom lip. Anger flashed in her eyes, and a burning fury lit up her expression.

Goosebumps rose on Aiyanna's flesh, and needle sticks pricked her scalp.

"I'll not be defeated by the gods. I'll destroy their precious guardians one by one, and then I'll have no one to stop me from returning Aghmach to my side."

Deidra's attention was drawn over Aiyanna's shoulder. The Vampryss appeared to have forgotten about her. Her eyes glittered, and a satisfied smile twisted her lips.

"Destroy the gods' precious guardians, and nothing will stand in my way," she murmured. She raised her hands aiming for the two guardians' unprotected backs.

"No!" Aiyanna shouted.

She reached Cameron at the same moment Deidra released an electric bolt of power. The lightning penetrated Aiyanna's chest.

A soft cry slid from her lips, and she stumbled backward, slamming into Cameron's back before she fell away. Her forehead smashed against the concrete, snapping a bone in her skull.

Her head throbbed, and her chest burned in agony. Knives were being stabbed methodically into her chest over and over again. Her back arched against the stinging pain.

"Oh god," she moaned.

Her body convulsed. The coppery taste of blood

filled her mouth and trickled from the corner of her mouth.

This is supposed to happen, isn't it? To be a guardian's true mate, she had to die and be reborn as an immortal. Although she'd read the prophecies, nothing could have prepared her for this moment.

The pain tore her apart from the inside out.

The impact took her breath away, but now, with every gasp, fire burned in her upper body.

Her thoughts rambled. Is this what it felt like to die? Visions of her past flashed in front of her eyes.

Cheyenne's face appeared; the mirror image of her own, and Aiyanna recognized sadness in her eyes.

She saw Harris, his face bitter and sadistic on that last day.

And then Cameron—

The crushing weight left her chest, and the pain eased. A light emerged behind her closed eyelids.

Not yet! Panic flooded her, and she forced her eyes open.

The mystic light remained, and she fought against the darkness descending over her.

She opened her mouth and croaked past the blood choking her. "Cameron." Her cry came out a raspy whisper, unheard above the wage of battle.

A tear slipped from the corner of her eye. She wanted to tell him she was okay...it'd be okay, but as she sank into oblivion, she realized she wasn't going to get the chance, at least, not in this lifetime.

Chapter Thirty-Six

A solid object slammed into his back and shoved him forward. Cameron staggered. Spinning around, he raised his blade prepared to strike, yet his eyes met Deidra standing on the pulpit. A malicious, self-satisfied smile twisted her lips.

His first thoughts were of Aiyanna, but he dared not take his eyes from the bitch.

"She must have truly loved you."

Confused, Cameron followed her gaze.

Aiyanna lay on the ground. Blood pooled out from beneath her body. His heart lurched, and a suffocating sensation tightened his throat.

"By the gods...*nay!*" he breathed. Dropping to his knees, he scrambled to her side.

Deidra was forgotten.

Cameron knelt beside her and gently pulled her into his arms. At his touch, she gasped. Flesh burns marred her chest, and her clothing seared and smoldered, melted to her skin.

An acute sense of loss smothered him, peaking to shatter the last shred of his control. Silent tears streamed down his face.

"Ye bitch," he shouted, looking over his shoulder, but Deidra only laughed at his pain.

Aiyanna struggled to breathe and coughed up blood.

"Doona leave me," he choked out.

"I love you," she whispered.

"Shhh, love. Ye're going to be okay." Cameron turned toward Devlin who had finished the last vampires and now faced Deidra. He needed the elder's help.

"Ye wilna win, Dee?" Devlin's face was a mask a fury.

Deidra smiled, bobbing her head toward Cameron. "All it takes is one at a time, Devlin, one at a time." She raised her hand to her lips and blew him a kiss. "Until we meet again, my dearest."

And then she was gone. Her solid form dispersed forming a bright red mist and floated out the door, vanishing into the night air. The crypt now stood empty with the exception of Cameron, Devlin, and Aiyanna.

Devlin walked toward Cameron, and Cameron read the sympathy in his eyes.

"Help her, Dev," Cameron begged.

"I'm sorry, Cameron. There's nothing I can do."

Aiyanna's body went limp in his arms, and she expelled her last breath. He shook her, tears coursing down his cheeks. "Nay, Aiyanna, doona go." He pulled her against his chest, and her head lolled sideways on his arm.

Devlin placed a comforting hand on Cameron's shoulder. "She's gone."

Cameron pressed a tender kiss on Aiyanna's forehead before he settled her gently on the ground.

He rose to his feet, inhaled a deep breath and glared at Devlin.

The elder retreated. His jaw tightened, and an impenetrable look of withdrawal came over his face. He held up his hands in front of him as if to halt Cameron's advance.

"She's dead because of ye." Cameron lips thinned with fury, and he reached for his knife.

"Doona do this, Cameron," Devlin commanded, taking another step back.

Cameron continued his advance. The sharp-silvered blade waved wildly in front of him.

****

"Aiyanna!"

Cara jumped at the shrill scream piercing the silence of the house. She spun around and peered in the direction where it originated. Cheyenne sat straight up on the couch, her eyes wide, distant.

"What's the matter with her?"

Cara's heart skipped at Fallon's muffled voice against her ear.

"Would ye stop sneaking up on me like that," Cara said, between gritted teeth. She swiveled around to find Fallon munching on a sandwich. "Is that all ye ever do? Eat?"

His expression turned into an exaggerated pout, and he shrugged a shoulder. "I was hungry. When a person's hungry, they usually eat." He took another bite then glanced at Cheyenne. "What do ye suppose is wrong with her?"

"I doona know. A moment ago, she was passed out cold. She sat up and screamed Aiyanna's name. I don't know what it means."

Fallon took the last bite. With his mouth full, he replied, "Beats the hell out of me, but I'll pop over to the cemetery and see what I can find out. They should have been back by now."

"Okay, but be careful," Cara said over her shoulder, as she walked to the couch.

"I dinna think ye cared."

Cara turned around to make a smart-assed comment, but he was already gone. Instead, to herself, she muttered, "Jackass."

She sat beside Cheyenne on the couch and caressed the woman's hair. "'Tis all right. Ye're going to be okay."

Cheyenne's expression didn't change. "Aiyanna's dead." Her dull, lifeless tone sent chills up Cara's spine.

Cara shook her head. "Aiyanna's fine. They're

no' back yet."

"I'm telling you she's gone. I feel it."

Cara remained silent, uncertain how to respond. It had been documented that twins held a bond with each other that they carried through life. This connection originated from sharing a womb together for nine months. Twins feel each other's emotions, happiness, sadness, and even pain. Was it possible they shared death? Cara's heart skipped, and she shut down the thought. She'd grown fond of Aiyanna and prayed nothing bad happened to her.

Damn! Why weren't they back yet?

****

"Whoa...Whoa...gentlemen, it seems as if I've arrived in the nick of time. What the bloody blazes is going on here?" he asked, staring at the knife Cameron brandished. "Put that down, Irish, before ye hurt someone."

"That's the plan. Now, get the hell out of my way."

He glanced over his shoulder at Devlin whose wary eyes watched Cameron.

Fallon peered back to Cameron who steadily moved closer. He held up a hand and placed it against the other man's chest. "Back down, Cameron." When Cameron didn't stop, Fallon jerked the knife out of his hands. "What is wrong with ye?" he asked, noting the man's glossy, swollen eyes.

Cameron swung away. "Just keep him away from me, or I'll kill the bastard."

In confusion, Fallon watched Cameron walk away.

And then he saw the reason for the other man's distress. Aiyanna's body, coated in blood, lie still and unmoving.

"Thank ye."

Fallon didn't turn at the sound of Devlin's voice behind him.

"Doona thank me. Thank Cheyenne. She woke up from a coma screaming Aiyanna's name, so I thought I'd pop over to see what was taking so long. 'Tis a good thing ye left a trail, or I would never have found ye in time. At least, no' in here." Fallon nodded to Cameron who picked up Aiyanna's lifeless body and held her against his chest. "How did that happen?"

"Deidra saw an opportunity," Devlin replied.

Grief rocked Cameron's large frame. Fallon recognized the sentiment and empathized with the other man.

"Ye havena told him?"

Devlin glanced at him. "It is part of the process, or have ye forgotten?"

Fallon suppressed the shiver coursing through him at the memory of his Lizzie lying lifeless in his arms. "I remember all too well." He stared toward Cameron. "But 'tis still a bitch."

"It'll be over soon, Fallon, and all will be as it should be."

"Have I ever told ye I hate it when ye use philosophy, Dev?"

Chapter Thirty-Seven

"Aiyanna," Cameron pleaded. "Come back to me, love."

From a distance, his voice begged her to return, but she had no control over the direction she traveled. She drifted where the winds took her, floating high above the world.

A deep, satisfying peace enfolded her.

She glanced down to the place she'd just left. Cameron's shoulders shook with grief over her broken, bloodied body.

"It's okay," she called. "I'll be back."

He didn't look up.

Cameron disappeared from sight, replaced by a vast river that glowed of an inner luminosity. She coasted onward until her feet touched solid ground. The unexpected landing threw off her equilibrium, and she stumbled. Her arms flailed helicopter style until she regained her balance.

Stars spun and rotated around her in a beautiful rainbow-colored swirl. Before her, a light glowed. A sphere emerged and grew larger and larger.

And then another...and another...

What was going on?

Unafraid, the illumination hovered in front of her. The globes shifted and altered until three figures emerged, their faces indistinguishable in the brilliance.

And then, the light faded.

Two men and one woman stepped forward. All of them wore silken robes tied at their waists by a braided golden cord. The woman's long raven hair blew in a soft breeze behind her. A pinkish-rose flush on her cheekbones accentuated green eyes of polished jade. The men, one with curling black hair, the other light brown, flanked her on the right. When they smiled, the glow in their faces warmed her, and the kindness she read in their eyes humbled her.

The woman held out her hand to Aiyanna who clasped it without hesitation. "I am Danu." With a dainty finger, she pointed to the men at her side. "And this is Dagda and Lugh."

Aiyanna bowed and murmured, "Gods of the Tuatha Dé Danann?"

"No child." Danu tightened her grip on Aiyanna's hand, preventing her from reaching her knees. "You do not kneel before us." She inclined her head toward the other gods. "It is us who should kneel before you."

"No!" Aiyanna replied, with semi-crazed fervor over her choking, beating heart. At their looks of astonishment, her face warmed, and she laughed. "Why don't we just call it even, then?"

Danu nodded and smiled. "Deal."

Aiyanna glanced around at the clouds that surrounded them. "Then I am in heaven?"

"You are in our heaven. This is our home, a place we call the Otherworld. But you cannot stay here."

"Why not? It's so peaceful here."

"Your place is beside your mate."

Aiyanna's nerves jumped in understanding. Her gaze shot to the goddess. "Cameron. So this is the process I read about."

Danu tilted her head to one side. Her eyes studied Aiyanna with curiosity. "You are smarter than most humans we have seen. The prophets chose well, but I must ask you a question." At

Aiyanna's raised eyebrows, she continued, "Why did you not tell Cameron of your impending death?"

Aiyanna shrugged. "I'm not certain. If he knew, I'm sure he would have told me. And then I spoke to Devlin. He told me this was part of the process."

Danu nodded. "Cameron MacLean is your soul mate, your life mate, and you are his life."

"I don't understand any of this. Why me? Why Cameron?"

"There is a fire in your blood that runs rampant through your veins and stirs his blood. Together, you make a powerful match. The Princess of Fire, mated to a Síoraí."

"Princess?" Aiyanna's mouth dropped. When she caught her breath, she waved a hand through the air. "I think you've got the wrong girl for that."

Danu smiled. "I believe we have chosen the right one."

"And what if Cameron doesn't want me as part of his life?"

"He will. When Cameron lost his family, he closed himself off from the rest of the world. It took a long time for Dagda to pull him from the shell he'd placed around himself. But once his internal light was freed, he became cocky, too cocky for his own good, you might say. We were afraid he had a death wish, but he has improved since Dagda threatened him."

"The god bolt?"

Dagda laughed, and Aiyanna turned, startled at the rich, temporal sound. "That man thought he was the king himself until I told him that every time someone knocked him on his as—," He hesitated and cleared his throat. "Anyway, if he was put down, I would duplicate the process using the method of my choice. He learned to fight rather quickly. It did my heart a world of good to see him go down at your hands. You are truly his mate and his equal."

Lugh slapped Dagda on the shoulder. "That she is."

"Why has all of this happened?"

"This has been fated, Aiyanna. Your destiny and his were decided before your births."

"His family?"

Danu's eyes darkened with sadness. "An unavoidable prerequisite, I'm afraid." Her brows drew together in an agonized expression. "They needed to die for Cameron to become who he is."

"I don't think he has ever gotten over their deaths. He blames himself."

"It is yer destiny to make him forget."

Aiyanna stared into a cluster of clouds behind the gods, searching for the owner of the soft, feminine voice.

She recognized the lilting tone in that voice.

"Sarah?"

Sarah stepped from the fog with two beautiful red-haired girls in her arms, one resting on each hip. "Aye, it is I."

"Why can't *you* tell him yourself?"

Danu clicked her tongue and sent Sarah a disapproving look. "Because Sarah should not be here as well she knows. She should not have contacted you as she did."

Sarah smiled at the goddess. "And ye need to understand the power of love. It crosses the boundaries between life and death. I will rest once I know my Cameron has found the love of a good woman, one that will take care of him and who will love him despite his flaws." Sarah turned back to her. Aiyanna read concern in the other woman's eyes when she asked, "Ye are that woman, are ye no'?"

Aiyanna smiled and nodded. "I'd like to think I am, but I don't know if he'll let me."

Sarah nodded. "He is stubborn, but he isna a stupid mon." She winked. "Thank ye, Aiyanna. I can rest now." She squeezed the girls in a hug. "We all can."

"It is time for you to go home." Danu's gentle voice pulled Aiyanna's attention away from Cameron's wife and children.

"What happens now?" she asked.

"You live a very long life of love with your soul mate."

"Will I see you again?"

Danu smiled gently and nodded. "When the time comes, we shall see each other again. You are the Princess of Fire, the woman who holds the blue flame. Our battle is not yet over."

****

Positioned on the floor, Cameron held Aiyanna to his chest.

He couldn't let her go.

Guilt ate at his insides, twisting and turning until he thought he might upchuck. It had been so easy to place the blame on Devlin, but it wasn't the elder's fault. He should have made Aiyanna stay home even if that meant he tied her to the bed.

History repeated itself. He couldn't save the woman he loved.

He choked on his laughter. How ironic. Hell of a time to realize he loved her. He never got the chance to tell her.

"Tell me now."

His heart skipped, and he glanced down at the sound of Aiyanna's fragile voice.

"Aiyanna?"

Her eyes were open, and she smiled weakly. "In the flesh, well, part of it anyway."

His arms tightened around her. Tears rolled down his face. "Oh, thank the gods! Thank the gods! Thank the—" he chanted.

"Easy." Aiyanna groaned. "I'm back, but I'm not feeling so hot."

Cameron loosened his grip on her. Barely.

"Well, are ye going to tell me or not?"

He pressed a tender kiss to her lips and leaned back. A glimmer of moonlight shone in her eyes. In a hoarse whisper, he declared, "I love ye, lass."

"I knew ye did," she boasted.

"Then why?"

"It's always nice to hear the words."

"I know," Cameron encouraged.

Aiyanna lifted her hand and caressed his cheek. "I love you, too, my valiant knight."

Cameron grasped her hand in his and brought it to his lips where he pressed a tiny kiss in her palm. His eyes twinkled when he said, "I knew ye did."

Chapter Thirty-Eight

Two Months Later

Cheyenne strolled down the steps, running her hand along the smooth oak banister. When she reached the landing, she stopped and stared out the picture window.

A little past midnight, the moon hung high in the sky, no longer tainted by the color of blood. The celestial body radiated a smoky grayish color. Luminous shadows of light speared toward earth, innocent beams of a peaceful full moon, undaunted by evil.

After two months, she still had trouble sleeping. Since her ordeal with the bitch Vampryss, her life hadn't returned to normal and probably never would. The memory of her captivity remained a nightmare that haunted her days and filled her nights with terror.

Cheyenne shivered at the memory of that night. The night her sister died. Everything in her told her Aiyanna was dead, but then Fallon returned and told them, "She's perfectly fine, although I believe she just told that half-wit Irish she loved him." He rolled his eyes in fabricated disgust. "What she sees in him, I'll never know."

Cara laughed at Fallon's dramatics, but relief had overwhelmed her.

Her sister lived.

Within an hour, Aiyanna came through the front door followed by a large, extremely handsome man.

He stood almost as tall as Fallon, and just as muscular. And when her sister looked into the man's face, her features sparkled of brilliance.

And Cheyenne came to realize that this was the man Anya loved.

Then Anya introduced her to the guardians of the Tuatha Dé Danann: Cara, Fallon, and then, finally, Cameron. Open-mouthed, she shook their hands, too stunned to speak. Who would have figured she would meet the famous guardians?

Fallon and Cara proved to be terrific, ordinary people, and Cheyenne found their company comforting. Fallon had a quick wit about him that made her laugh.

After two days, Fallon declared he'd been away from his wife too long. He'd winked at Aiyanna and said, "Give me a call when 'tis time for the wedding. My Lizzie loves to cry at happy occasions."

Aiyanna and Cheyenne kissed his cheeks, and then he disappeared, vanished into air. She'd glanced toward Aiyanna in surprise and received a shrug and a smile, along with a quick, "Don't ask."

Cara left a couple of days after that. Her travels took her to the west coast. With a cynical laugh, she commented that she was going to get her some rays. The weather in this part of the country wasn't doing a thing for her complexion. Of course, no one believed her. Sunshine was still lethal to her.

Cheyenne sighed and forced her attention back to the present.

Tomorrow, Aiyanna and Cameron were getting married, and she vowed to make it a happy day. She would find a way to get past her inner conflict and make it memorable for her sister. Aiyanna deserved that much.

Over the past two months, Cameron joined their small family. Tomorrow was just legality. Even Starr, who never had a good thing to say about anyone, took a liking to the rough and tough guardian.

And her sister, well, she was absolutely, positively smitten.

Aiyanna went back to work while Cameron enjoyed his newfound freedom from the guardian *"curse"*. He left the house every morning to walk the parks and enjoy the sunlight, but he always returned before Aiyanna got home from work.

The man was a glutton. He ate everything in the kitchen cupboards and the fridge and even seemed to have taken quite a bit out of her sister.

Aiyanna's happiness thrilled Cheyenne. She deserved it after what the last asshole put her through.

Turning from the window, she strolled down the remaining stairs.

She missed meeting one the guardians, the one called Devlin. He left from the cemetery after their fight with Deidra. No one knew how to get in touch with him, but Cheyenne hoped he received his invitation.

She rounded the corner into the kitchen and came to a sudden stop, her heart doing a tipsy turvy, topsy curvy in her chest, half in fear, the other in *"damn."*

A man stood in front of the kitchen sink. He stared out the window, concentrating on something outside.

As if sensing her presence, he turned and smiled. "Hey, I hope ye doona mind I made myself at home."

This must be Devlin.

"Devlin..." she began, her tone hesitant as she tested the waters. When he appeared okay with her use of the name, she took that as confirmation. "You know you're welcome anytime."

"Thank ye," he commented, leaning across the

sink to peer out the window at the evening sky. "The moon is beautiful on nights like this, and the stars light up the sky."

She walked over to stand beside him and followed his gaze. "Yes, it is, and they do."

Out the corner of her eye, she checked him out. Not only did he have a sexy voice, but his body radiated exquisiteness. Tall, he stood a good six and a half inches above her. He wore a tight, sleeveless black T-shirt and black jeans with what looked like sharp-toed leather boots. But what stood out even more than the deep, perfect indentations of his muscles were the knives strapped to biceps and the ancient hilt of a sword on his hip. He had gold bands on each forearm, decorated with ivy vines and doves. The doves seemed a bit out of place on his masculine frame.

She cleared her throat, turned and walked to the cabinet where she grabbed a glass. Stepping beside him, she reached for the tap and switched on the faucet. She filled the glass half way and took a sip. He glanced down at her, and she asked, "Can I get you anything?"

He turned and leaned back against the sink, his beefy arms crossed over his massive chest. His brows creased in confusion, but he politely shook his head. "No, thank ye just the same."

Oh, he was delicious, delectable, and Cheyenne couldn't stop herself. She set the glass on the counter and stepped over to him.

His sapphire blue eyes captured her gaze. Her hands moved across his chest where his heart beat against her palms, fast and furious. He appeared unaffected by her touch. In fact, just the opposite, he grabbed her hands and gently pulled them away.

"What are ye doing?"

"I want you. Is that so hard for you to understand?"

His jaw clenched, his eyes slightly narrowed. "What about Cameron?" He asked. His voice was rough with anxiety.

Her body stiffened in shock. "What about him?"

Something clicked in her mind, the thought freezing her brain. She took a quick breath of utter astonishment and stepped forward. "Do you know who I am?" she asked in a hoarse whisper.

His eyes narrowed, and his back became ramrod straight. "Of course, I know who ye are, but what I doona understand is what the hell ye're doing?"

Her arms wrapped across his shoulders. "Then please, don't push me away!" she whispered, dropping her head against his chest. "Devlin."

Chapter Thirty-Nine

The way she said his name dissolved his anger.

Anger gave way to a compulsion to hold her tight, to take her as his own, to protect her and to love her.

What the hell was wrong with him?

He could never have this woman...his friend's chosen.

When her arms crept up around his shoulders, his head shot up. He peered down at the crown of her head and longed to plant a soft kiss in the part of her long, silken black hair.

Her body rested supple against him, fit snugly against him.

The sweet, light smell of jasmine filled the air and rose in his nose. He longed to nuzzle her ear with his nose, to nestle against the sexy flesh of her neck.

He wanted to taste her.

All of her, but he wouldn't. He couldn't.

His arms rose, and he clasped her wrists in his hands. He lowered her arms from around his neck. Her fingers relaxed and uncurled then clenched in his grip. He gave her a soft push away from him and released her hands.

She leaned forward and pressed her lips to his neck. Her tongue swept across the tender area below his neck. Shivers of eroticism raced over him. His body reacted instantly to the sensation. In the next instant, her teeth clamped down on his neck, and he shuddered in desire.

What the hell?

This time, he gripped her shoulders and thrust her away, perhaps a bit more violently than he intended. She stumbled back a step.

He stared down at her paralyzed, unable to move, to think or to breathe. Shock sustained him for an instant, and then the importance of what took place sank in. She stepped forward and lifted her face until their lips were scarcely an inch apart.

"What the hell do ye believe ye're doing, lass?" Devlin asked, his voice a choked whisper.

"I think I'm going to kiss you."

"Nay, ye're bloody well no'."

"I am." She licked her lips.

Panic surged through Devlin.

Heat, a burning fire, tingled over his body where their bodies touched. The curves of her body intimately pressed against him.

He ached to cup her breasts, to caress every inch of her.

He pulled away, but not before he read desire in her eyes. Her fingers bit into the flesh of his upper arms, but he pushed her away.

"Ye will stop this now," he demanded, his breathing ragged.

Cheyenne leaned into him again. Her lips curved into a soft smile. "Why?"

"Hey man, what are ye doing here?"

Devlin flinched when Cameron's voice rang out in the room.

He glanced toward the doorway where his friend strolled into the kitchen.

His mind floundered.

Cameron never hesitated, walking to the refrigerator where he opened the door and withdrew a carton of milk.

Devlin glanced at Aiyanna, who smiled brightly and shrugged as though to say they'd been caught doing nothing wrong.

Had the whole fucking world gone crazy?

Devlin gazed to Cameron, who swiped the back of his hand across his mouth, wiping away a milky mustache before his attention turned to him.

When Cameron's eyes lit on him, his brows drew together in a frown. He glanced first at Devlin to Aiyanna, and then back again, his eyes sharp and assessing.

A chill speared up his spine at his friend's intent look. Was he acting guilty? Would Cameron recognize his discomfort?

Cameron's brows rose, and he asked, "What's going on?"

"Nothing," Devlin answered, perhaps a little faster than necessary.

"Nothing, huh?" Cameron's gaze passed over Aiyanna. "Shy? What have ye been up to?"

A knot formed in the pit of Devlin's stomach, and he captured her eyes with his. Her face brightened when he asked, "Shy?" His voice choked. "As in Cheyenne? Aiyanna's sister?"

She nodded. Her lips curved as she stretched up on tippy toes and pressed her hot lips against his. "Yes sir, that's me." She leaned up beside his ear and whispered, "Has anyone ever told you how hot and sexy you are?"

Devlin's heart fluttered, and he struggled to find his voice.

Cheyenne stepped away and winked at him. "Goodnight," she said in a soft voice, before she turned and moseyed from the room.

Devlin turned to Cameron whose face remained pinched in confusion. "Umm, did I miss something? What was that all about?"

"Twins? They're fucking twins?" Devlin's voice rose with each word, each question.

"Aye, I thought ye knew..." Cameron hesitated,

but only for a moment before understanding filled his expression. He chuckled. "That's right. Ye dinna return to the house after the cemetery. Ye never met Cheyenne."

"No, I dinna."

"Oops, sorry about that, man." Then, Cameron's eyes flashed, and he grinned warily. "Listen, Dev, I'm sorry about that night. 'Tis just that I was upset about what happened to Anya—"

"Doona worry about it. I understand what ye were feeling."

"Thanks."

"No' a problem. By the way, congrats on the wedding. Ready to take the big step again, eh?"

"Aye, I canna see my life without Anya in it."

"It seems that women tend to have that effect on us men."

"Oh, hell aye, but with Aiyanna, 'tis different. With Sarah, I loved the lass with a passion. She made me happy, but with Anya, a fire burns inside me when I'm with her."

"The bond ye two share has been cemented by the power of yer love. I'm happy for ye," Devlin murmured, as jealousy stabbed through him.

"Now, I understand how Fallon feels. The food, the sunlight, 'tis hard to explain."

"Doona try, and *doona* rub it in," Devlin grumbled.

Cameron chuckled and nodded in understanding. "In other words, doona be a pain in the ass like Fallon."

Devlin grinned. "Ye got it."

"And what about ye? It looked like ye and Cheyenne were hitting it off?"

"By the gods, man, I thought she was Aiyanna." He grunted.

Cameron nearly choked; his brows rose in surprise. "Ye thought Shy was Aiyanna?"

"She looked like her. I thought Aiyanna had turned into a harlot, and then ye walked in and dinna say a word, I thought the world had gone crazy."

Cameron laughed. At the look on Devlin's face, he stopped and coughed. "Sorry, my mistake. I left Aiyanna sleeping upstairs, so I knew it wasna her."

"Havena ye ever gotten them mixed up?"

Cameron nodded. "Once. I did once."

"And what happened?"

Cameron rubbed his cheek as though in remembrance. "I got smacked twice."

Devlin chuckled and walked over to him where he slapped Cameron on the back. "And I am quite certain ye were deserving."

"Thanks, although I expected a wee more sympathy from ye."

"After what I just went through, I doona think so."

"My bud," Cameron teased. "Deserting me when I need ye the most."

"I've always got yer back, man."

"I know." Cameron yawned. "Well, I'm off to bed. Ye're welcome to any of the rooms upstairs. If ye're nice, Cheyenne might offer to share hers."

Devlin frowned. "Shut up! She could have told me who she was."

"Maybe she thought ye already knew," Cameron said, defending Cheyenne.

Devlin could have argued that point but decided against it. Instead, he said, "Maybe."

Cameron hesitated at the doorway, glanced back and said, "Goodnight."

"Yeah, right, imagine that one." Devlin grumbled. Thoughts of Cheyenne's warm body next to his pretty much guaranteed his night wasn't going to be a peaceful one.

****

296

"Where did you go?" Aiyanna asked sleepily, when Cameron crawled back into bed beside her. She cuddled up against him, her arm slung across his midsection.

"I went to get a drink. Devlin's downstairs. I was in the kitchen with him."

Her head rested on his chest, but at his words, she tilted her chin and looked into his face. "How is he?"

Cameron pressed his lips to her forehead and chuckled. "I believe he was fine until yer sister gave him a premature heart attack."

Aiyanna's brows shot up. "Premature heart—" Her voice rose, eyes narrowed. "What did she do?"

"She put the moves on him."

Aiyanna relaxed, her eyes twinkling. "And what is wrong with that?"

Cameron stretched out an arm, drawing Aiyanna's head back to his shoulder. "He thought she was ye." He chuckled. "What would ye think? His friend's fiancée put the moves on him. He thought ye'd become a woman who walked the streets."

"What?" Her head shot up again, eyes wide. "He did not!" And then, she thought of Cheyenne. Her cheeks flushed. She knew her sister. She could be a bit outspoken at times. *Oh no!* "She did not!"

"She did. In Dev's defense, he dinna come back to the house that night and dinna know ye were twins."

"Oh, my Lord. Poor Devlin." Her lips curved up, and the wheels began to turn. "Think about it. Wouldn't they make a handsome couple?"

Aiyanna shrieked when Cameron rolled her onto her back. "Leave it alone, love. Now what's this about poor Devlin? Bloody hell to him? What about poor me?"

Aiyanna smiled, and her hands moved slow,

caressing his arms across his shoulders. "Oh, baby, what can I do for you to make it all better?"

Just before his lips closed on hers, she heard, "Let me show ye."

Chapter Forty

Cheyenne draped an arm across Aiyanna's shoulders. They stared at the reflections of each other in the mirror. With identical faces, Aiyanna's champagne gown of organza left little doubt as to the bride. Cheyenne's maid of honor gown was a simple shade of peach and added a tint of color to the only two woman of the wedding party.

"You are absolutely beautiful," Cheyenne commented, in a weak and tremulous whisper. Her eyes filled with tears despite the loving smile she'd pasted on her lips.

"So are you." Aiyanna smiled in return.

A knock sounded on the door.

"Aiyanna?" Devlin's voice, deep and sensual, resonated through the solid wood door.

"We'll be right out," Aiyanna called over her shoulder. She grabbed Cheyenne's hand and gave it a tight squeeze.

"Cameron's waiting for you," Cheyenne whispered.

Sadness poured out in those words, and Aiyanna turned to her sister. "Shy, there's a man out there for you. I know there is, and when you find him, you'll be just as happy as Cameron and me."

Cheyenne's brows drew together in an agonized expression. "You worry too much about me, sis. This is your time, not mine." Cheyenne murmured, and then smiled, tugging Aiyanna's hand, leading her to the door. "Come on. Your man is waiting."

Before they reached the door that would

transform her life, Aiyanna stopped. When Cheyenne turned in question, Aiyanna's eyebrows rose, understanding that her sister's wide-eyed innocence was merely a smoke screen.

"What's the matter?" Cheyenne asked. "Getting cold feet?"

Aiyanna giggled. "Not on your life. I was wondering...what do you think about Devlin?"

"What about him?"

"I heard the two of you hit it off."

"Ladies!" Devlin called again. This time, his tone held a hint of impatience.

Cheyenne winked. "You gotta love a forceful man." She tugged again. "Come on before the man breaks the door down."

Aiyanna giggled at the image of Devlin doing exactly that. She drew in a deep breath, fighting the butterflies that swam cockeyed in her stomach.

"All right already, we're coming," Cheyenne called out.

Outside in the hall, the soft melody of *Amazing Grace* floated up the stairs.

Devlin's tight expression relaxed into a smile at the sight of them. For a moment, his eyes locked with Cheyenne's. He lowered his gaze, but not before Aiyanna recognized the desire in his eyes.

A flash of excitement coursed through her. So, he did want Cheyenne.

Hmmm...

He bowed in front of her. When he stood, he offered her his arm. She placed her hand on his jacket. He covered her hand with his own and gave her a heart-stopping smile.

She offered him a small, timid smile and apologized, "I'm sorry for making you wait."

He patted her hand, winked, and escorted her down the stairs.

Aiyanna and Devlin walked down the staircase

side-by-side, Cheyenne following close behind.

With each step, Aiyanna's heart beat faster, her stomach twisted, and her knees shook. If Devlin hadn't been by her side holding her up, she would have taken a nosedive down each step. One step at a time, she moved, guaranteeing each foot planted firmly in place before taking the next step. She breathed a sigh of relief when the hard wooden floor at the base of the stairs hit the soles of each foot.

Elizabeth O'Callaghan, Fallon's wife, waited for them in the kitchen. Fallon and Liz had arrived yesterday afternoon giving Aiyanna and Cheyenne the opportunity to spend some time with the first Síoraí wife. Liz, a woman of great courage and love for her husband, made her feel welcome in the Síoraí family. Fallon and Liz shared an unusual relationship...one that overflowed with love.

Liz rushed forward and breathed out in a rush, "Hold on to her, Devlin. My goodness, she looks like she might collapse at any moment."

Devlin winked. "Like you on your wedding day, Lizzie."

She laughed. Her hand rested on her swollen stomach. "I probably would have if you hadn't been holding me up. Don't you remember?"

"I remember well."

Liz turned to Aiyanna. "Are you okay?"

Aiyanna nodded; her tongue froze in her mouth.

Liz drew Anya in her arms. "You look stunning, Aiyanna," she whispered in her ear. When she stepped back, she winked at Devlin, and said, "I'll tell them we're ready."

And then she disappeared.

Cheyenne led the way through the kitchen. They stopped in the doorway leading outside to the back yard. On cue, the music altered into the solitary melody of the harp playing the Wedding March.

Devlin patted Aiyanna's hand and offered her a

charming smile. "Cameron is a lucky man, lass. A verra lucky man."

Outside, night had transformed the skies. Ten large Victorian style lampposts provided just enough light to create a soft, romantic backdrop for a wedding.

The cornucopia of pink cherry blossoms entwined with ivy garlands that adorned a natural wood wedding and garden arbor temporarily distracted Aiyanna. Beneath the tresses of gossamer ribbons and bows, her gaze met Cameron's. Her heart thudded before settling back to its natural rhythm.

Her breath caught in her throat. Cameron, handsome in his midnight black tux, stood beside the trellis. His eyes burned of golden nuggets and glittered of love. When his gaze met hers, his lips curved into a breath-taking smile.

The Goddess Luna stood beside him. The high priestess volunteered to administer the ceremonial vows. Dressed in a long shimmering white gown, Luna presented the picture of an enchantress, a gorgeous visualization of the Otherworld. Long, blonde tresses fell to her waist. A circlet of golden oak leaves surrounded her head.

Devin placed Aiyanna's hand into Cameron's. Before he released them, he gripped both of their hands in his and whispered a prayer before he bowed in respect and stepped away.

Aiyanna and Cameron were getting married at midnight with the moon sparkling down on them. As though in acceptance, the stars twinkled.

Their vows were the simple, traditional words spoken a million times by countless couples. For them, this ceremony only reinforced the immortal bond they'd already formed.

"Do you, Aiyanna Grey, take Cameron MacLean to be your husband, to live together by the gods' ordinance—in the holy estate of matrimony? Will you love him, comfort him, honor him, in everlasting life, for richer, for better, for worse, in sadness and in joy, to cherish and continually bestow upon him your heart's deepest devotion, forsaking all others, keep yourself only unto him as long as you both shall live?"

"I will." She stared into his eyes. "Forever." The last word choked out in a nearly unintelligible whisper. She blinked to clear the tears that blinded her.

And then, Luna turned to Cameron and repeated the promise.

When it was his turn to reply his words rang out clearly, "I will, forever."

The rest of the ceremony blurred for Aiyanna. She only had eyes for the handsome man who stood at her side.

With Cheyenne's assistance, the marriage ceremony quickly morphed into the reception. To Aiyanna's surprise, the gods and goddesses of the Tuatha Dé Danann made their appearances. Although their attendance was brief, they wished the bride and groom a long lifetime of happiness.

At one time, Aiyanna caught the subtle looks that passed between Devlin and Cheyenne. A secret smile curved her lips when she thought of what a handsome couple they'd make and vowed to help them to find their way into each other's arms.

"What are ye smiling about, wife?" Cameron's voice sent a burst of warm air to tickle her ear.

She giggled. "Nothing, love. Nothing at all." She was certain Cameron would tell her to butt out and mind her own business, but, by her way of thinking, Cheyenne was her business.

A loud *clink* of a knife hitting a wineglass caught everyone's attention, and they turned toward the goddess Luna who smiled and raised a wine glass. "I would make a toast to the bride and groom. Cameron, Aiyanna, may the gods grant ye long life and happiness." She chuckled. "Oh, we've already granted the long life."

The crowd laughed.

In the next moment, her face turned serious. "And to all of you, I promise you that this madness will end soon. All the pieces have not yet been added to the puzzle. Evil will always have their playground, but the Vampryss Deidra does not belong amongst it. She will make her appearance again, stage her schemes, and destroy many in her thirst for vengeance, but the gods of the Tuatha Dé Danann have chosen our protectors well. I have faith in *all* of you." She nodded. "Now, enough of the pep talks, and on with the party."

Aiyanna caught the stress the Goddess placed on 'all', and couldn't help but wonder if there was a hidden meaning. Yes, there was a battle to be fought, and they would fight it, but more importantly, Cameron would be at her side for the rest of her life, which meant forever.

Cameron's arms encircled her, one hand in the small of her back. He pulled her close. His uneven breath brushed her cheek. The warmth of his arms was so male, so strong, masculine and so unmistakably Cameron. "What do ye think? Is it time for bed yet?"

Aiyanna twisted and glanced up into his face about to tell him that would be rude to leave in the middle of their party. Her words stilled in her throat at the look of undisguised desire in his expression.

Cameron didn't wait for her reply. Turning to the crowd, he cleared his throat. "Can I have your attention, please? The wife and I want to thank all of ye for coming. 'Tis time for us to retreat for some alone time. Please stay and have a good time. We certainly intend to."

The small group erupted into laughter, and Aiyanna's face flamed with heat. She hid in the crook of Cameron's shoulder.

He laughed and led her through the crowd amidst congratulatory pats on the back and kisses on the cheek.

Inside, Cameron picked Aiyanna up into his arms.

"What are ye doing?" she asked, when he walked up the stairs.

"I believe 'tis customary for the groom to carry the bride across the threshold."

"The threshold, yes, but through the house? I'm not believing that one." She chuckled and wiggled in his arms. "Put me down before you hurt yourself."

He shook his head and pressed a kiss to her lips. "Keep squirming like that, and I wilna be blamed for my actions." By this time, they'd reached their bedroom door. "Open the door, love, and let us in."

Aiyanna laughed at his gruff imitation of the big bad wolf from the three little pigs' fairytale. She reached down, turned the knob, and pushed the door wide open.

Once inside, he released her legs. Her body slid down the length of his. She wrapped her arms around his neck and pulled his lips to hers.

His mouth covered hers hungrily, and his passion aroused hers. But before she lost all inhibitions, she needed to tell him something. She reached up her hands and pushed him away.

She read concern in his eyes when he asked, "What's the matter?"

"Nothing. I have a wedding gift for you." Aiyanna walked to the closet where she reached inside and brought out a large wooden frame, the picture covered by a sheet.

"A picture? Of ye? Are ye naked?"

Aiyanna giggled. "And what if I were to tell you

it was? Where would ye hang it?"

He looked behind him and then raised his gaze to the ceiling above the bed. When he peered back at hers, his eyebrows raised a fraction, and a cocky grin lit up his face.

She laughed. "Not an option, dear one." She set the picture down and leaned it against the dresser before she strolled back to him. She grabbed his hands and led him to the bed where she motioned with her head for him to sit.

She sat beside him.

"Ye look serious," Cameron said. He picked up her hand and pressed a kiss in her palm.

She caressed his cheek, and her eyes glowed with love. "It is. You know, Starr always told Cheyenne and me that things happen for a reason."

****

Cameron had a hard time concentrating on her words. Being close to her like this, her tender touch, the love and caring he saw in her eyes stirred emotions from a time long ago.

"There's a reason why I'm here," she continued. "A reason you and I were brought together." She inhaled and released her breath in a soft *whoosh*. "I'm supposed to be here, beside you. It's destiny. I don't know where we go from here, but as long as I have you beside me, I'll never be afraid again."

"Aiyanna?" His voice came out a whisper. He swallowed the ache that formed in his throat.

"No, don't say anything. Just listen." She stood and walked over to the painting. She picked it up and flipped it over. Cameron's heart paused a beat, and he stared at a hand-painted portrait of the family he had years ago.

He raised his eyes to hers. "Why?"

"I don't want you to forget. I know you want to, but I won't let you. Without this woman and these two little girls, you wouldn't be the man you are. I don't want to forget what they sacrificed so that I wouldn't."

"Aiyanna, our life is ours. They are part of the past and best left there."

"They are part of you." She cleared her throat. "Sarah came to me and asked me to teach you to love again, to help you to overcome your guilt. To help you see that their deaths weren't your fault."

Cameron's pulse leapt. Heartache ripped through him, and he murmured, "I should have been there for them."

"You couldn't. Destiny took you away that night. Everything you've been through was meant to happen. Otherwise, we wouldn't be together now."

"Sarah told ye this."

She nodded. "No one controls their own destinies, my love." She gently set the picture back down. "Not even you. You've helped me to deal with my past. We have both felt the touch of darkness and overcame it. Whatever comes next, we'll handle it as long as we're together. Don't forget, we have forever now."

Aiyanna told him how the gods granted her immortality. The way it was supposed to happen. He'd been angry at first, remembering his anguish at her death, but as the meaning of her words registered, he'd gotten past his anger.

Their lives bound forever in eternity as avowed by the Legacy of the Síoraí.

Cameron held out a hand toward her, and she slipped her hand into his. He pulled her down onto his lap. "I love ye."

"I love you, Cameron MacLean." She smiled. Her eyes twinkled. "Now, how would you like to light up the darkness, my love?"

"Och, love, let's set it afire."

A word about the author...

Victoria Noxon is a hopeless romantic. Her passion for reading began at an early age, so it seemed quite natural when this obsession transformed into a love for writing. She writes contemporary, historical, and dark paranormal stories about strong, sexy heroes and the beautiful, intelligent heroines who rule their hearts during the day and their bodies at night.

A mother of four, she resides with her loving, supportive husband of twenty-five years in Upstate New York, where the number of cows far outweighs the number of high-rises. When she's not reading or writing, she works full-time at a local area hospital.

For more information, check out Victoria's website at: www.victorianoxon.com